IT

STARTED

ON THE

UNDERGROUND

BY

CORRINA BRYANT

For my grandad, Fred, who made me believe I could do this.

ACKNOWLEDGEMENTS

Special thanks to my amazing daughter,
Jodie, for her support and inspiration.

My two brilliant friends, Vicki and Lesley,
for taking the time to read the first draft and give me
valuable feedback and insight.

My boys, Elliot, Dylan, and Dom,
who make me so proud, and Jason, for his encouragement
and for being my rock in life.

CHAPTER 1

On reflection, it was a mistake to tell Poppy my boyfriend had died. I didn't actually have a boyfriend, and the man she thought was my boyfriend wasn't dead—well, not as far as I knew anyway.

Poppy used to be my manager and the nicest person in the office. This wasn't difficult because there were only four full-time employees at Thames FM, where I was the general assistant/dogsbody. There were also a couple of freelance presenters who thought they were local celebrities, plus the occasional over-enthusiastic student volunteer. But it was Poppy that everyone loved.

Poppy was one of those people who was always smiling and always looked amazing, and as much as I would have loved to call her my friend, really, we were just colleagues. I didn't have any actual friends—except Kai, who I'd known since school and was like a brother to me. I did have another friend once, but she was mean to everybody all the time, and it made me feel grubby. When I found out she talked bad about me, too, I stopped hanging out with her.

My other colleague, Gary, was the main station presenter, and he had the final word. He had some serious personal hygiene issues, took fag breaks every five minutes, and liked to compare Thames FM to the BBC.

In reality, Thames FM is a small local radio station with a handful of listeners, most of whom are in their late eighties and unlikely to see another Christmas.

The only other member of staff was Warwick, the head of sales. He didn't return calls, was never in the office, and was often 'Missing in Action,' but he did meet his sales targets, which kept the station on air. Basically, he could do whatever he wanted.

Local radio was a dying institution. Gone were the days when reporters rushed to report live from the scene of a crime. They no longer showed up at village fetes to draw the raffle or interview the local mayor opening a new bus shelter. Nowadays, pretty much everything was pre-recorded and sandwiched between regurgitated links in an attempt to make it sound live. However, occasionally Thames FM did go live. For example, when I had to pretend to be a listener and win the family ticket to the local pantomime each year. Gary insisted on this annual humiliation so that he could take his latest girlfriend and two kids—one from his first marriage and one from his second. He asked me because he was also under Poppy's spell and didn't want her to think less of him. I was also pretty good at impersonations. Middle-aged housewife from West London being my speciality.

I'd worked at Thames FM for nearly five years. My main duties were photocopying (because Gary didn't trust computers), filing, answering the phone, and ordering stationery and kitchen supplies. I also started a station Instagram account out of boredom. It had twenty-six posts and seventy-three followers. I'd suggested a weekly 'What's on' guide for listeners, but that idea went down like Poppy's diamond earring when it fell in her coffee. I did manage to fish it out, but I almost gave myself third-degree burns in the process.

'Who do you think we are? Charity Radio?' Gary said.

'I just thought we could help promote local events and support the community,' I said in a rare display of defiance.

'If anyone wants to advertise their event, they can bloody well pay for it.' He sighed dramatically, like an exasperated teacher talking to a pupil. 'If you want to be a do-gooder, donate to Great Ormond Street or something.'

'But I thought we got funding from the local arts council to help—'

He interrupted me. 'To help keep us bloody afloat, not to give away free adverts. Jesus!' Gary said and went outside for a fag break.

The day my life started to unravel, I was wearing black skinny jeans and a baggy grey sweatshirt over a black fitted vest top. My hair needed washing, so I'd scraped it back into a tight ponytail, and I was wearing my glasses because I'd forgotten to order new contact lenses. Basically, I blended in with the streets of London and the weather on that day—grey. Kai would never have left the house looking like that. Kai was a guy who was so pretty he should have been a girl or at least gay, but he was neither. He loved extravagance, especially when it came to clothes, and he didn't take money very seriously. Not because he had lots, but because he was a 'life is for living' type of guy. My dress sense was 'apathetic,' according to my only living relative, Mad Auntie Jean, who was my late mum's sister. They couldn't stand each other.

I wore my clothes until they fell apart and bought them mostly from the cancer research shop. I hated trying things on in there though, because it took effort, and it smelt rank. I was not really that bothered with what I looked like, which was lucky because I had hair with its own personality. Kai's hair, however, was his pride and joy. It was dirty-blond, shoulder-length, and fell in soft curls around his cherubic face. He was obsessed with mousse and gels and was always moaning about the 'wrong type of air,' saying it made his hair frizz.

Kai and I also had very different opinions on public transport. I was happiest when I was people-watching and listening to other people's conversations. I especially loved the underground because it was a great place to be if you were nosey like me. Since losing his driving licence, Kai liked to Uber everywhere, but if necessary, he would rent an e-bike, but only if there was not a hint of a breeze. Our biggest difference, though, was that Kai had grown up wanting to travel the world, whereas I had always been happy in my little corner of North London. But despite our differences, we were drawn to each other at school. The two oddballs in class who started talking when Kai asked me if I knew why pecan nuts looked like brains. I said I didn't but that I liked the question, and that was it. Friends for life, or so I believed at the time. Oh, one more thing. Kai was straight-talking, whereas I tended to waffle.

Poppy and me arrived at work at the same time. I opened the door for her, resisting the urge to bow.

'Morning,' Poppy said, her chestnut-brown hair swinging from side to side, brushing her dimples. Some hair stuck to her painted lips, and she pulled it away with her perfectly manicured nails. Gary was sitting at his desk, chewing his.

'Morning, gorgeous,' Gary said, the 1980s being his vibe.

Poppy flashed him a smile, and I was disappointed she didn't have a witty comeback.

'Hi Gary,' I said brightly. He went back to scrolling on his phone.

I hung my jacket up on the broken coat stand in the corner, catching it as it fell and propping it back up against the wall—a daily ritual. My desk was littered with yellow post-it notes stuck onto piles of paper. All had different instructions. *x 20 Urgent, x 10 Asap, x 6 Double Sided.* I carried them over to the copier. The orange warning light indicated a paper jam, and the toner symbol was flashing.

'It's not working,' Poppy said. 'I think we might need to get the engineer.'

I removed the jammed paper, replaced the toner and completed the copying, placing it all on Gary's desk ten minutes later. He didn't look up. So far, this was a very typical day.

Thames FM studios were in a small, seventies office block on the outskirts of Hammersmith in West London. There was a dry cleaner and an off-licence on one side, a dingy-looking pub and a cafe called *The Good Cafe* on the other, where the coffee was average. The nearest tube station was Barons Court, which was on the District Line (my favourite line) and the Piccadilly Line, but I liked to mix it up and use all the underground lines and different stations when I could. My life wasn't very exciting.

I lived in Kings Cross, in the same two-bedroom flat I grew up in. My parents bought it off the council, and although it wasn't particularly homely, it had been a good investment. When they died within six months of each other in 2021, I was advised by their solicitor to stay put until their estate was finalised. As their only child, I'd assumed the family home would be left to me, but it turned out there were other beneficiaries, including a crowdfunding scheme for 'Statues for Britain' and a rabbit rehousing scheme, plus a mystery family friend who'd apparently, 'been a great support to both of them over the years.'

So, although I lived in the flat, I didn't own it, and my parents' Will stipulated that if I ever moved, the flat should be sold and the funds distributed accordingly. As I was very much single and lived a lifestyle that offered little chance of meeting a partner, I expected I'd live here until I was carried out in a box. However, even without rent to pay, after paying the utility bills, the council tax and my travel, I had just about enough left to feed myself.

The day itself dragged like a geography lesson— my least favourite subject. Gary's nose-picking habit had repulsed me even more than usual, and I had a strong urge to go home and shower to wash away the image of wet nasal discharge on his stubby pinky finger.

I left the office at exactly five o'clock. I knew this because Thames FM was on all the time in the office and another load of train strikes were announced on the news. It didn't affect me directly because I got the tube, but it meant the underground would be busier than usual on those days. I didn't enjoy sharing space and air with halitosis or armpits, but on the bright side, being up close and personal was great for earwigging.

I walked to Gloucester Road to get the Circle Line home. It was a longer walk, but I was more likely to get a seat at this station; also, the Waitrose next door did good yellow sticker markdowns at that time of day. I bought a small pack of pre-prepared runner beans and a vegetable lasagne ready meal for one, costing £3.07. The portion size was tiny, but would make a nice meal with some leftover garlic bread I had in the fridge.

However, as it turned out, I didn't end up eating the lasagne or the beans because my night took an unexpected turn.

I was waiting on the platform and noticed a couple standing just along from me. He was in a dinner suit, wearing very shiny shoes and a brand-new white shirt. I assumed it was new because there was no way it could be that white if it had been washed, even in Vanish Gold Oxi. His hair looked Brylcreemed like Elvis, and he had a bow tie hanging undone around his neck. She was extremely pretty. Her hair was piled on top of her head, and soft, bouncy ringlets framed her face. Her lips were full, and she was wearing a lot of unnecessary eye makeup. Her dress was bottle-green and layered, pulled in tight at the waist. Thin straps fitted over her shoulders, which were glistening, and even from a distance, I could smell her perfume. A shawl hung halfway down her back, and I remember thinking it was funny that she was wearing this glamorous outfit with dirty white trainers. Then I saw she was carrying a pair of strappy silver sandals in one hand and a large diamanté clutch bag in the other.

When the train came in, I followed them onto the carriage and sat opposite. It was difficult to take my eyes off them—her in particular. They looked like they could be famous, but I guessed they weren't because if they were, they probably wouldn't be travelling with the general public. However, Kai did often say I could be sitting next to Prince William, and I still wouldn't recognise him.

By the third stop, I'd managed to glean they were meeting their friends, Livvy and Max, for cocktails, then going on to a VIP dinner and dance. It sounded very glamorous, and I felt quite excited just listening to them.

'Don't put your foot in it like last time,' she said. 'Seriously, Liv will kill me if she knows I've told you.'

'Relax, I won't.' He winked at her.

'I mean it. Don't get drunk and blurt it out. Promise me.'

He pretended to slur his words. 'So Liv, I hear you, and Max tried a threesome the other week? Didn't go too well though, apparently.' He started laughing.

'Stop it!' She slapped his thigh with her bag. 'I told you, nothing happened. She couldn't go through with it.'

'And you believed her,' he said, raising his eyebrows.

'Yes, I do, actually. Now do your tie up.'

'I don't know how,' he said, shifting his body to face her.

'What makes you think I can do it?' she asked him. 'I've never worn a bow tie.'

He pulled out his phone and started tapping the screen. Moments later, they sat, heads together, watching a 'how-to' YouTube video. She told him to face the other way and put her hands around either side of his neck. Several other passengers were now also watching them.

'Hold up the phone so I can see it,' she said, and for the next three stops, she tried but failed to tie the tie. 'You'll have to get Max to help you,' she said, letting go. She pulled the black silk tie away from his collar and handed it to him.

'He's gonna think I'm a right idiot,' he said.

'I could do a shout-out on the carriage?' she offered. 'See if anyone knows how to do it?'

'No, don't draw attention to us. Just in case.'

If you don't want to be noticed, don't look so gorgeous and travel by public transport, I thought, wishing I could tie a bow tie and be the hero of the hour. Where was Kai when I needed him? I was pretty confident I'd be able to follow the YouTube instructions. I mean, how hard could it be? But I didn't offer to help because I didn't want them to know I'd been listening. That would have been embarrassing, and I'd been called a nosey parker before—and much worse on a couple of occasions.

When the train pulled into Kings Cross, I didn't get off. I hadn't planned to stay on, but I just found myself sitting there, watching the doors open and close. I felt invested in this couple and his bow tie now. I needed closure. A few stops later, we pulled into Monument Station. The couple got up, and I followed. I wanted to see where they were going, check out Liv and Max, and check he got his tie tied.

The station was busy, and by the time we reached street level, the rush hour commute home was in full swing. They weaved their way in and out of the traffic, and I stayed close, which was easy to do unnoticed in my drab outfit. They came to a stop outside The East Hotel and Restaurant. Doormen stood on either side of the entrance, wearing identical top hats and long tailcoats. They pulled a brass handle, each in perfect unison, and I glimpsed a world that was very different from any I'd ever seen. Everything was either coloured gold or covered in black velvet. Huge chandeliers hung from the ceiling, and beautiful people sat at every table, laughing and drinking from glasses filled with colourful fruits. A large black piano sat on a small raised circular stage in the middle of the room. I recognised the music playing, but before I could identify it, the doors swung shut in my face. I walked away, feeling like I'd been turned away at the gates of the Willy Wonka Factory, one of my favourite movies. The original, not the 2023 movie *Wonka*, which was, frankly, a bit of a let-down. I should have just headed home then and there, but I wanted to be part of that world, just for one night.

I turned down a small side street and took off my sweatshirt. I twisted my hair into a bun and swapped my glasses for sunglasses. I rooted around in my bag for some lipstick, applied it heavily, added a dash to my cheeks, and then headed back, holding my head high.

'Good evening, madam,' one of the doormen said, tipping his top hat. I nearly looked over my shoulder to check it was me he was talking to.

'Good evening,' I said, feeling like I'd won the lottery as I walked in, finding myself amongst the glamour and the glitz.

I couldn't see the train couple at first, but then I spotted her. Bottom perched on a bar stool as she bent down and switched her trainers for her party shoes. She was talking to another glamorous woman, who I presumed was Liv. From a distance, they looked like squawking parrots. Every time one of them stopped talking, they dipped their head to sip their cocktail delicately through a straw, and then the other one perked up and started talking. I moved to a table nearby and scanned the room. I saw the guy from the train return with his friend. His tie was tied, and I felt pleased.

'You did it,' the lady from the train said, reaching over and wiggling it straight.

'Max did it—thank God,' he laughed and slapped his friend on the back. 'You obviously go to far more black tie events than me, mate,' he guffawed, and I thought, *surely that can't be his actual real laugh?*

'Can I get you a drink, madam?' A waiter hovered over me, one hand behind his back.

'A cocktail, please,' I said.

'Would you like to see the cocktail menus?' he said, whipping an array of menus from a gold stand on the table and offering them to me like a bouquet. He had a slight French accent, which I wasn't wholly convinced was genuine. I scanned the list, unable to focus on anything other than the price. I settled on an Old Cuban, which I ordered in my best Kate Middleton voice.

'Do you wish to start a tab, madam?'

'No, thank you,' I said. 'I'm not staying long.'

He produced a small hand-held device, prompting me to reach into my handbag, which had a large ink stain on one corner and a busted zip, meaning the lasagne and green beans were both on display, yellow stickers facing up. I handed over my bank card and waited for my seventeen pounds worth of Bacardi, champagne, mint, and lime to be shaken to within an inch of its life, judging by the man behind the bar and his biceps.

'You must visit the loos here,' Liv said to her friend. 'Trust me, they're incredible. Honestly, you could fit my entire flat in there.'

'Darling, I think we need to make a move. We need to get a good position,' Max said.

'I'll be five minutes,' the train lady said, wiggling off of her stool and trotting towards the sweeping double staircase.

The dubious French waiter appeared at my table with my drink. Foliage was trailing down the side of the glass.

'So sorry. Could you possibly give me a few minutes.' I smiled. 'I just need to pop to the ladies,' I said, nailing my polite, confident new persona.

'Of course, madam,' he nodded and retreated backwards with a slight bow like he was a royal courtier.

I headed down the stairs, through a heavy mirrored door and into a huge room with vintage sinks fitted along two of the walls. There was a dusty pink Victorian-style confidante sofa in the middle. The seats were connected but faced different directions, and a small brass plaque told me that two hundred years ago, these were used for secret, hushed conversations in public places. There was a selection of hand creams and soaps that were beautifully displayed and a huge fresh flower display on a glass table. It smelt divine—like a candle shop. An archway led to a corridor of identical toilet cubicles, and I dived into the first vacant one. I locked the door and, after a few seconds, flushed for authenticity. At the basins, I took time to lather my hands and it didn't take long for the train lady to appear at one of the sinks along from me. She touched up her makeup, then sat on the confidante to make a call.

'We're here and about to go in. I've got the flags; Liv has the paint. I'm assuming we'll get arrested, so keep your phone on.'

It was one of the few times in my life where being unremarkable was an advantage because I don't think she even noticed I was there.

I know this story makes me sound a bit crazy, but honestly, I was just entertaining myself. Things only started to get complicated when I had to explain all this to the police.

CHAPTER 2

I followed her back upstairs, keeping my distance. She picked up her shawl from the back of the chair, slung it over her arm, and collected her trainers from the floor in one slick move.

'Let's do this,' she said.

'Let's change the world.' Liv high-fived them all and handed them a gold invitation with calligraphy writing.

The group of four walked away from the bar area. My entertainment was over. I wasn't getting into the party, and I wasn't going to witness them changing the world or get arrested.

I dived into one of the group's vacant stools and the barman appeared like a genie with my cocktail. I sipped it slowly. The longer I could make it last, the better I would feel about spending so much money on a single drink. Everyone around me was living their best life in this world I didn't belong in. Perfectly manicured nails gesticulating conversations and wavy sunshine-blond hair dazzling in the light from the chandeliers above. The outfits would make Kai pee his pants. I couldn't wait to tell him about this. He would want every last detail and probably ask me questions I couldn't answer, like 'Was she wearing Louis Vuitton?' Then, he would laugh and tell me I was a let-down when I told him I had absolutely no idea.

As I sat indulging my love of people-watching, I felt a little bit excited. I had almost witnessed a live protest. I started fantasising. If I worked for the BBC or Sky News, I could have called the news desk and told them something big was about to go down at a top London hotel. Maybe I would even have had my reporting debut. But Thames FM didn't care about live reports anymore. The reality was I had an exclusive breaking news story but nowhere to break it.

I didn't know exactly what the train couple and their friends were planning. I'd only heard them mention flags and paint, and they didn't look like your typical protestors, but on reflection, I should have probably alerted security. I thought about it, but then how would I explain what I was doing there? If I told them the truth, I could find myself getting arrested for stalking!

I sat and waited for the drama to unfold. The two guys now sitting next to me were being very loud, and their language was vulgar. After another half an hour, nothing had happened, and I was getting hungry. The menu prices were astronomical and I'd finished my drink long ago, so I left and went home. It was too late to cook the lasagne and the beans, so I made some marmite on toast and went to bed.

The next morning, I turned on the radio (not Thames FM because I wasn't very loyal, and Gary insisted on playing nineties hits in the morning that stayed in your head for days).

'Last night, a top London hotel was targeted by a group of environmental protestors who threw paint over guests attending a charity event. The activists stood on dining tables and waved flags, demanding the government act to stop what they called 'the final nail in the world's coffin.' Police officers made several arrests, and the suspects were led from the scene, shouting at onlookers. A spokesperson for The East Hotel in the City of London said they were extremely sorry for the distress caused to both the guests and organisers of the event. They confirmed there would be an internal inquiry, and a review of their security procedures is already underway. Guests confirmed no bag checks had taken place.

As I travelled to work that morning, I couldn't stop smiling. I had an exciting story to tell and something interesting to say. Even Poppy might be impressed. I was on time (timekeeping wasn't my strong point), and when I walked into the office, I had a small spring in my step.

'Good morning,' I said to Gary. 'Do you want a coffee?'

He gave me a kind of *'who are you?'* look and held his mug up above his head for me to take. When I placed his mug back on his desk, I did an Oscar-worthy yawn.

'Oh, excuse me, I had a bit of a late one last night,' I said.

Gary didn't react; he didn't even flinch.

'I was at The East Hotel in the city,' I added casually. I could practically see the cogs whirring away in his mind as he registered what I'd just said. He looked up.

'You were at The East?' Gary said, disbelief written all over his unshaven face. 'At the event with the protest?'

'I wasn't at the protest, but I was in the bar with the protesters—before they protested,' I said, leaning against his desk in a bid to keep the conversation going. Poppy would be arriving any minute because, unlike me, she was never late, and I wanted her to see me talking with Gary.

'Morning, everything okay?' Right on cue, Poppy walked in.

'E...e...e...' Gary looked mildly embarrassed.

'Eve,' I said.

'Eve was just telling me she was at The East last night.'

'Where the protest was?' Poppy asked.

'Yeah, I know. Crazy, eh?' I shrugged my shoulders in a kind of casual, *'Get me, I'm actually quite cool,'* kind of way.

'I didn't know you...'

15

'Went out?' I offered.

'No, no, I wasn't going to say that.' Poppy said, colour rising in her cheeks.

'It was a last-minute thing.' I smiled. I didn't want her to think she had offended me. To be fair, the five-star East Hotel and I weren't an automatic pairing. Similar to *Swan Lake* and heavy metal, or meat and quinoa.

'I heard on the radio that the protestors threw green paint at the guests?' Poppy said.

'I don't think we specified the colour of the paint,' Gary said.

'I wasn't listening to us,' Poppy said.

'Great,' Gary said.

'Yeah, it was pretty crazy,' I said, feeling my bra tighten as my chest expanded with pride.

'What happened?' Poppy said. 'Did you get paint thrown at you?'

'No, no, I was just having cocktails at the bar.' I swished my hair like she did when I said this.

'Oooo, get you. Who were you drinking cocktails with on a school night?' Poppy said.

I'd prepared my answer in anticipation of this question.

'I was on a date,' I said, with confidence that I wasn't wholly feeling.

'Really? Who with?'

'Just someone I met,' I said.

'How did it go?' Poppy said, 'I hope the protesters didn't spoil it?'

'It was good,' I smiled, 'and no, they didn't.'

'Can you two continue this conversation another time and preferably not at my desk?' Gary said.

'Sorry,' Poppy said, smiling at me.

For the rest of the morning, I felt really happy. Poppy was being ultra friendly and I could just tell she was dying to ask me more.

'Sooooo, tell me more about last night,' she said as soon as Gary went for his next fag break. 'Was your date of the male or female variety?'

'Male, of course!' I said. I didn't mind that she thought I might be a lesbian, but we'd worked together for five years, and I regularly talked about my celebrity crushes with her. All were male, except for Alesha Dixon, but everyone thought she was beautiful, didn't they? 'He's gorgeous,' I said.

'You got a picture?' Poppy asked me. 'Or can I stalk him on Instagram?'

I nearly faltered but managed to save myself.

'We've only just met.' I laughed. 'I don't want to scare him off. He does have a George Michael beard, though.' I added this detail because Poppy had a photo of George on her desk and I figured it was a good physical feature for my pretend boyfriend to have.

'I'm really happy for you, Eve,' she said, sounding so genuine that I nearly confessed then and there. But confessing that I was actually at The East on my own because I'd followed a couple I'd admired on the train wasn't cool. Neither was telling her that there was no date. Especially, if I wanted her to like me and consider me a normal human being.

'It's early days, but I think he's special,' I added for good measure as Poppy made her way back to her desk.

'That's great,' she said, checking her phone, her voice trailing off.

Gary came back in and the interest in my life vanished as quickly as it had arrived. But just when I thought my moment in the spotlight was over, Gary burst out of the studio, one finger up his nose. He wrenched it out before speaking.

'Eva, I need you to do a live interview in six minutes.'

'It's Eve.'

'I'll come to you straight out of the news. I'll introduce you as a witness. Okay?'

'A witness to what?'

'The protest—duh.'

'But I didn't really see anything. I was just there,' I said, my heart going a lot faster than it should be for a semi-healthy adult.

'Exactly. That's what I want. Having a witness will help us be seen as a serious news provider.'

I swallowed a laugh.

'Can't you find someone else?'

'Why would I find someone else when I have someone who was there standing right in front of me? I'm going for a wazz,' he tutted loudly. 'I'll meet you in the studio.'

'You okay?' Poppy said, pushing herself over to my desk on her wheely chair. 'You don't have to do it, you know.'

'He's not going to take no for an answer, though, is he?'

Poppy squeezed my shoulder. 'You'll be great.' She smiled at me. 'Just say what you saw.'

This was the moment I realised Poppy really did care about me, and we were actual friends, as well as colleagues.

I sat opposite Gary, willing this to be over. My hands were sweating, and I felt a little faint.

'Thames FM has managed to track down a guest who was at The East Hotel last night. She has agreed to speak to us exclusively and is here with us now. Hello Eva, I know you were at the hotel with *a friend*,' he over-emphasised the word *friend*, 'and witnessed the drama unfold. Can you tell us, did you actually see the protestors before they carried out their attack?'

'Yes, they were sitting at the bar.'

'And what were they doing?'

'Having a drink.'

'Were they acting suspicious in any way?'

'No—not that I could tell.'

Gary paused, his eyes boring into mine until I looked away.

'Can you tell us what happened when they threw the paint over the guests?'

I froze. I didn't know what to say. Gary glared at me over the microphone. I was going to make him and the station look stupid if I said I didn't see the actual protest, but I couldn't make it up—live on air.

'There was just a lot of confusion,' I said.

'Did the activists say anything?'

'Yes, but I couldn't hear what.'

'And was the paint throwing indiscriminate or targeted?'

'I don't know. I didn't get any paint thrown at me.'

'Can you confirm if your bag was checked by security when you and your guest arrived?'

'No, no, it wasn't.'

'Do you have any sympathy at all with the protestors?'

What was Gary doing? Expecting me to give a personal opinion live on air on something I knew nothing about.

'I...I...' I stammered. Gary shook his head in a warning.

'I think people should be allowed to enjoy an evening out without feeling threatened,' I said. Gary nodded his head at me. 'But I also think governments need to listen to what the protestors are saying.' Gary threw his arms up in the air.

'And finally, what did you and the other guests do after security had intervened?'

I looked across the table at him. I didn't have an answer to this.

'I left and went home.'

'That was Eva, who was at The East Hotel last night and witnessed the protest. This is Gary Jones, reporting for Thames FM.'

'Don't give up the day job,' Gary said, following me out of the studio.

'Leave it,' Poppy said. 'It's nerve-wracking going live. Especially when it's going out on multiple stations.'

'What do you mean multiple stations?' I said, my stomach dropping.

'We offered it to the local radio network in return for a credit,' Gary said. 'I told them we had a reliable witness who was there on the night. I would have got more from a bloody tortoise.' He rolled back his eyes. 'She sounded half asleep until she decided to stand up for people who break the law,' he said, talking about me as if I wasn't there.

'Sorry,' I said, 'you made me nervous with all your questions. I told you I didn't really see anything.' Gary sighed so loudly, that it was almost a groan. 'And you shouldn't have asked me what I thought. You put me on the spot.'

'Any sane person would have said no of course they didn't have sympathy with them. That's what you were supposed to say.'

'But climate change is real,' I said.

Gary shook his head and laughed. He was so condescending I felt like I was six years old. I felt the need to scream, but in an open-plan office, privacy was hard to come by.

'Excuse me,' I said.

I sat on the toilet seat and pushed my fist into my mouth. This whole thing had got out of control very quickly.

'Are you okay?' Poppy knocked on the toilet door.

'Yep. Won't be a minute.'

'Gary's an arse, don't worry about him.' I unlocked the door and came out. I squashed next to Poppy in the sink area, and we both looked into the mirror at one another's reflection. 'I've made you a cup of tea. It's on your desk.'

'Thanks,' I said. 'That's really sweet.' My heart lifted a little.

'In a few hours, you can go home, enjoy your weekend, and forget all about it,' Poppy said.

I didn't reply because I was trying not to cry, and it made me feel pathetic, but I felt overwhelmed by what had happened.

'What are you up to? Anything nice?' Poppy asked.

'I'm going on a surprise date,' I said, the words coming out of my mouth before I could stop them. I don't know why I said it, but Poppy never asked me what I was doing at the weekend, and I didn't want to disappoint her by saying I had no plans—at all.

'With your new man?' Poppy said. 'Can you ask him if he'd be up for an on-air interview?' Poppy said.

'I don't know if he—' I started to panic ramble.

'I'm winding you up,' she laughed, throwing her head back, her eyes twinkling. 'God, your face was a picture.' She laughed again. 'Ignore me. I have a sick sense of humour.'

By the end of the day, my interview had gone out on several local stations across the country. Gary was acting like he was Rupert Murdoch; I was feeling sick with fear that I was going to get found out.

On Saturday morning, Kai came over, and as usual, he wanted to go window shopping. I didn't.

'Pleeeeeeeease,' Kai said, pushing past me, pulling off his jacket, and flinging it dramatically onto the sofa. 'I've had a really boring week. I need to do something fun today.'

'How can you have a boring week? You literally work in entertainment?'

'Corporate entertainment is not entertainING,' he said, emphasising the *ing*. 'Basically, I arrange for people in badly cut suits to have forced fun.'

I looked outside at the ominous sky.

'Why don't we stay in and play Scrabble?'

'You know, if it wasn't for me, you would officially be a recluse. If you died, no one would even know until they investigated the foul stench coming from inside your flat.'

'That's nice,' I said.

Kai squeezed me tight and kissed me on the top of my head.

'You know, one of these days, I'm going to surprise you and book a trip to a sun-soaked island,' I said.

'If you do that, I'll eat my hat,' Kai said. 'Although, not my Givenchy baseball cap, because that was my best eBay win ever.'

'I bet it's a fake,' I said, then clocked his latte-coloured trousers embroidered with partridges, white collarless shirt, and burgundy silk scarf knotted around his neck. 'Oh, my God, what are you wearing?'

'You have to look rich if you want to be treated like a VIP,' he said. I raised my eyebrows. 'Don't blame me for the screwed-up world we live in,' he added.

'You look like you're going to Scotland to shoot pheasants with the gentry,' I said.

'Don't be bitter. Jealousy is the biggest destroyer of friendships,' he said, filling up the kettle. 'Right, you go and get ready; I'll make tea.'

'I am ready,' I said.

'We're going pretend designer shopping, not gardening,' Kai said, looking me up and down.

'I don't own any posh clothes. I work for Scrooge Radio, remember?'

'You don't need to own them. You just need to look like you can afford them,' he said, heading for my bedroom before I could stop him. 'I hope you've made your bed.'

'I've been busy,' I said, running in after him, shaking the duvet and pushing yesterday's twisted knickers underneath the dressing table. I scooped a pile of clothes up off the floor and kicked several pairs of shoes into the corner of the room.

Kai opened my wardrobe and started sliding the hangers dramatically from one side to the other.

'So I'm thinking smart and sexy. The type of outfit you'd wear to a court appearance,' he said.

'I'm not planning on any court appearances,' I said, 'unlike someone else I could mention.'

'That was a misunderstanding,' he said. 'I'm dyslexic. It wasn't my fault I couldn't read the *no entry* sign.'

'And the other two times?' I said.

'Who needs a car in London anyway?' Kai said.

'I did try telling you that when you dragged me around that Jaguar dealership,' I said.

Kai ignored me, sending me out to make the tea instead. When I returned, he'd managed to pull together what he called an *'it'll do'* outfit comprising a long black skirt, a black jumper, and a large buckle belt that I'd forgotten I had. He told me I needed to accessorise with a pair of sunglasses, which he said I should wear the entire time to hide my 'unmade face.'

'Otherwise, we'll be rumbled,' he said.

'Charming.'

'And please let me do something with your hair?'

'No.'

'You have to wear a hat then.'

'No, again,' I paused. 'Could we not go for cocktails instead of window shopping?'

'Cocktails?' Kai said. 'Since when have you drank cocktails?' I went to answer, but he interrupted me. 'Plus, it's not even midday yet.'

'This week, actually,' I said, regretting my words as soon as I put them out into the world, knowing a Spanish Inquisition was incoming.

'You went out? Where did you go, who were you with, and why didn't you tell me?'

'It was a kind of ad hoc thing.'

'You don't do ad hoc things.'

'Yes, I do!' I protested. 'Okay, I haven't before now, but it's the new me.'

'I kind of preferred the old you. She was less annoying,' Kai said. He paused. 'And the with?'

I'd dug myself into a hole and quickly needed to find my way out. Either I had to tell Kai the truth—*I was drinking cocktails alone after I'd followed two strangers I saw on the train to a hotel bar*—or the lie, which, thanks to Gary, had now been shared with half the country. *I was there with a 'friend,'* and that Kai would never believe because he knows me.

'I'll fill you in later,' I said, buying myself some time. 'Now, get out while I change.'

'Seeing as you're now into "ad hoc and cocktails," maybe we could go on an "ad hoc" trip to Ibiza and drink Pina Coladas?' Kai said as he walked out.

'You're only saying that cos you've got no one else to go with,' I shouted after him.

'True,' he shouted back.

The first shop we went to had a guard on the door. Kai nodded at him, put his arm around my waist and led me to the back of the store.

There were security cameras everywhere, and I felt guilty just by being there. A ridiculously tall woman with flawless skin and perfectly applied lipstick approached us. She was wearing a bodycon dress that looked like it had been painted on, and her bottom looked very pert—much to Kai's obvious delight.

'Good afternoon,' she said, looking at Kai.

I smiled, too scared to speak.

'Hey,' Kai said. *Hey?* I thought.

'Are you looking for anything in particular today?' she asked.

Kai dragged his eyes away from her and snapped back from a drooling, weak male to a professional, rich man.

'I have a VIP event tomorrow and my agent has just told me there's going to be a load of paparazzi there. I have absolutely nothing to wear,' Kai said in what I have to say, was quite an impressive American accent. The sales associate, Georgina (according to her badge), went to speak, but Kai butted in, 'I need something that screams 'Look at me.'

'I understand, sir. You can trust me,' Georgina said, eyeing Kai up and down. 'I'm guessing thirty-two, thirty-two for the trousers and thirty-eight for the jacket?' She left before Kai could reply.

'Shall I leave you two to it?' I said.

She returned before Kai could reply, holding a deep burgundy suit. 'Please, sir, this way.' She led Kai to the changing rooms, and I followed like a puppy, half expecting him to invite her in to help him undress. Georgina selected a baby-pink shirt from a clothes rail, unlocked one of the changing rooms and hung it on the wall inside. She turned to me. 'Would you like a drink, madam? Champagne, tea, coffee, herbal?'

I declined, earning me a glare from Kai before he disappeared inside. I sat down and was instantly swallowed by an ink-blue velvet sofa. Minutes later, a second sales associate appeared, arms full of clothes. He was followed by two men who looked identical. The same body shape and the same flawless complexion with a hint of orange. They were both wearing very short chinos with long socks and sliders. Their caps were worn back to front, their polo shirts done up to the top. One of them sat on the armchair opposite me, and the other went into the changing room. His friend asked for champagne, which was brought to him on a silver tray with a small terracotta bowl of Bombay mix. I was gutted.

'Hun, what time is the premiere tomorrow?' his partner asked from behind the changing room door.

'The reception starts at five; screening is at six,' he replied through a mouthful of the mix, which he washed down with a swig of his champagne.

'We don't want to arrive too early, though.'

'But I don't want to miss seeing Paul.'

'Remind me, what's he been in again?'

His friend turned and offered me some Bombay mix.

'What's that programme called that we all binge-watched in lockdown?'

'Ermmmm, I'm not sure,' I said, picking up a dried, crusty green pea with my thumb and forefinger.

'Paul Mescal and Daisy whatsherface—lots of sex scenes.'

'*Normal People*,' Kai shouted from behind his dressing room door.

'Thank you, changing room one,' he shouted out to his companion. '*Normal People*.'

'And what's this one about?' his friend said from changing room two.

'Something to do with him going on some holiday with a kid. I think it's a bit dark. He's battling addiction and stuff.'

'God, can't we see something fun for a change?' his friend shouted back. 'All this doom and gloom isn't good for my complexion.'

Kai opened the door, and I lifted my sunnies. I had to admit it: he looked pretty damn gorgeous.

'Wow,' my new friend said, gulping more of his champagne.

His friend opened his door, wearing just his boxers and showing off a hairless, toned six-pack.

'Don't mind me,' he said, looking directly at me, then at Kai. 'Oooo, yes, that's very nice.'

'How does it feel, sir?' Georgina said, entering the room and making it feel like some weird fetish party and not a changing room.

'How much is it?' Kai said.

'£995,' Georgina said. 'Adjustments are complimentary.'

I watched Kai's Adam's apple move up and down.

'Darling, what do you think?' he beamed at me.

I could barely see a thing through my sunglasses.

'I think it's...nice.'

'She hates it,' Kai said to Georgina, flouncing back into the dressing room. The bolt slammed shut across the back of the door. Georgina glared at me, and my new friend turned his back. His friend returned to his changing room.

Five minutes later, we were back on the street. Once we'd turned the corner, Kai burst out laughing.

'I can't believe you turned down the champagne,' he said.

'I didn't know how much it cost,' I protested.

'It's complimentary, you idiot,' he said, slinging his arm around my shoulders.

'Oh, is that for everyone, or special treatment for Georgina's VIP guests?' I said, letting my sarcasm hang.

'Everyone, you idiot. You gotta admit she was very—'

'Sexy?' I said.

'Striking,' Kai offered.

I raised my eyes. Kai was a flirt. He knew it; I knew it.

'You looked good in that suit,' I said.

'I know,' Kai said. 'Shame we haven't got a premiere to go to.'

But the one thing I did have was my surprise date story ready for Poppy on Monday.

CHAPTER 3

My Saturday nights were usually spent sprawled out on my sofa in my pjs, eating nachos with salsa, watching old episodes of *Friends*, and texting with Kai. Tonight was no different.

Kai: *You forgot to tell me about your 'Pretty Woman' moment drinking cocktails.*

Eve: *Are you suggesting I work as an escort in my spare time?*

Kai: *You need to improve your dress sense if you're considering a career change.*

I liked it with a laughing emoji.

Kai: *Want to go for a stale, cold, overpriced pizza at that place in Battersea Park tomorrow?*

I replied with a thumbs-up emoji.

Kai: *Why are you only communicating with emojis?*

I replied with another thumbs up, then turned my notifications off. When Kai was this bored, he didn't stop, and it was the episode where Joey speaks French—my favourite episode.

I met Kai at Sloane Square underground station at the top of Kings Road, otherwise known as Glamour Central. It wasn't the sort of place I usually hung out because the shops and restaurants catered only to the wealthy, but you were almost guaranteed to see someone famous as long as you could recognise them. Despite it being November, it was a warm and sunny day. The world's weather seemed pretty crazy lately, and while I didn't support throwing paint at people in posh hotels, I did think maybe the train couple and their accomplices, Max and Liv, might be onto something.

I had overdressed in jeans and a hoodie because I never trusted the forecast, especially when it didn't make sense. Also, Kai wouldn't be able to convince me to do more pretend pretentious shopping dressed like this. Although, when I saw him, I realised posh shopping wasn't in his day plan.

'Are you auditioning for a part in a pasta sauce advert?' I said as he appeared at the top of the escalators, wearing denim dungarees, a red and white striped tee shirt, and black Doc Martens.

'I see you got dressed in the dark this morning?' he said.

'Touché,' I said.

'I thought you'd like the European vibe—as you're of Maltese decent.'

I laughed. Kai loved to bring up the fact that my grandmother, Nanna Sultana, was from Malta, which made me a quarter Maltese. I'd never met her or even been to Malta, but when I was growing up, my dad used to joke that this was why I loved Maltesers chocolate. I believed him at first, but then I tried a sultana and was nearly sick.

'Pass me your phone,' Kai said. I did as I was told, and he typed in my pin.

'Hey, how come you know my pin?'

'I don't know your pin. I know you.'

'I'd forget it if it wasn't 1234,' I said sulkily. 'So, why are you dressed like an Italian?'

'I am dressed like a European, which is what I was until the government stripped me of my identity. But they can't stop me from seeing the world.'

'Where are you off to?'

'Who knows, one day I might just decide to leave grey, crime-ridden London behind.'

'Send me a postcard when you get there,' I said.

'Sure thing. I'll address it to the girl who lives in a tiny corner of the planet. Open brackets, you'll find her watching TV, close brackets,' Kai said.

'Very funny, haha. One of these days, I'm going to surprise you and call you from the Caribbean, telling you I'm selling coconut water on the beach,' I said.

Kai laughed. 'I won't hold my breath. Don't want to die young,' Kai said, handing me back my phone. 'Email address?' I typed it into the screen. 'Right, you're all set. Follow me.'

He led me around the corner to several green and white bikes parked on the pavement. He told me to scan the app on my phone to unlock it.

'What are you doing? I can't ride one of those,' I said.

Kai laughed. 'Don't be boring, Eva Diva,' he said, knowing this would trigger my adventurous side.

Five minutes later, I was whizzing over Albert Bridge (the prettiest bridge in London, in my opinion) and heading towards Battersea Park. That's another thing: Kai always got me to do things and go places I wouldn't otherwise do and go. I always complained, but annoyingly, he was usually right, and I enjoyed whatever it was he'd persuaded me to do. Sometimes, I thought he knew me better than I did.

When we got to the park, Kai said he wanted to go to the children's zoo for petting therapy and visit the sacred gold Peace Pagoda for some inner peace.

'I need to eat first; otherwise, my rumbling stomach will ruin any peace you're seeking,' I said.

'You're being bossy,' he said.

'If I eat, my bossiness will evaporate,' I said, which got me my own way for a change.

We found an outside table at the pizza cafe, and Kai sat down, closed his eyes, and lifted his face to the sun. His leg started jigging up and down. An affliction he had that meant he couldn't sit still.

'Can you go order? I need to top up my tan,' Kai said.

'You're doing your leg thing?'

'That doesn't affect my sunbathing.'

'Just try and sit still for thirty seconds.'

'Stillness is for the idle,' he said, switching legs.

'Shall we split a Margherita?' I said.

'I thought you were hungry?'

'I am, but I'm also poor, and I want ice cream for afters.'

'Okay, but get extra mushrooms, peppers, and sweetcorn?' Kai said.

'So you want a green feast?'

'Fine, but don't tell anyone I eat vegetarian food.'

I stood up, and it was at that moment I heard someone calling my name. I spun around and saw Poppy waving madly at me. She was holding a lead with a ginger fluffy thing with four legs on the other end, jumping at her feet. My instincts told me to pretend I hadn't seen her. I looked like I was homeless, and Kai looked ridiculous. She also might ask me about my surprise date in front of Kai, who definitely wouldn't play along or worse still, she might think Kai was my date and ask him about the protest. But Kai didn't have a George Michael beard. All this was going through my head, but it was too late to plan my escape because I was staring right at her. I lifted my arm and waved in response.

'Who's that?' Kai said.

'No one.'

'It's a sad day when you start waving at nobody,' he said.

'Oh my God, Eve.' Poppy was now at our table. 'What are you doing here?'

I silently cursed Kai for indirectly making me dress like I was clearing out a garden shed.

'Oh, you know, just out in the park.' Poppy looked at Kai, who beamed at her like a demented cat. 'This is my friend, Kai, who is just about to go and order us a pizza.' I kicked Kai hard under the table. 'What about you?'

'Owwwww,' Kai said, getting up. 'What was that for?'

'Don't forget the extra toppings,' I said as he walked away, limping dramatically.

'I live around the corner, so I always walk Nevil here.'

'I didn't know you had a dog,' I said, bending down to scratch Nevil's ears so I could avoid eye contact with Poppy for a little bit longer.

'I didn't know you had friends who wore Doc Martens with long socks,' she laughed. 'Nevil's not mine; I borrow him sometimes.'

I carried on fussing over Nevil, trying to think up ways to make her leave before Kai came back.

'So, is Kai your new boyfriend?' she said, her eyebrows knitting together.

'Oh my God, no,' I threw my head back and laughed. 'Kai? Absolutely not. I mean, no. Crikey, no way. He's not my type at all!'

Poppy's smile faded a little, like the sun had gone behind a cloud. She picked up the ginger fluff ball.

'You're cute,' I said to Nevil, reaching my hand out and getting a warm, sandpapery lick in return.

'So, who is he?' Poppy said, placing Nevil back down on the floor. 'You've never mentioned him before.'

I wanted to say, *'That's because you've never shown any interest in me or my life until this week.'* But instead I said something bad that I regretted for a very long time afterwards.

'He's just a family friend. A bit of an oddball, to be honest. I actually feel sorry for him and hang out with him, sort of as a favour to his mum. To give her a break. He can be quite awkward. Especially around strangers.'

'Ohhhhh, is he on the autistic spectrum?' Poppy whispered it like it was a swear word. 'Shame, he's very handsome.'

'Is he?' I said. 'I've known him for years; he's a bit eccentric, but that's not his fault,' I said, looking up and staring straight into Kai's eyes.

'Anyway, we need to go. See you on Monday,' Poppy said, scooping Nevil back up. 'Goodbye, Kai. Nice to meet you.' She spoke slowly, as if talking to a child and waved in his face.

I turned to Kai. His cheeks were red. His eyes glazed with a mix of sadness and confusion.

'Sorry, I'm such an embarrassment,' he said, throwing the pizza box on the table. 'Enjoy your lunch.' He pulled his jacket off the chair; the chair crashed to the ground with the force. Some of the other customers stopped what they were doing and stared over at us.

'Don't be like that,' I said. 'I didn't mean it. I can explain. Kai, come back.'

'I'm not hungry,' he shouted without turning back. 'Save some for your boyfriend.'

As I watched him walk into the distance, I sat down, feeling embarrassed and ashamed. I had a really horrible feeling in my stomach, and it didn't go away for a very long time.

I must have messaged Kai over fifty times that afternoon, alternating between texting and repeatedly calling, leaving voicemail after voicemail. It was harassment and borderline stalking, but I just needed him to let me explain. He might understand. He might even laugh at the fact that I'd actually had to make up fake dates to get my colleagues to like me. I tried one last time.

If I come posh window shopping with you next weekend, will you forgive me? (Laughing emoji.)

I waited thirty minutes. He didn't reply, so I went to bed. I'd lost my best and only real friend in the world. I was an awful person, and I felt really miserable about it.

On Monday morning, I dressed to match my mood in a pair of jogging bottoms, a loose-fit tee shirt, and hair up in a messy bun. I didn't even care about impressing Poppy today. I pushed my feet into my trainers and grabbed my denim jacket. I was late to work and didn't care about that either. When I arrived, I didn't apologise. Poppy was on the phone and didn't make eye contact. I sat at my desk, turned on my computer, and started reading the listeners' song requests from the weekend that had just passed. Our listeners couldn't grasp the fact the shows were pre-recorded and that we didn't sit there reading their emails all weekend. Bless them.

I'd suggested to Gary on more than one occasion that when asking for requests on air, we say they need to be emailed in advance, but he wasn't having it.

'That isn't how live radio works,' he said, sighing loudly.

'But we're not live,' I argued.

'Yes, but the listeners don't know that, do they.' He sighed louder.

'But—'

He didn't let me finish. 'Leave the programming to me and you concentrate on doing what you do best. Photocopying.'

'I—'

He put his hand up to silence me, and I walked away, which probably made him think he'd won. The alternative was stapling his hand to the table with the staple gun, which might have lost me my job and got me a restraining order. So, I didn't bring it up again. Instead, I replied to every email, apologising and telling them we'd play their request the following weekend to make up for it.

'Eva, you're late again.' Gary said, coming out of the studio.

I didn't feel now was the time to correct him again on my name, so I let it go.

'Sorry.'

'Right, two things. Firstly, we're doing the family panto ticket competition this morning, so I need you to call the studio just after the ten o'clock news, okay?' He didn't wait for my answer. 'You need to be excited and gushy when you win, okay? Not like last year when you acted like you'd won a funeral for your granny,' he carried on before I could respond. 'The answer to the question is 'donkey,' okay? What's the answer?'

'Donkey.'

'And remind me of your name again? Only kidding,' he said. 'Don't let me down, Eva—you'll break my little girl's heart if you do.'

'It's Eve.'

'Actually, I'm gonna call you Sandra, okay, and can you change your voice a bit? Don't want anyone to recognise your voice after your brilliant crime interview on Friday.'

I went to speak, but he interrupted.

'But don't go full-on Essex on me, cos we're a local station. Maybe channel your inner Posh Spice. Make our listeners think we're high-end, okay?'

'She's not actually posh,' I said. He ignored me and started looking at his phone. 'What's the other thing?' I said. He looked at me blankly. 'You said there were two things.'

'Oh, yeah, the police want you to call them about the protest at The East.'

My legs felt like jelly as I stumbled into the kitchen to make a coffee. I say kitchen, but really, it was a cupboard with a worktop that supported a tiny fridge big enough for a pint of milk and a couple of cans of Coke. There was also a grubby kettle and a microwave alive with remnants of Gary's daily Greggs steak bake. I had never been in trouble with the police before and I felt guilty already. Poppy poked her head in.

'Morning.'

'Hi,' I said, cupping my hands around my mug, scalding my hands in the process.

'So funny seeing you at the park yesterday,' Poppy said.

'Yeah.'

'And I was kicking myself after I left cos I didn't ask you.'

'About?' I looked at her blankly.

'Your surprise date? Where did you go?'

'Ohhhhhhh yeah, we went to a film premiere.' I tried to add some enthusiasm to my voice.

'Really?' Poppy gushed. 'What film?'

'One with Paul Mescal. It was good, but a bit dark—about addiction and stuff.'

'How come you got to go to that? Is this new man of yours an actor or something?'

Stupidly, I hadn't prepared an answer to this question, which was an obvious one if I'd thought about it.

'He's a photographer,' I said. 'Got me in on a press pass,' I silently congratulated myself on my quick creative thinking.

'That's so cool,' Poppy said. I could almost see her face turn green with envy. As she turned her back on me to make herself a tea, I made a mental note to put some thought into my boyfriend's back story so I'd be ready for Poppy's questions next time.

'Gary wants me to win the panto tickets again, so I need caffeine,' I said, changing the subject.

'Good luck,' she said, sounding a bit irritated.

I waited at my desk. My stomach felt like I'd swallowed ten ice cubes, and the coffee wasn't touching the sides. At ten o'clock, I dialled the studio number.

'Hold the line, please, caller,' Gary said. I put my phone on speaker and placed it on my desk.

'That was *Take That* with their nineties hit 'Relight My Fire.' Talking of lighting fires, it's that time of year when our thoughts turn to Christmas, and that means,' he did a dramatic pause. 'It's pantomime season. Oh no, it isn't; oh yes, it is. *SFX: Fog Horn*. It's behind you, *SFX: Fog Horn again*— only it's not, because it's in front of you.' Gary laughed at his own joke. 'As always, our friends at The Palace Theatre have offered us a family ticket to see their festive production, which this year is—drumroll please... *SFX: Drum roll. Shrek the Musical. SFX: clapping and cheering.* The prize includes a ticket for two adults and two children, a programme and four ice creams. Wow—and this is all thanks to our friends at Best Gig Tickets. First on the line, we have Sandra. Hello Sandra.'

'Hello.'

'And where are you from, my love?'

'Hammersmith.'

'Hammersmith? We're practically neighbours!' His laugh was grating. 'Can you come a bit closer to your phone, please, Sandra?'

'Is that better?'

'Perfect. Now, are you ready? Don't be nervous.'

'I'm ready.'

'What is the Donkey in *Shrek* called? *SFX: Loud ticking clock.* 'Take your time, Sandra; you have thirty seconds to answer before we move on to our next caller.'

'Ooooo, I think I know,' I said with as much enthusiasm as I could manage. 'Is it, is it—Donkey?'

SFX: Celebration horn played in my ear.

'Congratulations, Sandra from Hammersmith. You and your family are going to see *Shrek* this Christmas, and it's all thanks to our friends at Best Gig Tickets. How do you feel?'

'Brilliant. Thank you very much.' I tried to add some variety to my tone, but my heart was heavy with fear. All I could think about was what I was going to say to the police and how I wished Kai would speak to me because he'd know what to do.

'So, who are you going to take with you?'

'My two girls.'

'Ahhh, now that's lovely. Are they there with you now?'

I glared at Gary through the studio window.

No, of course, they're not because I don't have any children, as you well know, and I am currently staring at you through the studio window. Plus, most children are at school at ten a.m. on a Monday morning. 'No, I'm at work.'

'And what is it that you do, Sandra?'

I glared at him again. What the hell was he playing at?

'I work at Tescos,' I paused. 'I'm on my break.'

'Well, tell your boss you're going to need an afternoon off from scanning the turkeys because you are our pantomime winner.'

SFX: More celebration horns blasted into my ear.

'I'm sure you'll have a brilliant time, and I hope your girls love *Shrek* as much as we do here at Thames FM. And now, we have a song from the show itself. "One Love",' by Antonio Banderas.'

'God, I hate this song,' Gary said, coming out of the studio and putting his fingers in his mouth, pretending to vomit. 'Better than last year, but your enthusiasm still needs work,' he said.

I didn't care what he thought, and I didn't respond. He went outside for a fag.

Poppy was quiet, head down, not talking. She stayed like this for the rest of the morning. It felt like I'd done something wrong, but I wasn't sure what. Was she jealous of my cool new boyfriend? Or had she found out what I'd done?

When Gary went to get his steak bake, I wheeled my chair over to her desk.

'Are you okay?' I said.

'Yeah, just busy.'

41

'Do you want a cup of tea?'

'No thanks.'

Poppy never turned down a cup of tea.

'You'd tell me if I'd done something to upset you, wouldn't you?' I said, cringing at how needy I sounded but desperately wanting to know she still liked me.

'It's nothing you've done. Not directly, anyway.'

'Phew,' I said, but the silence still hung between us. She stopped typing and looked at me.

'I know you didn't have a choice, but it really annoys me that Gary does that every year. Takes the prizes and makes you pretend to be the winner. It's not like he can't afford to take his kids to the pantomime.'

This was true, but Gary was also the boss.

'I'm sorry, you're right. I hate doing it,' I mumbled, feeling like I was five years old and was being told off in front of the entire class.

'It's not your fault,' Poppy said. We sat in silence for a while; then, she seemed to snap out of it. 'Ignore me. I'm just being grumpy. Tell me more about your handsome photographer. How did you meet him again?'

'On the train,' I said, which was as close to the truth as I could make it.

Detective Inspector Michaela Andrews called me again that afternoon and invited me to go to the police station to give a statement. Although 'invited' makes it sound like it was a nice thing and that I had a choice. She wasn't very friendly on the phone and said, 'When can you come in?' not 'Would you be able to come in?' We agreed on nine a.m. the next day, which would mean I'd be late for work again, but seeing as this was all Gary's fault anyway, he couldn't exactly complain, and I just wanted it done and over with.

That night, I struggled to sleep. *Should I tell the police I'd followed the protesters to The East or that I was in the bar drinking alone?* Both options made me look bad, but neither was illegal. Well, maybe the following one was, but only if I had a motive—which I didn't. I got up and made a cup of camomile tea, which was disgusting but distracted me from my overthinking. I wished I'd never done the stupid interview with Gary, I wish I wasn't such a pushover, and I wish I'd never told him I'd been at The East that night. Why did I want to impress him and Poppy anyway?

I must have dropped off eventually because I woke up feeling like I'd been hit over the head by a green ogre riding a donkey. I was sweating, and the sheets were tangled around my legs. I had a cold shower—not through choice, but because the boiler was playing up, and I was still shivering when I walked into the police station, clutching a hot chocolate from *Pret a Manger*. A luxury I couldn't afford but deemed necessary under the circumstances.

DI Andrews was small for a detective inspector. She had nice, smooth skin, small hands with short, well-kept nails, and not a hair out of place. She was wearing jeans and a jumper, which was a little disappointing, as I'd been expecting her to be in uniform.

'Good choice,' she said, nodding at my hot chocolate. 'We only have a vending machine here, and I wouldn't recommend it.'

I followed her down a bleak corridor reminiscent of school and into a small room comprising a table and two plastic chairs. The sign on the door read *Interview Room 1*. DI Andrews pulled out a chair for me to sit on.

'I just need to ask you some questions about the night in question.' I nodded. 'You are here voluntarily and as a witness, not a suspect.' I nodded again. 'This shouldn't take long, and just so you know, I'm recording this interview. She put a mobile phone on the table. 'Right, whenever you're ready, can you tell me everything that happened that night?'

I told her how I'd been sitting at the bar and noticed the couple with their friends. I said I'd ordered a cocktail and while I was waiting, I'd gone to the ladies and overheard a conversation which mentioned paint and getting arrested.

'Do you often go to bars alone?' DI Andrews said.

'I was waiting for someone.'

She nodded her head slowly.

'So you said in your radio interview that you saw the protestors throw the paint. Can you tell me about that?'

I dug my fingernails into my wrists, which were on my lap under the table.

'I didn't actually see it happen, just the aftermath.'

I was trying to be as vague as possible, but she kept pushing me to be more specific, which I appreciate was her job, but it made telling the truth, whilst not admitting I'd lied on live radio, extremely difficult.

'And what did the aftermath look like? From where you were?'

'Just as you would expect.'

'Such as?'

'Surprise, confusion,' I trailed off.

Next, she showed me some photographs and asked me to point out the train couple and their friends. I identified all four of them, which was when I realised they'd done this before. They were known to the police and had form. The glamorous public school act was exactly that.

'Can you confirm if you've been contacted by the protestors or threatened in any way as a result of your interview on the radio?'

'No. Why will they try and find me?' I said, slightly freaking out.

'Not necessarily, but possibly, if they think you're going to testify against them. I wouldn't worry too much, but obviously, let us know if anyone intimidates you.' I nodded. 'Great, I think we're done here. Unless there's anything else?'

'Will my identity be kept anonymous?'

'Yes, unless it goes to court, in which case you might be called as a witness.'

'I don't want to do that,' I said.

'If the judge feels it's necessary, you won't have a choice.' She breathed in through her teeth. 'Failure to attend can result in a fine or a prison sentence, although both would be unlikely.'

I thought she was joking at first, but the look on her little pixie face told me she wasn't.

'It's a crazy world when a witness can be threatened with prison simply for being in the wrong place at the wrong time,' I said.

'Just doing my job,' she said, opening the door wide, inviting me to leave.

I didn't want to go to work; I wanted to go home and curl up in bed. I hated Gary for making me feel like this. It was his fault I did the stupid interview, and now, because of him, I'd lied to the police and was expecting a brick through my window at any moment. I really needed Kai that day.

'You look smart,' Poppy said as I hung my coat up, catching the stand with my free hand.

'It's my police interview look,' I said.

'How was it?'

'I told them what I saw, and the inspector said I might have to go to court to give evidence.'

'Do they want to speak to your date? I assume he does actually have a name by the way.'

I hesitated.

'They said my statement was enough,' I said, ignoring the second half of the question.

'So when are we going to get to meet your mysterious photographer then?'

I shrugged. She was persistent; I'd give her that.

'It's a bit early for that.'

'At least tell me his name and show me a pic,' Poppy said. 'I'm excited for you.'

'Greg and I don't have one,' I said.

'Greg?' She smiled. 'As in sausage rolls?' I felt heat rise up my neck and into my face as I cursed myself for picking a name synonymous with pies and Gary's lunch. 'Ahhh, you're blushing. Does Greg have Facebook or Instagram?'

'I don't do social media,' I said, sounding hideously superior. 'But I would if I had enough friends,' I self-deprecated. 'I'll try and get a pic next time I see him,' I said, wondering why I kept saying things that made my life more difficult. How was I going to take a picture of a gorgeous man with a George Michael beard called Greg, who didn't exist?

CHAPTER 4

The thought of going home and being alone with my thoughts was as appealing as being trapped in a confined space with Gary, so I detoured to Barons Court station. As I made my way up, down, and along the grid of residential streets, I dragged my feet and sent telepathic messages to Kai to forgive me. I stared inside people's homes, all lit up and welcoming; it was like watching a live movie. Children played on living room floors, cats washed themselves on window sills, lights turned on and off, curtains were drawn, and televisions flickered. A man in his basement kitchen was cooking. All these people going about their everyday lives made me feel a longing to be part of something. I just didn't know what.

When I got to the station, I tapped in with my phone, slamming hard into the barriers when they didn't open. I reversed to try again and backed into the most delicious-smelling man I'd ever smelt, although I could count how many this was on one hand.

'Sorry,' we both said at the same time.

I looked at my phone accusingly, which was when I realised I'd been trying to tap in with my Boots loyalty app. I started frantically swiping, but my phone timed me out. I glared at the screen, which told me my face couldn't be recognised, and feeling increasingly flustered, I entered my wrong pin. I delved into my bag, rooted around for my purse and snagged a nail. As I studied the damage, people started shouting. I looked up at a queue of agitated people, slammed my debit card on the reader and when the barriers eventually opened, I burst through them like my life depended on it.

I apologised to Mr Aroma again and watched him walk down the stairs to the west-headed platform. I was headed north, but with nowhere to be and a lonely night ahead of me, I figured a small diversion couldn't do me any harm.

He was dressed impeccably. Kai would have loved his outfit. Straight cut, heavy faded black chinos, a pair of well-loved tan leather boots, and a grass-green linen shirt, finished off with a casual coffee-coloured blazer. He also had a bit of a stubble, which was when the idea came to me. Could Mr Aroma be my new boyfriend? His facial hair wasn't as defined as George Michael's, but it was enough to justify my 'he's got a George Michael beard' comment to Poppy. Obviously, I didn't mean 'literally become my boyfriend,' but if I could somehow take a picture of him, I could show Poppy, and it would give me a reason to message Kai again.

It was a simple enough plan and relatively easy to implement. I just needed to pretend I was on the phone, aim the camera, and get a perfect side-angle shot of this man's very impressive jawline. I could also take a full-body shot from behind to show the whole outfit. It was all going to be so easy, but just as I was about to take my first pic, the train came in, and the waiting crowd surged forward, so instead of a quick snap and run, I found myself on the same carriage as the nice smelling man, going the opposite way to home, obsessing about how to get a photograph.

I stood with my back to the doors, confident he hadn't spotted me, or if he had, he hadn't registered I was the stupid cow who had got stuck at the barriers. I managed to position myself for the perfect shot, but this time, just as I was about to take my picture, a bald man holding a Subway food bag stood right in front of me. All I managed to get was a close-up of a meatball marinara and a shiny head, reminding me I hadn't eaten all day—the sub, not his head.

The smell of fast food filled the carriage. Using both hands, he proceeded to demolish his food like a locust. He wiped the grease off his chin with his sleeve. It was gross and pretty inconsiderate and the sort of thing I saw day in, day out on the tube. I couldn't think of a more unpleasant place to eat. Kai had read me an article once about how no food or drink is allowed on public transport in Japan. Apparently, it's frowned upon to even talk loudly, and the playing of music is banned. The article asked the question: *Are the Japanese repressed or civilised?* Kai loved stuff like this and it led to the type of conversations I only ever had with him. It made me miss him even more. In my current predicament, the no-eating rule could have helped, and the no-talking would mean I wouldn't be in this predicament, but then again, earwigging was my favourite pastime.

The train was getting busier with each stop, and as I travelled further away from home, I decided I needed to get off; otherwise, I was going to end up at Heathrow Airport. As it pulled into Turnham Green, I got up to leave, and so, too, did Mr Aroma. My mission was back on; all I had to do was follow him, and for the second time in a week, I found myself following a stranger.

Two roads later, I watched him disappear into a pretty Victorian terrace house. It had a space-blue front door and shutters at the windows. If I had to pick a house that belonged to this man—with his cool clothes and delicious aftershave—this would be it. It was picture-perfect, and so was he, but my mission had failed.

I headed back to the tube station, deflated. The only positive being I'd managed to shorten my evening. The temperature had dropped dramatically, so I went to the platform waiting room. The only other person was a woman crying into her phone.

'I know it was the right thing to do,' she sniffed, wiping her nose with the back of her hand. 'He was in so much pain.' She dabbed her eyes and looked down at the floor, rolling her feet back and forth under the bench. 'I swear to God, if I find out who did it, I'm gonna slash their tyres and key their stupid f-ing car,' she paused, 'and I don't care if I get arrested.' She looked up and saw me staring at her. I gave her a sympathetic smile. 'No, I'm at the station. I left the basket at the vets. I couldn't bear to take it home empty. I told them to donate it.' She sniffed again. 'Yeah, okay. Will you come to the funeral?' Another pause. 'Just in the garden.' Pause. 'Okay, I'll text you when I'm back.' She ended the call.

'My cat got run over,' she said.

'Oh, I'm sorry,' I said. 'What was its name?'

'Louey.'

I smiled.

'That's a nice name.'

'He was an ugly little thing, and he hated me, but I loved him.'

Fortunately, I was saved from having to come up with an appropriate response to this because the train came in.

When I did eventually get home, I opened the fridge and stared inside, hoping a magic fairy had left me a risotto or a pizza. But all that was on offer was a half can of sweetcorn, a lump of crusty cheese, and the out-of-date lasagne and green beans. I made cheese on toast, squirted a dollop of salad cream in the middle, and sat down in front of the TV, hoping an episode of *Friends* would cheer me up. But it was *'The One With the Invitation,'* which everybody knows is the worst one, so my mood flatlined.

Another restless night meant another morning where I overslept which meant another day where I was late for work.

I arrived out of breath, hair unwashed, and wearing a sweatshirt with a large coffee stain in the middle.

'Sorry, I'm late.'

'It's fine; just breeze in whenever it suits you. It's not like you get paid to be here or anything,' Gary said.

'Ignore him. He's in a bad mood,' Poppy said.

'I'm in a bad mood because the staff treat this place like it's...'

'Sorry, but my cat died,' I said.

'Oh no,' Poppy said, 'I didn't know you had a cat.'

'He got run over, and I had to take him to the vets to be put down. That's why I'm late.'

'You should have called to let us know,' Gary said, his voice softening a little.

'Sorry,' I said.

'What was his name?' Poppy said.

'Louey,' I sniffed. 'He was an ugly little thing, and he hated me, but I loved him.'

It worked. Nothing more was said about my timekeeping, and Gary didn't bother me for the rest of the day.

That night, I decided it was time to turn over a new leaf. For the rest of the week, I made a big effort to get to work before nine, dress in clean clothes, and not tell any lies. I even invested in some hairbands and practised the high-swingy-Poppy-look, but it didn't suit my face or my hair, which was more mud-brown than Poppy's chestnut locks. My skin was pimple-free but pale; my eyes more dishwater grey than Mediterranean sea blue. If there was a face that represented England in November, mine was it.

I still hadn't heard from Kai, but I was confident he would forgive me eventually. The police hadn't contacted me again either, so it was time to put the whole incident behind me and move on. What had happened that night had been a momentary lapse of judgement, and I'd learnt my lesson. The only remaining issue was my new boyfriend Greg, who, as far as Poppy was concerned, was still very much a part of my life. It was because of him that Poppy and me had become proper friends, and she'd been making such an effort. She'd even bought me a coffee a couple of times from the Good Cafe. Having a cool boyfriend had elevated my status, so I didn't want to just tell her it was over. Also, with Kai still ignoring me, Poppy was my only friend.

Poppy talked to me about 'Greg the photographer' more than anything else, which meant no matter how hard I tried, the 'no more lying' resolution was hard to stick to. I referred to my notes daily, sometimes hourly, to make sure I didn't slip up. So far, I'd told her he was divorced, lived in Chiswick, went away for business quite a lot, and liked to surprise me by taking me to new places. On my evening commute, I looked for people who were dressed up and travelling in pairs; then I'd sit as close to them as possible and listen to their conversations, noting down where they were going and what they were doing. This gave me new and exciting dates to tell Poppy about the next day. For example, the other night, I'd heard two guys discussing a restaurant called The Place, which was always fully booked. When I got home, I googled the restaurant, downloaded the menu, and the next day, described my meal in great detail to Poppy.

'The food was amazing. Quite pricey, but Greg put it on expenses.'

'I can't believe you managed to get a table. I've been trying for over a year to go there—apparently, Ed Sheeran went there the other week,' Poppy said. I inwardly gloated that Poppy had inadvertently added a bit of showbiz glamour to my story.

'Really?' I said. 'I thought I recognised some people in there, but I'm useless with names and didn't want to embarrass myself.' I threw my head back and laughed. Poppy joined in.

'You'd have recognised Ed, though. Reddy blond hair, guitar, bit scruffy?' Poppy said.

'No, I don't think he was there.' I laughed freely.

Sometimes, I would go past my stop and find myself getting caught in rush hour, trying to get back across London, but it was worth it for the variety of dates I'd told Poppy about. Now Poppy was a real friend; she'd started asking me more intimate questions, making me uncomfortable. She found it hilarious.

'So...have you slept together yet?'

I felt the heat rise in my cheeks.

'You can't ask me that!'

'Oh, don't be such a prude. What's the big deal?' She winked at me. 'C'mon, tell me everything.'

'It's private,' I said.

'I'll take that as a yes then,' she said, raising her eyebrows and smirking.

I briefly considered describing a made-up sex life with Greg but decided that was a step too far. My lack of actual experience would almost definitely give me away, so I just accepted Poppy thinking I was a prude. It was less risky that way.

Poppy kept asking me to show her a photo and my excuses were beginning to sound flakey—even to me.

'C'mon, you must have a photo. He's a photographer, isn't he?'

'Yesssss, which means he's behind the lens, not in front of it,' I said.

'I'm not asking for an official portrait; I just want to see what he looks like.'

'I think he's worried about his ex-wife knowing he's met someone,' I said, wishing Poppy would stop going on and we could change the subject.

'A selfie will do—no need for anything pornographic,' Poppy said, laughing. 'I'm beginning to think you've made him up.' I laughed back. 'I mean, he sounds too good to be true, this new man of yours, and you seem determined to keep him hidden.'

'Okay. I'll take one next time I see him,' I said.

'Promise?' she said.

'Promise.'

I hadn't seen Mr Aroma or anyone that fitted the bill since that day, despite going back to Barons Court station at the same time several times, hoping to see him, but I had come up with a plan. I was going to go back to the house in Turnham Green with the blue door and do a stakeout. It was the only way to get Poppy off my case. She was getting suspicious, so I had no other choice.

I calculated that I needed to get to Turnham Green by seven a.m. if I was to catch him leaving for work. This meant I needed to leave my flat at six a.m., which would give me an hour to watch the pretty house with the blue door before I needed to leave for work. It was going to be cold and dark, and I didn't yet have a plan for how I was actually going to take the photo, but I needed to prove to Poppy that my boyfriend was as real and as gorgeous as I said he was.

I admit my behaviour had become a bit extreme over recent weeks, but I'd been in a tailspin since falling out with Kai. The way I saw it, I was keeping myself busy and enjoying some attention thanks to my pretend life. It was no different to when a child has an imaginary friend. People find it endearing, especially if the child doesn't have siblings. It stops them from being lonely and my imaginary life was doing this for me, too. I was an adult orphan and an only child.

My alarm woke me up, and as tempted as I was to hit the snooze button and forget all about my plan, I felt I'd committed, even if it was only to myself.

I brushed my teeth to Taylor Swift on Radio 1. I used to feel guilty when I didn't listen to Thames FM in the mornings, but I couldn't stomach Gary's voice being the first one I heard each day, and it's not like he knew who I brushed my teeth to. I looked in the mirror, relieved I was having a good hair day.

To give me confidence, I'd dressed up a bit. I was wearing my black jeans from Oxfam, a white shirt, and a rusty-red, chunky knit sleeveless sweater I'd bought from eBay. I pulled on my black boots instead of my trainers and put on some mascara and a deep reddy-pink lipstick that I also rubbed onto my cheeks.

It was a really nice time of day to be up and about. The streets were quiet except for a few dog walkers encouraging their pets to do their business, a couple of fluorescent joggers, and a cafe owner sweeping the steps in preparation for the morning rush hour. I resisted the urge to buy a coffee, deciding to wait until I was at Turnham Green. It was quite mild for late November, but the air felt damp. It was the kind of weather that made your hair go frizzy but not bad enough for an umbrella, so my good hair day was already over.

I got a seat on the tube and settled down in a corner seat, already regretting fighting my caffeine urge. I could be waiting for Mr Aroma for a long time, and as Turnham Green was suburbia, I couldn't be sure the cafes would even be open yet. My stakeout had the potential to be a miserable experience.

At Hammersmith, the train announced it would be waiting a few minutes on the platform until its scheduled departure time. I was anxious to get moving because I didn't want to miss my man. Especially now that I'd made all this effort. I strained my neck to look at the digital clock on the platform, and that's when I saw them: Poppy and Gary together on the opposite platform. I slunk down low in my seat, whipped my sunglasses out of my bag, and pushed them quickly onto my face. How would I explain where I was going at this time of the morning? It wasn't until we had fully left the station that my breathing returned to normal. I stopped to consider why they were together so early in the morning. I imagined several reasons, including some I didn't want to think about. However, none of them were right.

CHAPTER 5

I tucked my newly washed hair into my oversized woolly hat and joined a queue of two at a small cafe called *Piccolos* outside Turnham Green station. Having bought an extremely strong latte, I made my way to the road where I'd seen Mr Aroma go into the house. When I had the front door in sight, I looked around for somewhere to wait. It needed to be somewhere that allowed me to see the house but not look conspicuous. It wasn't a busy enough road for a bus stop, and there were no trees or hedges, so I settled on a skip outside a house on the opposite side of the street. I stood behind it and peered over an old oven, trying not to stare at the congealed grease.

While I waited, I tested out my phone camera, making sure I was near enough. I adjusted the settings and practised zooming in and out while keeping an eye out for my target. I was just finishing the dregs of my coffee when a man wearing a yellow hard hat approached me.

'Morning. Are you lost?'

He had an Eastern European accent, and I guessed he was Polish because he sounded exactly like my neighbour, Rafal, who liked to walk his cat on a lead.

'No. I'm just waiting for someone.'

'By my skip?'

'Sorry,' I said, apologising for nothing being a lifelong affliction of mine.

'Not a problem,' he said, 'but mind yourself, okay?' He lifted a large plank of wood out of the skip and leant it against the top. 'A wheelbarrow is coming.'

I looked behind me and saw another man, also in a hard hat, running towards me at full speed. He was pushing a wheelbarrow caked in dried concrete and full of rubble. I moved out of the way, but not quickly enough to avoid being engulfed by a dust cloud, temporarily blocking my vision. I walked away, wiping my eyes and coughing. Then, through the fog, the blue door opened and, like a mirage, out walked Mr Aroma, holding the hand of a small person.

He turned left and I followed on the opposite side of the street. It was difficult not to cough loudly because I felt like I'd swallowed the contents of a small brick. He looked as good as he had the first time I'd seen him. Today, he was wearing a knee-length navy coat, a university-style scarf, jeans, and a pair of retro Adidas trainers that even I could appreciate. This guy was one hell of a good dresser.

They turned left again at the bottom of the road. I crossed over and followed, still at a distance. I'd watched enough cop shows to know this was key to going unnoticed. I checked the time, I couldn't be late for work again, but also I couldn't leave empty handed. All I needed was one good photo. I momentarily considered explaining my predicament to Mr Aroma on the basis that maybe he was a nice guy and would just let me take his photograph, but I reconsidered after thinking about how I would explain my predicament.

Excuse me, but I wonder if you could help me? It's a long story, but I was wondering if I could take your photograph? I've told my friend, well, actually she's my colleague—and a friend now—that I have a boyfriend who looks a bit like you. I need to show her a picture to prove I haven't made him up, and I was thinking you could be my boyfriend? Not my actual boyfriend, just my pretend one? I really like your trainers, by the way...

I mean, if someone came up to me and asked to take a picture because I looked like their made-up girlfriend and they liked my dress sense, I would be a little freaked out. Although this scenario happening in reverse was extremely unlikely to ever happen.

A hospital-blue sign read *Western House Nursery and Primary School.* He went inside, following lots of small people clutching their grown-ups' hands. I stopped just outside the entrance and started reading the school noticeboard. The Christmas fair was coming up, new term dates had been confirmed, and donations for the school auction were now being sought. All I had to do now was wait for him to come back out. I bent down, tied, and retied my shoelaces, keeping an eye out for my target. I moved to the wall and sat, scrolling on my phone until I saw him. He was also scrolling, which gave me the perfect opportunity to set myself up unnoticed. I waited until he was closer, then stepped out in front of him, and—*click, click, click*—took several selfies of me, grinning, with him in the background. I got so close for the last two pics that I hoped it might even look like we actually knew each other. He stepped off the pavement and moved around me.

'I'm so sorry I didn't see you there,' I said, apologising for nothing again. Although I guess, in this instance, I was sorry for using him, even though he didn't know about it. The way I saw it, he'd just done a total stranger a small favour, and I comforted myself by believing good karma was sure to come his way.

I waited until he was out of sight, then checked the pics. They were good. I hadn't managed to get all of his outfit in, but they were good enough to show Poppy, and he even looked like he was kind of smiling in one.

I power walked back to the station, and it wasn't until I was back on the platform that I spotted him again waiting for a train. I took full advantage of my good luck and managed to get a full body shot for Kai, plus a few extra side profile shots for Poppy. He turned to look at me only once and I quickly looked away, then blended into the morning rush hour crowd. When the train arrived, I got on a different carriage—just to be on the safe side. I was smashing this undercover operation. Just call me Miss Marple.

I wasn't late for work—but I nearly was, so I didn't have time to go to The Really Good Cafe and buy Poppy her oat milk latte. I'd started doing this a couple of times a week because that's what friends do, but usually, I only bought Poppy one because they were nearly £4 each, and I could get a yellow sticker dinner for that.

'Morning,' I sang out to an empty office.

Neither Poppy nor Gary were there. I looked up at the studio, but the red 'recording' light was on, which meant it was a 'no-go' zone. Gary must be in the studio, and Poppy must be out at a client meeting or in the studio with Gary. This was when I remembered seeing them in the early hours.

Poppy came out first. She wasn't smiling and looked flustered. Gary followed her out, an unlit cigarette already hanging out of his mouth. He walked past my desk without making eye contact and went outside.

'Everything okay?' I said.

'Yes,' Poppy snapped. She sighed dramatically and put her jacket on. 'I'm going to get coffee.'

Many scenarios were running around my head. Had they had an argument? Had I interrupted something? Were they in a relationship? This last thought was particularly unpleasant and couldn't possibly be true. I made myself a cup of tea, sat at my desk, and waited. Gary came back in first, his cigarette breath polluting the office air.

'Has something happened?' I said.

'Was it you?' Gary said. 'Did you blow the whistle?'

'Blow the whistle?' I had no idea what he was talking about.

'Did you tell Bob about the pantomime tickets?'

'Who's Bob?' I said.

'Our chairman!' Gary spat the words out.

'I thought that was Robert.'

'Jesus, are you trying to wind me up because I'm not in the mood.'

I didn't reply straight away. I was confused. I didn't understand what I was being accused of, and when Gary was in this mood, I was too nervous to ask.

I have never even spoken to the chairman ever. He showed up once a year at Christmas with a tin of chocolates instead of a bonus and expected us to be grateful. That was as far as my relationship with him went. He probably didn't even know my name. Mind you, neither did Gary, and I worked with him every day.

The door opened, and Poppy came in carrying a coffee— just one. She put it on her desk, took her jacket off, and sat down without saying a word.

'She said it wasn't her,' Gary said.

'I told you,' Poppy said.

'So who was it then?' Gary said. I could see spittle coming out of his mouth.

I looked at Poppy, then at Gary, then back at Poppy. They both looked at me. I felt like I was on the film set of *Who Framed Roger Rabbit*—not the best film, but 'a classic' according to Kai.

'Someone told Bob about Gary using you to win the pantomime tickets for himself. We were both summoned here early this morning for a meeting,' Poppy said.

'Meeting? Is that what you call it? More like a rollicking!' Gary said.

'Apparently, if Ofcom finds out, the station will be fined,' Poppy said.

'And then heads will roll,' Gary said.

Heads will roll? Why was everyone talking in weird language?

'I told Bob it wasn't your idea,' Poppy said looking at me.

'There were no other callers,' Gary said. 'How would it have looked if we'd announced the competition and then no one called? I made an executive decision for the sake of the station's credibility. I couldn't care less about some stupid bloody pantomime. If I'd wanted to go that much, I'd just buy the bloody tickets.'

Poppy looked at me and raised her eyebrows.

'Bob has given us a warning,' Poppy said. I nodded. 'Obviously, we can't do anything like that again.' I nodded again.

Gary walked off into the studio. The recording light switched back on.

Poppy and I worked in silence. After a few minutes, I found the courage to ask.

'Why were you in the studio when I came in?'

'We were listening back to the call. Don't worry, Bob doesn't blame you.'

I was worried, though. As boring as my job was and as vile as Gary could be, I needed it, and since Poppy and me became friends, it was so much better. It would be typical if, after five years of wanting her to like me, I lost my job just as I had started to enjoy it, especially for something that wasn't even my fault.

'Who told him?' I said to Poppy. 'No one else knew.'

Poppy shrugged her shoulders, then started sipping her coffee, and reading something on her laptop.

When Gary went out for his next fag break, I stood up and leaned over my desk to hers.

'Guess what?' She looked up. 'I have a picture of Greg. Do you want to see it?'

'Sure.' She held out her hand for my phone. I passed it over, disappointed she hadn't leapt over her desk, especially considering what I had done to get it.

'He looks nice,' she said, passing back my phone. Literally, that was it. I almost told her the truth so she could appreciate the effort I'd gone to.

I'd sent the one with the full outfit to Kai with a witty comment: '*Saw this guy on the train and thought you'd appreciate his on-point outfit.*' It was unopened and unread. All that effort had been for nothing.

The atmosphere in the office was strained for the rest of the day, and I felt like I was in an episode of *The Traitors* with no one trusting anyone. I knew Poppy hadn't approved of Gary winning the tickets and using me, but she was the station manager who loved her job, and there was no way she'd risk the station getting into trouble. It wasn't Gary himself because why would he drop himself in it? Obviously, I knew it wasn't me either, but I also knew Gary thought it was me because I was the obvious culprit. I felt like I was fifteen again and back at school, being accused of cheating in the biology exam.

We had to sit in alphabetical order, and that meant I was next to Izzy Shepherd, who was the most popular girl in the school, and she wasn't too happy about it. I tried to become friends with Izzy when she first joined in Year Eight, but it became obvious very quickly that she only liked cool people, and nothing about me was cool.

The teacher told us we could start and demanded total silence. I started to read the paper and then watched as Izzy laid her forearm across her desk in an attempt to hide her answers from me. I wouldn't have cared that much, but she was taking up so much room that I barely had space to write. I moved my chair to the edge of the desk, which earned me a glare from the teacher and a loud *shhhhh*, which was way more distracting than my chair and caused everyone to look up. I tried to lay the question paper and the exam paper out in front of me, but there still wasn't room, and I remember panicking because everyone else was scribbling away like their life depended on it, and I'd barely finished writing my name.

'Can you move up a little bit, please?' I whispered to Izzy.

'Evelyn, pick up your papers and come and sit here, please,' the teacher said.

I tried to protest, but this got me more even glares and more tuts. Needless to say, I failed the exam and when I tried to explain to the teacher what happened, I was met with a finger on the lips. Before I handed over my exam results to my parents, I tried to explain to Mum what had happened.

'You need to grow up and take responsibility. You can't make excuses every time something doesn't go right in your life,' Mum said.

'But I didn't have any space to write; what was I supposed to do?'

'You should have put your hand up, and then the teacher could have sorted it out.'

'But we weren't allowed!' I said. 'Can't you just be on my side for once?'

'You're being silly. I'm not on anyone's side. It's not a football match.'

I called Kai and ranted down the phone to him for ten minutes. He didn't interrupt and only spoke when I stopped to pause for breath.

'Don't worry about it. Izzy may be a triple P, but she's dull as dish water.'

'What's triple P?' I said.

'Pretty, popular, and perfect.'

'Great,' I sighed.

'And I'd pick you over her any day,' Kai said.

'Thanks,' I sighed down the phone. 'I don't believe you, but I appreciate you saying that anyway.'

'Hey. I'm Team Eve, okay?'

'It's not much of a team. You're the only one in it,' I said.

I left on the dot at five p.m. and headed for Gloucester Road. It was a yellow sticker kind of day. I was tired from my early start and sick of Gary's accusatory glares. Despite the fact I had an empty weekend ahead of me, I was relieved it was Friday. I settled on some mushroom arancini and a bowl of chopped microwave-ready vegetables. They were just on the turn, but at 74p, it was a cheap way to get my five a day.

The train was relatively quiet until it pulled into South Kensington, and there was hardly any standing space on the platform. People waited five deep for the doors to open, which was typical for South Ken. Home of the Natural History Museum and the Science Museum—two of London's biggest and most iconic tourist attractions.

When I was in primary school, I'd been on trips to both museums, but neither of them since. I remembered sitting in a large room on the floor, eating my packed lunch, which was most likely a marmite sandwich, a bruised apple, and a soft digestive biscuit. The only other thing I remember was wishing I had Isobel Mathews's packed lunch because it was from Marks and Spencers and could have fed half the class.

The doors opened, and bodies forced their way onto the carriage. The noise level went up by several decibels and I found myself staring at the bottom—literally—of a man wearing Levi jeans hanging off his hips, revealing a pair of off-white Calvin Kleins. Three arms held on to the rail, their armpits directly above me. The doors closed, and the train pulled away; several student lanyards swung in my face, risking potential hypnosis.

'Guy the Gorilla was cool.'

'He was a dude.'

'That moon rock blew my mind, man. What the hell.'

I was sat next to a young guy who was chewing gum loudly. He had a large pair of earphones around his neck and was wearing the same student lanyard.

'Hey man, what's up?' one of the guys standing above him said.

'Leave it out.'

'C'mon, we were just kiddin. Don't be so sensitive, yeah.'

'Whatever. You're crap, mate.'

He pushed his headphones onto his ears, and a few stops later, his mates got off. As they pushed past him, one of them bent down towards him.

'Whatever your beef, turn off the dog and bone and write it out, yeah? Works for me every time. See you tomorrow bro.' He got off waving his phone in his hand. 'Ditch it, mate.'

Before going home, I went to a gift shop in Kings Cross station and bought a notebook. It had a silver dragonfly on the front. Not only was listening to other people giving me content for my nonexistent social life, it was also giving me life tips.

CHAPTER 6

The advice from the student to 'write out my beef' turned out to be pretty good. After the dry arancini and out of date vegetables, I turned my 'dog and bone' off and sat down with pen and paper. Turning my phone off wasn't a big deal; I could go days without getting a message from anyone, and since Kai had stopped communicating with me, I'd only had two messages. One from the dentist reminding me to book a check-up and one from Specsavers offering me a free hearing test. I replied, telling them I was thirty-two, not eighty-two, and to stick to what they knew best.

My writing therapy evolved into a letter to Kai, which was cathartic but made me feel guilty all over again. I wrote down things I would never say to him in real life, and the words spilt out of my pen so fast I could barely read my own writing. When I got to the end, a big fat teardrop fell on the page, washing away my name. It was like I was erasing myself from Kai's life.

Kai,

I'm writing you a letter you'll never read—about things you'll never know. I'm doing it as a kind of therapy (advice from a cool guy I overheard on a train.).

It's been a hell of a strange few weeks. Honestly, you wouldn't believe me if I told you. I don't think we've ever gone this long without speaking to each other since Year 7.

I know what I said was bad, and I'm really, really sorry. I want to be able to explain to you, cos then maybe you'd forgive me, but to do that you need to reply to my messages or call me. You're my best friend; you're the person I want to call when I've had a crappy day, the person I think of first when I get a yellow sticker bargain on a Charlie Bigham's fish pie—that's only happened once, but it was so good, and I knew you were excited for me. No one makes me laugh like you do, and honestly, I think of you as the brother I never had, and I couldn't ask for a better sibling.

I don't know why I said what I said. The lady you met in the park is Perfect Poppy from the office, who has finally started being my friend. When we saw her, I wanted her to think I was cool and that I hung out with cool people, and you must admit, you were dressed particularly badly that day (pasta advert—remember?) I know that shouldn't matter, and it really doesn't (to me), but I panicked because I'd told her I had a boyfriend (I don't, by the way), and I didn't want her to think he was you—not because I wouldn't want you to pretend to be my boyfriend, but because she would have started asking you awkward questions and then you would have blown my cover.

The thing is, I've got myself into a bit of a mess and I could really do with your advice to un-mess myself.

I know this probably doesn't make any sense, and as you're never gonna read this anyway, it doesn't really matter. I'm sorry I hurt your feelings. Please, please forgive me. I really miss you, and I really need you right now cos I know you'll tell me what to do.

*Love, Eve (your **best** friend) x*

I put the notebook in my bedside cabinet, lay down, and stared at the ceiling, listening to the world going on outside. How did people who lived in the countryside bear the silence and the darkness? I loved the noise of the city; it gave me comfort. Cars beeping their horns, police sirens, people, music, dogs barking. It made me feel less alone in what, lately, felt like a very lonely world.

I had lived in this flat all my life. It was on the first floor and had two bedrooms. Mine and what used to be my parents.' When they were alive, they never came into my room, and I never went into theirs. I still don't. The last time I did go in there was to sort their clothes and belongings, which I'd taken to the charity shop over several weeks. Dragging black bin liners down the stairs and carrying them along the street, my arms aching under the weight. It had felt like a pilgrimage. The only things I'd kept were their books, some paintings, and the furniture, so the flat looked pretty much the same as it did when I was growing up.

I'd made a few small changes to the lounge area—the only room that had any personality. I bought a bonsai tree for the table to bring harmony and peace and a rubber plant for wealth and happiness. I wasn't convinced either was working and, as a result, didn't recommend leaving life goals to plants. I hung some fairy lights around the mirror. I'd also invested in a couple of throws from Camden Market, which covered the two matching two-seater sofas. I'd bought a second-hand rug from Facebook Marketplace and, with the help of Kai, managed to lift up the elephant-heavy, solid oak coffee table and place it underneath. There was one photo up. It was of Kai and me at our school prom. He was wearing a red suit with a black shirt, looking like John Travolta. I was wearing a frilly yellow dress I'd bought from a charity shop. It wasn't my colour, and it was too small, but that night had been the highlight of my entire school life. I hadn't wanted to go and had negotiated with Kai to stay an hour.

'But what am I supposed to do if you end up dancing with Izzy Shepherd all night? I'm going to feel like a spare part,' I'd argued.

'I won't dance with Izzy Shepherd at all, let alone all night.' He laughed.

'I heard she fancies you,' I said.

'Well, I don't fancy her,'

'Yes, you do! You told me you thought she was pretty, remember?'

'She is pretty, but she's also boring. I'd much rather spend the night with my best friend.'

'Really?'

'Really, and anyway, who's to say you're not going to be whisked off your feet by—' Kai paused.

'Surely you can think of someone who'd consider dancing with me?' I said.

'Barry,' Kai said.

'Barry the Sheep?' I said. 'Is that all you can come up with?'

Kai swallowed a laugh. 'He's not that bad. You're being mean.'

'He literally looks like a sheep,' I said.

'Okay, he has sheep-like features, but what's wrong with that? Sheep are nice,' Kai said.

'It would never work. I don't like the countryside, it's too dark.'

'Please come. You are literally in every school memory I have. You have to be there.'

'Fine. One hour max.'

'Deal—but I bet you stay longer,' Kai said.

It had been such a fun night. I stayed until the end, and Kai and me danced together non-stop. Stupid, idiotic dancing that meant neither Izzy nor Barry came anywhere near us. In the breaks, we'd queued for the photo booth, choosing a different prop each time, and this picture was my favourite. Me with a fake moustache, Kai with Elton John glasses.

I'd made the kitchen more spacious by getting rid of the small extendable table, which we'd only ever used at Christmas and birthdays. I didn't want to be reminded of these occasions and how little I'd had in common with my parents.

We hadn't been an unhappy family, just a small one, and I had lived my life very separately from them. When I was at school, I made my breakfast, left the house, came home, went straight to my room, ate whatever I could be bothered to cook, and then went to bed. My parents lived alongside me, not with me. At the weekends, I always used to hang out with Kai. My parents never asked me where I was, who I was with, or what time I was coming back, and I never told them. They didn't come to parents' evenings, sports days, certificate assemblies, or school productions, not even when I was the narrator. They just weren't those types of parents.

The kitchen was functional and clean; Mum had been meticulous in her cleaning. The bathroom was blue. Blue floor tiles, blue walls, silver fixtures, and fittings. I'd actually felt more lonely living with my parents than I did living on my own. But I missed having people in my life who cared about me, which I think they did in their own way.

I woke up fully clothed. It was six a.m. on Saturday morning. I had a splitting headache and the whole weekend ahead of me with nothing to do, nowhere to go, and no one to see. It wasn't a nice feeling.

I took two paracetamols, had a bath, and then dressed in joggers and a jumper. I went to the 24/7 supermarket and bought some eggs, a tin of baked beans, and a loaf of bread. I cooked breakfast, washed, dried, and put away the dishes. It was eight-thirty in the morning, and I was already staring out of the window, wondering what Kai was doing.

I typed out a message.

Eve: *Am I forgiven yet?*

I deleted it.

After a couple of hours of watching Saturday morning kids' TV and drinking more cups of coffee than I should, I went out, taking my new notebook with me. I wandered around Kings Cross station, walking aimlessly into shops and back out again. At the top of the escalators was the communal cafe space, and I found a table to do some people-watching. On the table next to me were two women, both wearing a lot of jewellery and clutching expensive-looking handbags. Kai would have identified the brand within seconds, but I couldn't even tell my Primark from my Chanel. One of the ladies had an extremely large cleavage on display, and I worried she might spill out of her top if she so much as breathed.

'Oh my God, that restaurant—it was honestly some of the best food I've ever had,' her Mancunian accent was loud but friendly. 'It was actually worth coming South for.'

'We spent so much,' her friend said. 'My nan would've had a heart attack if she knew how much it cost.' She twirled her hair around her finger. 'Last night, Brasserie on the Hill, today, a Tesco's meal deal.'

They both cackled loudly.

'That starter was honestly to die for. I didn't even know what a scallop was!'

There were more hysterics.

'Oh my God, the truffle and parmesan.'

'And what was it again? Oh yeah, pumpkin and hazelnut. How do they come up with these dishes?'

'I can't believe you ordered the pigeon!' She mimicked a bird flapping its wings.

'It's not like the pigeon you see on the streets!'

'Course it is—and they're minging.'

'Well, you had the duck—quack quack.'

More laughter.

'I would have quite happily just had the dessert, though, wouldn't you? I mean, I thought I was gonna have an orgasm.'

'Stop it.'

'I mean it. Tell me you didn't get a tingling down there in your lady garden when you tasted that chocolate?'

A train announcement drowned out their laughter.

'That's us.' They got up, falling over each other in their high heels and headed for the escalators. I wrote down the name of the restaurant and all the dishes they'd talked about. Kai would think this whole conversation was hilarious. He was missing out on some really fun stories by ignoring me.

Before heading home, I went to the outdoor food market and bought some falafel and baklava, then sat in Lewis Cubitt Square behind the station. Another one of my favourite places to people-watch. The water fountain feature was half-heartedly doing its best, and a couple of kids were being pulled backwards by their anorak hoods as they attempted to run towards the water. I saw a group of people wearing the same black hoodie, with the words *Funky Choir* written on the back in large orange letters. They were singing as they walked.

Crossing the square, there was another group following a lady carrying a flag on a stick. She was telling them about the Kings Cross fire in 1987. She commanded them to follow her to the memorial.

73

Maybe I should join a group and make some new friends. Usually, I was perfectly happy with my own company, but not having Kai around was making me really miserable. I belonged nowhere and had no one.

A young couple walked past me. He was pushing a pushchair. They sat down on a bench opposite. The child started arching his back, desperate to get out and explore the fountain, but they weren't watching. I knew what they were doing from their position. I saw it on the underground day in day out. Humped back, eyes down, head tilted towards the ground. I watched. How long would it be until they lifted their heads from their phones and set their son free to play and chase pigeons like the other children? People watching had made me realise how many people were more interested in other people's lives than they were in their own.

I spent the afternoon struggling to lift myself out of my mood, ignoring the doorbell twice. My neighbour, who was never in, had an ASOS addiction, and I was on first-name terms with her delivery courier, but I wasn't in the mood to make small talk with him today. I felt bad after chatting to him for so long last time because he had eventually told me he had a delivery quota and barely had time to pee. I offered him the use of my loo after realising he must have felt sorry for me.

On Sunday morning, I made the stupid mistake of going to the Natural History Museum. Only a tourist would think this was a good thing to do on a Sunday morning. As I joined the winding queue and watched all the smug people who had pre-booked their time slot walk past me, I nearly changed my mind. But I was here now, and I had nothing else to do. As it turned out, queuing for a museum was a great place to find out why I should never run a marathon or have children, thanks to the two mummies I was standing behind.

'I am literally a marathon widow. The kids have forgotten what he looks like. Honey, don't wander off, cos I am not losing my place in this line to come and find you.'

'When is it? Stay with me, please, princess.'

I wasn't sure if Princess and Honey were the children's actual names or just terms of endearment.

'Not until April. Honestly, I can't wait for it to be over. He's obsessed. He runs every morning before work, whatever the weather. He gets up in the dark, puts on this ridiculous Lycra outfit; he even wears a head torch. He's lucky he's not been murdered.'

'What's murdered?' Honey said.

'Nothing, darling.' She kissed her on the head, then carried on. 'He goes to the gym in the evening on his way home. He's given up drink and looks at me like I'm the devil if I so much as sniff a bottle of wine.' She paused. 'At the weekends,' she paused again for dramatic effect, 'he goes off for hours on what he calls "*his coastal runs.*"' She used air quotes.

'Bloody hell. You sure he's not having an affair?' This joke didn't look like it went down too well, judging by the glare Honey's mum gave Princess's mum. 'I'm joking, obviously,' Princess's mum said, punching her friend's arm.

'What's an affair?' Princess said.

'You'll find out when you're older,' her mum said.

'I bet he's looking fit, though?' her friend said.

'He's skinny. I preferred him when he had a bit more to cuddle.'

'Awwwhhhhhh.'

'And he wasn't constantly complaining about his knees, his toes, and his feet. He's spent £300 on a pair of moulded running shoes. Honestly, he had them moulded around each foot?'

'Nooooo?'

'Yeah, straight up, and obviously, he can't take them back cos they've been tailored to order, but they've made his toenails black.'

'Ouch.'

'It's not ouch; it's gross.'

'So what you're telling me is that your husband of ten years has black toes nails, dodgy knees, gets up in the dark, and gets in late. Doesn't drink and spends his weekends running at the seaside–alone? And he's spending more on his running shoes than you've ever spent on a single item of clothing?'

'Well, technically, two items, but yeah.'

'You should consider Tinder.'

'What's Tinder?' Princess said.

'Something for grown-ups,' Princess's mum said. 'I did threaten him with that the other day,' she said, raising her eyebrows.

'What about sex?' Princess's mum lowered her voice.

'Shhh...not in front of the girls.'

'They don't know what sex is,' Honey's mum said.

'Mummyyyyyy, what's sex?' Honey said in a voice that seemed to ripple and cause everyone in the queue to stop talking.

'It's how babies are made,' Princess said, 'Isn't it, Mummy?'

'Yes, darling. Right, who wants some raisins while we're waiting?'

'I need a poo.'

'Oh, darling, can you wait?'

'I really need a poo.'

Princess and her mummy left the queue and ran to the front, leaving Honey begging her mum to play eye spy, which they did until, finally, we all found ourselves at the front.

The museum itself was nowhere near as entertaining as the queue had been, and I couldn't even find Guy the Gorilla, although his stuffed friends were definitely the most interesting thing I saw. It was claustrophobic, and the directions were confusing. I kept finding myself back in the same exhibition room. Having had several pushchairs ram my ankles, I left and walked to Hyde Park to kill more time before going home to research Brasserie on the Hill.

A petite woman got on the train wearing all black. Her hair was pinned in a very tight bun. She was carrying a huge case that was taller than her, which I guessed was an instrument. At Leicester Square, she heaved the case onto her back and got off. I watched her walk along the platform. A professional musician, off to perform in a concert. I thought about her for the next few stops, thinking how life as a musician must be a strange one. Working late, then sleeping late, and eating at unsociable hours. How did she spend her days? Maybe some exercise, life admin, probably rehearsals, auditions, then back to work in the evening. These thoughts keep me going until Kings Cross. I was expanding my hobby. It wasn't just listening to strangers who kept me entertained; I was now starting to imagine their lives, too.

It had been such a miserable weekend that I was actually looking forward to Monday. At least I had lots of stories for Poppy when she asked me about my weekend. Not lying was harder than lying, so I'd given up sticking only to the truth because doing so meant I had nothing to say. My borrowed lies made my life sound full and interesting.

CHAPTER 7

When I woke up on Monday morning, I felt the best I'd felt in a long time. Writing the letter to Kai had felt like I'd had a wardrobe clear out. Everything that was taking up space in my head that I didn't need had gone on the paper, and I felt a sense of achievement for having made it through the weekend. I wouldn't describe my mood as happy exactly, but I was happier. It was a cold day, but the sky was a bright blue, and I was looking forward to telling Poppy about my romantic meal out at Brasserie on The Hill with Greg. Also, I had my trip to the Natural History Museum to share, although I hadn't decided yet if Greg came with me or not. Maybe I needed to introduce a new friend. Could I handle having two made-up people in my life? Probably not.

I was trying to ignore the fact that Christmas was fast approaching, but it was everywhere. Perfect families wearing paper party hats were already being displayed on every billboard and featured in every TV advert. I liked the decorations and the window displays, but for me, Christmas was a day usually spent watching TV with Mad Auntie Jean and messaging Kai, who entertained me with his family arguments and weird gift stories and always seemed to feature a detailed account of his dinner—potatoes not crispy enough, veg overcooked, lumpy gravy, and dry turkey. But this year, I wouldn't get to know how bad his Christmas dinner was unless he decided to embrace the season of goodwill and forgive me.

I'd given up my seat to a heavily pregnant lady at Leicester Square, which was eight stops before Barons Court, and was stood next to two Virgin Airlines cabin crew, who wore matching scarlet-red suits. I'd become a bit of an expert at recognising airlines by their cabin crew uniforms. Qatar, maroon with gold detail. British Airways, navy blue, and Easyjet, charcoal grey with orange accessories. When the train pulled into the next station, a lady with a tiny baby in a papoose strapped to her chest got up. She smiled at the pregnant lady.

'It's the greatest love you'll ever know,' she said, which, for some reason, brought tears to my eyes.

At Barons Court, I joined the queue at the bottom of the stairs to exit, still thinking about the lady with the baby. I looked across to the opposite platform and did a double-take because Mr Aroma, aka Greg, was getting off the train, looking as perfect as I remembered him. His hair was slicked to the side, and he wore a posh wax jacket with a corduroy collar. I pushed my way up the stairs, stopping at the top and pretending to root around in my bag for something. When he was in front of me, I seized the opportunity to get a few new pics. They weren't that good, but I did manage a nice side profile one, thanks to congestion at the barriers. It never hurt to have a few spare pics of my made-up boyfriend on my phone, just in case.

I followed him out of the station towards Hammersmith Road. Despite my previous dalliances with stalking, this wasn't that because this was also the way to Thames FM, and it didn't last that long anyway. When we came to the main crossing, 'Greg' crossed over and disappeared into one of those flashy-looking corporate buildings with mirrored glass everywhere. He looked back over his shoulder before he went in, and I wondered if he sensed he was being followed. Had he felt like how girls feel when they convince themselves an axe murderer is following them, and it ends up being some innocent guy just going about his day? I crossed the road and walked away quickly. I was just an innocent lady on my way to work.

I bought Poppy and me a coffee and got to work five minutes early. Today was going to be a good day. Baggage gone, headspace freed.

'Thanks,' Poppy said when I walked in, taking her coffee from me.

'You're welcome.' I smiled. 'How was your weekend?'

'I'm exhausted,' Polly said, running her hand through her hair, letting it fall in perfect waves around her face. She didn't show any signs of exhaustion whatsoever. No dark circles, no dull skin, no break-outs.

'I wish I looked as good as you when I'm tired,' I said, cringing inwardly at my gushing words.

'Bless you,' Poppy said, sipping her coffee. I wasn't sure if she was referring to me buying her the coffee or my compliment, but either way, I'd been blessed.

Poppy sat down at her desk and started to read something on her computer. She didn't even ask about my weekend. I'd memorised an entire menu and spent a day staring at stuffed mammals for nothing.

I tried a couple of times that morning to engage Poppy in conversation, but she seemed distracted and a bit agitated by my interruptions.

'I do want to talk to you,' Poppy said, 'But I need to catch up with some emails and stuff first. Then we can have a chat, okay?'

I wasn't sure what Poppy meant by *have a chat.* Did she mean a mate's chat, now that we were proper friends? Or did she mean a chat about work? It was confusing having a friend at work.

I answered all the weekend emails, did some more pointless tree-killing photocopying for Gary, and, as soon as he went out for a fag break, I wheeled my chair over to Poppy's desk.

'Is now a good time for our chat?'

Poppy sat back in her chair.

'Yes, why not.' She searched her desk for her notebook and flicked it open to a blank page. 'So, after what happened last week with Gary and the competition, Bob—Robert, the chairman, came up with a suggestion.' I nodded. 'Gary explained the reason he got you to win the tickets was because there weren't enough callers...'

'But, there were ...' I started to protest.

'It doesn't matter,' she cut me off, and I fell silent. 'What it has done is highlight the fact that we need to raise the profile of the station and let more people know about us.'

'Great idea,' I enthused.

'So, Bob has allocated a small marketing budget.'

'Amazing,' I said, already predicting the extra workload coming my way.

'And I've recommended you manage it,' Poppy said, beaming with pride like she'd just offered me a Caribbean cruise. 'What do you think?'

'Me?'

'I need you to come up with a plan for how best to use the extra money and then put together a proposal. If possible, by the end of the week.

'But I don't know anything about marketing.'

'You don't need to know anything about marketing. Marketing is just another way of making a noise. Just come up with some ideas on how to get the Thames FM name out there.'

'How much money?' I said, already feeling out of my depth.

'£500.'

'£500?'

'I know, don't look so disappointed. We need to impress him, okay?'

£500? What was I supposed to do with that? The way Poppy had bigged it up, I thought we would at least have enough for some banners or something. We'd be lucky if we could secure a five by five centimetre advert in the local paper for £500.

I sat at my desk with a notebook in front of me and a pen in my hand, not writing anything at all.

'How you getting on?' Poppy said.

'Great. I've had a few ideas,' I said. 'Just working through them.'

By mid-afternoon, I'd written four words.

Stickers

Pencils

Flyers

T-Shirts

None of these were groundbreaking, and we probably couldn't afford all of them, but at least I could start getting some quotes. The first person I thought about messaging was Kai. He put together goody bags for his corporate clients all the time. But Kai wasn't talking to me or communicating in any way, so I was going to have to do it alone. By five p.m., I'd done some fun doodling and made a pretty chart with lots of columns, and now it was time to go home.

Hammersmith station was busy. A combination of school children, commuters, and people going out for the evening, all coming together at the same time. I squeezed onto the carriage and found a spot to lean against the glass. A lady got on with three young children. A little boy in a pushchair and two girls wearing navy blue school uniforms. Two identical book bags hung from the pushchair handles. Both had *St Mathews C of E Primary School* written in gold across the back.

'I'm tired,' the boy said.

'I know, darling. Just a few stops, and then we'll be home, okay?'

'I'm really tired.'

'You can have a rest and a biscuit when we get home, okay?'

'I don't want a biscuit.'

'Mummmmmmmmmy,' one of the girls said. 'Our class is running the biscuit decorating table at the Christmas fair. Can you put your name down to help, Mummy? Pleeeeeeeeese.'

'I'll try.'

'Miss Simpson says every mummy has to help.'

'What about daddies?'

'Don't be silly, Mummy; Daddies can't decorate cakes.'

She didn't attempt to argue but closed her eyes and let the children's words float past her.

'Can we have pocket money for the fair, Mummy?' the other daughter said.

'Miss Simpson says the mayor is coming, and the school choir is going to be singing Christmas carols, and there's going to be a raffle with prizes.'

'What's a raffle?' her sister said.

I'd listened to a lot of conversations over the years and especially these past few weeks, but this was the first time I thought maybe I was meant to be here, on this train, listening to this nice little family, because they had just given me exactly what I needed.

I never usually even thought about work after I'd left the office. Only how I could impress Poppy, but by the time I opened my front door, my mind was spilling over with ideas. I worked late into the night, and by the time I finished, it was past midnight. I did my best to make my presentation look professional. I'd done a lot of research and with lots of help from Mr Google. I was feeling pretty proud of myself.

The next morning, I showered and washed my hair, pulled on my black jeans, a pale blue shirt, and a white fitted cardigan. It wasn't exactly an outfit Poppy would wear, but it was as close as I could manage, and it made me look smart-ish. She'd given me this opportunity, and I wanted her to know I was taking it seriously. I was capable of more than just photocopying and answering emails.

I resisted the urge to buy coffee and went straight to the office. I didn't have a printer at home, so I emailed my presentation to myself. I was in the middle of printing an extra copy when Poppy walked in, holding a single coffee.

'You're early,' she said. 'I would have got you a coffee if I'd known you were here.'

'Don't be silly,' I said. 'It's fine.' She looked at the printer. 'I'm just printing off the proposal.'

'You've done it already? That's great. Can we catch up after lunch? I've got loads to do this morning.'

'Sure.' I smiled, feeling a little crushed.

I paper-clipped both copies and left them on the side of my desk while I replied to some listener emails. I checked the post and did a stationery order. I emptied my filing tray, cleaned the kitchen, and chased up some invoices. By four p.m., Poppy still hadn't asked to see the proposal. I'd heard her on the phone to her sister and seen her do a Tesco online shop on her computer when I was on my way back from the loo.

'Can I show you my ideas now?' I said, feeling like a child pestering her big sister to play with her.

'Five minutes, and I'll be with you.'

Five minutes turned into thirty, and then eventually, at 4.40 p.m., Poppy wheeled her chair over to my desk.

'Right, let's see what you've got.'

I took her through my five-page proposal, page by page. Telling her how much of the budget I thought we should spend on each thing. I showed her my mock-up flyer where I'd copied and pasted a photo of Gary as 'the voice of the station' so people could put a face to the voice. I'd included the Thames FM logo and surrounded it with some of my favourite listeners' quotes that I'd lifted from emails. '*I wake up to Gary every morning.*' '*Gary plays the hits from my childhood,*' '*Gary makes the school run fun.*'

Poppy nodded, not commenting. Next, I showed her a list of some of the local schools in the area that were advertising their upcoming Christmas fetes. I told her I wanted to start contacting them and asking if we could come and have a stall. Finally, I asked her if I could read out my closing paragraph. She nodded.

'*By having a presence in the community, we can let local families know about Thames FM. By offering stickers and pencils, we can attract potential listeners by engaging with them and their families, inviting them to write down a request for a loved one. This will also encourage them to listen for longer and stay tuned in.'*

I waited for Poppy's reaction. Okay, it hadn't been rocket science, but it was a feasible idea that could potentially bring in some new local listeners.

'I know it's not much, but for the budget, I think this is the best way to promote the station.'

Poppy picked up the papers and started looking at them again one by one.

'Thanks, Eve. This is great. Leave it with me.' No gold star, no pat on the back. No discussion. She changed the subject.

'What you up to tonight? Anything nice?' she said, folding the proposal in half and putting it in her bag.

'Yeah, I'm going for dinner with my boyfriend,' I said without thinking. I was still annoyed all my menu revision had gone to waste and saw this as an opportunity to use it.

'Nice. Where's he taking you?'

'Brasserie on the Hill.'

'Oooo, very posh. Lucky you. Well, enjoy and take some pics of your food. I love it there.'

I didn't understand why people took pictures of food. Was it to make other people jealous? Was food envy even a thing?

'Of course, I will,' I said.

The yellow sticker selection that day was disappointing, especially as I was supposedly having dinner at a top London restaurant. I splashed out and bought a chicken parmigiana ready meal for £4.25 and two loose potatoes for chips. It was a celebration dinner for one.

CHAPTER 8

'Eve! Guess what? Bob loved our idea,' Poppy said as soon as I walked in.

'Does he want me to go through it with him?' I said, ignoring my palms that had started sweating at the thought. 'I can explain how—'

'No, no. I've done that already,' Poppy said, cutting me off. 'But it's good news. You can go ahead and start reaching out to the schools.'

'Did he say anything else?' I said, fishing for a compliment. I was disappointed not to have been invited to the meeting, and yes, damn it, I wanted some credit.

'Just to keep him updated on the feedback.'

'Yeah, of course I will.'

'This is totally your baby, but please don't go over budget.' Poppy put her hands together in prayer. 'Oh, and Bob said no to the tee shirts. He said no one will wear them, and his wife campaigns against disposable fashion, so...' she trailed off like she didn't know what to say next. 'Apparently, there are some hanging around from a few years ago that were offered as prizes in an on-air quiz. I'll ask Gary; he might know what happened to them.'

Just two weeks later, I was getting ready for my first school fair. I'd had to pay extra for fast-track printing and postage on the giveaways that Poppy had approved after I argued (in a very nice way) that I couldn't change the date of Christmas or the school fairs. Despite the extra work, I was excited about running my own project, and knowing that Poppy believed in me gave me the confidence I needed. This whole thing had come about at the perfect time in my life, filling my empty evenings and distracting me from my thoughts. I owed Poppy more than she knew, and I was determined to make my little project a success.

My first school was Western House Primary School in Turnham Green. Obviously, I knew this was the school that 'Greg's' daughter went to because that is how I knew they were having a Christmas fair, but I wasn't going to take any pictures. This was purely professional. It was also a local school, and this was all about increasing awareness of Thames FM, and Caroline, the head of the PTA, had been very friendly on the phone and practically begged me to come. I was wearing a navy blue Thames FM tee shirt that Gary had found in his garage. I'd washed it twice, once in antibacterial detergent, so it was still a bit damp, but it made me feel important.

When I arrived, Caroline, who had requested I call her 'Caz,' greeted me with a lukewarm cup of tea and showed me into the school hall where there were lots of busy people setting up their stalls.

'I've put you over here by the stage. You'll get a great view of the carols later.'

'Great,' I said.

'This is for you,' she said, thrusting a red felt Santa hat at me. All the stallholders get one. Put it on.' I did as I was told. Caz wasn't the type of person you argued with.

I lay out my table with the flyers, pencils, stickers, a notebook, and a pen for any dedications. I'd also bought an empty coffee jar and cut a small gap in the lid so the kids could post their requests. Who knew I was so creative?

While I waited for the fair to open, I wandered around the other stalls. There were lots of people selling homemade cake, a lucky dip stall, some second-hand toys, arts and crafts, homemade candles, homemade Christmas cards and decorations, and, of course, homemade jams and pickles. All the stallholders were wearing Christmas jumpers and their Santa hats, and there was a buzz of anticipation.

When I reached 'Santa's Grotto,' a quick peek revealed a broom cupboard draped in red cloth, a rocking chair covered in fake snow, and a large hessian bag that looked to be full of presents. A sign next to the cupboard read £2 *small gift included*. An elf approached me.

'Paying to see Santa doesn't seem right to me,' he said. 'Bet it doesn't happen in Lapland.'

'I guess it's a fundraiser,' I said, shrugging.

'Not for the North Pole, though, is it?' He winked at me and disappeared inside the grotto/cupboard.

Having interacted with a winking elf, I returned to my table where a group of children were being squeezed onto the stage. They were all wearing their red and grey school uniform and handmade Christmas crowns. Caroline was guiding them into position and instructing them to 'smile, lift their chins in the air and put their hands behind their back.' I thought she must be ex-military. If she wasn't, she'd missed her vocation in life.

Four of the youngest children were sitting on the front of the stage, holding bells in one hand and maracas in the other. 'Jingle Bells' started playing from two large speakers on either side of the stage. The wannabe musicians started shaking their instruments. The choir started, the doors opened, and people flocked into the hall. The grand opening had been choreographed to perfection.

After three songs, the choir took a break, which was when I started making eye contact with parents, offering them a friendly smile to go with a free pencil and a sticker. I'd memorised a spiel about Thames FM, but most people said one of four things: 'I've never heard of Thames FM,' 'I don't listen to the radio,' 'I only listen to Radio 2,' or 'I think my gran listens.' I responded to each one by thrusting a flyer into their hands, encouraging them to tune in, convincing them we played a great variety of music for all the family, and offering them a free request on the radio.

A little girl with pigtails, wearing a spotty top, flowery leggings, and glittery wellie boots, stood in front of me.

'I like your outfit,' I said, wondering what planet her parents were on dressing her like this.

'She dressed herself this morning, didn't you, Lily?' A man came up behind her, put his hand on her head, and started stroking her hair. I looked up and felt adrenaline enter my bloodstream as I stared up at 'Greg' and his George Michael beard. There was a flash of recognition across his face.

'Would you like a sticker, Lily?' I said, peeling one off the wax paper and offering it on the end of my finger like it was something unpleasant. She peeled it off and stuck it to her spotty top. 'What about a pencil?' I said, shaking the pencil pot like it was a jar of sweeties.

'What do you say, Lily?' her dad said.

'Thank youuuuuuu.'

'You're very welcome,' I said. 'If you want a request played on the radio, you can write it down and pop it in the jar.

'I can't write,' Lily said.

'Oh, well, maybe your daddy could write it, or I can write it if you want to tell me your favourite song and who you want it played for?'

'Ummmmmmmm "Wheels on the Bus" for Mummy.'

Me and 'Daddy' laughed.

'I'm not sure we have that one, but I'll see what I can do,' I said.

Caroline appeared, phone in hand.

'Smile,' she ordered, taking several pictures of me, Lily, and her dad.

'Photos are for internal use only, but if you're happy for them to be used for school publicity, you can opt in. Just fill out the form on the school website.' She breezed off into the crowd, and Lily and her dad wandered to the next stall. I let my shoulders drop and sighed out the air that had been building in my lungs. I had considered that I might see him from a distance but not that we would come face to face. But I'd got away with it; my Santa hat had been a master disguise.

The rest of the afternoon was noisy. Children cried, ran around, ate sweets, and were reprimanded by their parents. The fete was closed with a lovely rendition of 'We Wish You a Merry Christmas,' performed again by the very sweet school choir and led by Caz. When they'd finished, Caz forced buckets into their hands, instructing them to 'shake these in people's faces until they give you money.'

As the nearest stallholder, a bucket very quickly made its way up close to my face.

'Please give us money for our school,' a cute girl with plaits said.

'It's falling down,' added her friend.

I put a tenner into one of the buckets, but her friend looked like she was going to cry, so I put a tenner in hers, too. I doubted I could claim this on expenses, but I comforted myself with the thought that I was contributing to the safety and welfare of the local children, and they were very sweet.

It was already dark when I left. On the journey home, I leaned my head against the train window and closed my eyes. I felt tired but happy. I had a jar of requests for Gary; I'd given away at least fifty pencils and over hundred stickers, plus I told a lot of people about Thames FM. It had been a success.

I wasn't hungry, thanks to the four Christmas biscuits and three butterfly cakes I'd consumed. The usual heavy feeling I had when I was going home wasn't there. I was looking forward to lighting a couple of candles, pouring myself a cheeky glass of wine, and getting cosy under my duvet in front of the TV. I'd cracked it. Being busy was the best way to fight sadness. Why didn't everyone know this?

A loud group of teenage girls got on at the next stop, forcing me to open my eyes. Although it was now December, they were all revealing their midriff. One of them sat down next to me, and two others stood in front of her. One of them balmed her lips, then passed it to the others—Covid a distant memory. I closed my eyes again, enjoying the motion of the train and listening to the girls' conversation.

'You sure we gonna get in without a ticket?'

'Trust me, yeah? Anyways, I helped look after my nephew yesterday, so got some good karma owing. Don't stress.'

'How do we know where to sit?'

'Just hang at the back, wait til the film starts, then move to an empty seat.'

'But what about when they check the tickets?'

'Jeez, we're not robbing a bank! Just wait til a large group comes in, join the queue for popcorn, tell them you've already had your ticket scanned, and they'll let you through. You just gotta act confident, yeah? It's not like the film isn't showing anyway.'

I looked around me to see if anyone else was listening to these girls blatantly announcing they were going to break the law. But it appeared I was the only one. Did young people really believe that as long as you'd done something good, it cancelled out anything bad you did? The girls got off two stops later, on their way to rip off the local cinema, with not a care in the world. How did these young people have the guts to do this stuff? I felt guilty when a store alarm went off because the sales associate had forgotten to remove a security tag!

I woke up on Sunday morning, missing Kai. I didn't want to spend the day on my own; I wanted to hang out with him, talk rubbish, wind him up, and go get cheap food. I couldn't believe he still hadn't forgiven me. It had been weeks now. I sent him a text.

Eve: *Miss you.*

It showed as delivered, but no reply.

Eve: *I'll come window shopping with you and buy you a doughnut if you forgive me?*

No reply.

Eve: *I'm not going to message you again.*

I made a cup of coffee and two slices of marmite on toast, then sat in the kitchen and stared out the window at the grey sky. All I could see were roofs and pigeons, and a wave of darkness crashed over me. The high of yesterday had gone.

When I'd finished crying, I tidied up. Either I could stay in and wait for the next wave of sadness or go out and find a distraction somewhere—like, say, the cinema.

The girls on the train were right. It was easy to get into a cinema without a ticket. But it wasn't that easy to feel good about it. I opted for the Paul Mescal film. I thought this was a good choice, as I'd already told Poppy I'd seen it. I'd checked online, and it looked busy but not fully booked. When I got there, I hung around outside until I saw a group of friends who looked about my age heading to the cinema. I followed them in, staying close. While they fumbled about bringing up their booking codes on their phones, I joined the popcorn queue. I ordered a small box of mixed salted and sweet and headed to the screen. When I got to the entrance, there was a member of staff checking tickets.

'I've had my ticket scanned already,' I said, overdoing *the ditsy, popcorn balancing, can't find my phone, oh here it is, whoops, it's out of battery, scarf trailing on the floor* act. 'I know where I'm sitting.' I flashed a smile and fluttered my red and swollen eyes, which potentially helped.

He nodded, and I walked in. Mission complete. Ten minutes later, I was sitting at the end of the row, watching the trailers, feeling super anxious. A bit of low-level stalking was one thing, but blatantly breaking the law was quite another, and I didn't feel good. Every time the door opened, I thought it was security coming to get me, and by the time the movie started, I was feeling sick. It didn't help that the movie itself was quite tense with lots of strobe lighting, and at one point, it made me and my popcorn jump. I scrambled on the floor in the dark, trying to pick up as much as possible. My hands were sticky, and my teeth kept sticking together. A loud 'Shhhhhh' from the lady behind drew attention to me, and people turned to stare. By the time the film finished, my heart was racing, my hands were sweating, and I had no idea what the film had even been about. The whole experience had been awful from start to finish, and I couldn't wait to leave. As soon as the credits started rolling, I grabbed my jacket and pushed my way through the double doors and out into the street. I power-walked to the station, desperate to get away from the scene of my crime. I wasn't cut out for life as a criminal, and I didn't like or recognise the person I was becoming. Following strangers, lying about my life, and sneaking into cinemas without paying—this wasn't who I was or who I wanted to be.

I leaned against the wall, the muscles in my legs refusing to cooperate with my brain. God, I was such an idiot. I staggered back out of the station and sat on a wall to catch my breath.

Ten minutes later, I was back at the cinema.

'Excuse me. I've just watched a film, and I'm really sorry, but I think I forgot to buy a ticket.' I smiled at the girl at the door. 'I've got a lot on my mind, and my job's really stressful. I'm in marketing.'

'Right, errrm, are you here to see another film?'

'No, I just wanted to pay for the film I've just watched.'

The girl looked behind her. 'I wouldn't worry about it,' she said.

'But I didn't pay,' I said, waving my purse around.

'It's fine. The till won't let you buy a ticket for a film that's already screened anyway, so don't worry about it.'

'But I need to pay,' I said. 'Can you call your manager?'

'Honestly, it's fine,' she hissed. A family was queuing to get their tickets scanned.

'Please, can you just let me pay?' I whispered it, but loudly, which defeated the point.

'I've told you I can't,' she said, shaking her head at me.

'Excuse me, what film are you watching?' I asked a little girl at the front of the queue who was dressed up as Elsa from *Frozen*.

'*Rainbow Gnomes*,' she said sweetly.

I went to open my mouth.

'It's sold out,' the girl at the door said. Then she moved in front of me and started checking the tickets of everyone now waiting.

Not wanting to cause more of a scene than I already had, I walked away. At the self-service ticket machine, I bought myself a ticket to see *Rainbow Gnomes* on Tuesday afternoon. I waved it in the air as I walked out, in case I was on CCTV. I already had my defence. I was under emotional pressure and had tried to pay retrospectively, but my custom was refused.

The high following my successful day at the school fair the day before had been swallowed up by the London smog and replaced by a fear that was totally of my own doing. I spent the rest of Sunday under my duvet, scared of what stupid decision I might make next.

95

CHAPTER 9

It was Monday morning, and winter was well and truly here. The windows in my room whistled as the icy cold air found gaps to blow through, and it was still dark when I left home. By the time I arrived at work, the sky was a piercing blue, and the sun was doing its best to melt the morning frost. My nose was running, and my ears were numb. Poppy, however, was radiating a healthy glow.

'How did it go? I meant to call you yesterday, but I was too hungover.' Poppy laughed while baring her teeth. 'I'm not proud.'

She was dressed in workout gear and spotless white trainers. A pair of large sunglasses were perched on her head, acting as a headband, and there wasn't a hair out of place. I didn't think a workout had yet taken place.

'I spoke to lots of five-year-olds and their parents and quite a few grandparents, plus a very grumpy Father Christmas.'

Poppy laughed. 'Poor you. I was going to come and keep you company, but I just ran out of time. I had a crazy busy weekend.'

The buzzer to the office went.

'I'll go,' Poppy said, walking towards the door, her hair swishing behind her. Moments later, she returned, followed by DI Andrews.

'There's someone here to see you,' Poppy said.

'Eve, can I have a word?' DI Andrews said.

Poppy looked at me, then back at DI Andrews, and then we all looked at Gary as he came out of the studio.

'Everything okay?' he said.

'The police are here to speak with Eve,' Poppy said with a sense of glee in her voice.

'If this is about yesterday, I can explain,' I said, forcing myself to smile.

'Yesterday?'

'The mix-up at the cinema?'

'It's about the protest at the hotel. We just need to clarify a few points with you.'

Poppy was back at her desk, shuffling papers. Gary, a creature of habit, had gone to the toilet to perform his morning ritual, as he was prone to do at this time of the day.

'Are you happy to talk here, or is there somewhere we can speak privately?'

'Don't worry about me,' Poppy said. 'We're friends.' She got up and wheeled her chair over to my desk, offering it to PC Andrews.

'Thanks, this won't take long.' She nodded at Poppy, who hovered like a fly. 'So we've listened back to your radio interview again, and you said you were there with a friend, but when we interviewed you, you said you were there alone.'

I nodded as bile made its way up my throat.

'The CCTV shows you arriving and leaving alone and shows you sitting at the bar but not talking to anyone else.' She paused, and I glanced up at Poppy, who was staring at something intensely on her phone.

'I was there on a date. It was a first date,' I added. 'We arrived and left separately.'

PC Andrews sighed and wrote something down in her notebook.

'So why didn't you tell us this before? We're going to need their contact details.' She said this without raising her eyes.

'Because,' I paused, 'because he's married.' Poppy took a sharp intake of breath. I had no idea how she would feel about this, but it was all I could think of to say. I wanted to tell DI Andrews the truth, but with Poppy listening, I couldn't. I'd waited five years for Poppy to like me. I couldn't lose her friendship already.

'We'll be discreet.'

'Can I get you a drink? Tea? Coffee?' I said, willing her to say yes.

'Tea,' she paused. 'Please.'

DI Andrews followed me across the office, both of us ignoring an unpleasant smell that was coming from the toilet.

'Is there something else you want to tell me?' she said.

I filled the kettle with water and turned it on, hoping the hissing would drown out our conversation.

'I was there alone. My date didn't show up. I didn't want to say anything before because I was embarrassed.'

'Right. There is no married man then?'

'No.'

'And were you at the actual event?'

'No.'

'Which explains why your name wasn't on the guest list.' She scribbled something down in her notebook. 'And you didn't see the protestors throw the paint?'

'No, I just heard them—one of them—in the toilets. Like I told you.'

'You could have saved me a lot of time if you had just been honest from the start.' She put her notebook in her top pocket.

'I'm sorry.'

'There's no need for the tea,' she said. 'I'll see myself out.'

When I sat back at my desk, Poppy was tapping her fingers on the table and grinning.

'You dark horse,' she said, beaming. 'I thought you said he was divorced.'

'It's not as bad as it sounds. They're separated,' I said. 'Getting divorced.'

'He told you that, did he?' She raised her eyebrows. 'And you believed him?'

I was about to defend him, but then I remembered this was my imaginary boyfriend, and we were talking about a made-up marriage in a made-up world that only existed in my stupid head.

'Of course, I believe him. His ex is a bit of a psycho. Stalks him and stuff.'

'You wanna be careful. If she finds out about you, you could end up in a black bin liner in the Thames.' Poppy laughed; I didn't. 'Oh my God, your face! Ignore me; I have a sick sense of humour sometimes.'

DI Andrew's visit had shaken me, and Poppy's jokes weren't helping. I needed some fresh air. Maybe something to eat to settle my stomach.

'Are you okay?' Poppy said as I got up and started to put my jacket on.

'Yeah, I just need some air and some food,' I said.

'I'll try and cover for you,' she said, 'but if you don't start doing some work soon, I think Gary might have a sense of humour failure.'

'I did work all day on Saturday,' I said, not meaning to snap, but I was feeling stressed.

'I know, and I want to hear more about it, but maybe get on top of the emails first and finish his copying. You can fill me in later. Gary's not fully on board with the marketing idea and thinks the money should have gone into programming instead. We need to prove him wrong.'

I took my jacket off and sat back down at my desk. I thought Poppy would ask me more questions about what the police had said and about Greg's wife, but she carried on like it was no big deal having the police turn up at work to question me. Either that, or she wasn't interested.

I found a bruised apple at the bottom of my bag and a squashed cereal bar, which is what I was eating when the office buzzer went again. Hoping it was the bulk toilet roll order I'd placed last week, I went to answer the door. I don't know what Gary did with it, but I swear he got through a roll a day.

I opened the door, but instead of forty-eight toilet rolls and a courier taking a photo of me to prove delivery, staring unsmiling right at me was 'Greg,' aka Mr Aroma. Could this day get any worse? As I searched for the right words to ask him *what the hell he was doing here?* Poppy appeared at my side.

'Greg! It's so nice to meet you. We were just talking about you!'

I stared at him, willing him not to speak and my legs to keep me upright.

'Wait there,' I said, shutting the door in his face. 'I'm taking a break. I'll be back in a bit,' I said to Poppy.

'You are in demand today,' she said.

'I just need to explain to him about the police and everything,' I said far too quickly to be coherent.

'Invite him in. It's freezing out,' Poppy said, heading for the door.

'No!' I shouted.

'What is going on?' Gary said, appearing again like a genie.

'Eve's boyfriend is here,' Poppy said.

'For fucks sake,' Gary said.

'I just need to sort something out,' I said.

'Can't you sort your private life out in your own time?'

'She did work at the weekend,' Poppy said.

'Waste of time,' Gary muttered as he headed to the kitchen.

'Ignore him,' Poppy said.

'I won't be long,' I said, pushing past her and opening the door.

Greg was still standing there. He hadn't moved. The door opened behind me, and Gary came out.

'Can you and your boyfriend do this somewhere else,' he said.

'Who are you?' Greg said.

'Her boss, so get on with saying whatever it is you need to say cos she's busy, and I pay her to be inside the office, not outside.'

The door opened again, and Poppy came out.

'Whoops, sorry, just popping over the road for some lunch. Can I get you anything?'

I shook my head.

'Greg?'

'He's fine,' I said.

I grabbed his arm and pulled him behind me. He shook it off with force. There was nowhere to go, and it was freezing. I hadn't brought my coat with me, and I didn't want this confrontation to last any longer than it had to. I walked around the side of the building, and he followed.

'Hi,' I said, hugging myself to keep warm.

'I'm calling the police,' he said.

'What? Why? I haven't done anything.'

'Are you mentally unwell?' he said. I shook my head. 'Because I think that maybe you need some professional help.'

'I'm fine,' I said.

'Then why have you been following me?'

'What do you mean? I haven't been—'

'You followed me home, I've seen you outside my house, you followed me to my daughter's nursery, you've taken photos of me, you followed me to my work, and then at the weekend, you show up again at my daughter's school.' He paused and took a breath. 'I want to know why?'

I swallowed down a lump in my throat.

'I can explain.'

'Talk,' he ordered like we were in a cop drama, and I was being forced against my will to reveal the identity of a criminal.

'How did you find me?'

'Because you were wearing a tee shirt with the name of your radio station emblazoned on the front, and you gave my daughter a sticker and a pencil with the name of your radio station on it.'

'Oh.'

'New to this, are you?'

'This?'

'Stalking men. Scaring my family. Are you one of those feminists who is trying to make men understand what it feels like to be a vulnerable woman?'

'No. Of course not.'

'Good. Because if you are, you have chosen the wrong man.'

'What do you mean?' I said. 'Are you threatening me?'

'Am I threatening you? Jesus.' He sort of laughed, but not in a happy way. More in a kind of '*I can't believe you just said that*' way. 'I mean because I'm a good guy. I'm married— happily married. I take care of my child, I do household chores, I respect my wife's career, I visit my mum—and my nan. Okay?' I didn't know what he wanted me to say, so I said nothing. 'Okay?' he said again.

'Yes. Okay. That's good. You're nice. That's why I picked you. Because you looked nice.'

'Picked me?'

'Yes, picked you to be my pretend boyfriend. I know it sounds weird, but it's not a crime, okay, and it doesn't actually have anything to do with you. Not really.'

I nearly cried several times during my explanation, but I did tell him the truth. As ridiculous as it sounded, I think he did actually believe me, and he seemed a lot less angry by the time I'd finished.

'So you pretended you went on a date, and when your friend asked you about it, you described a man that looked a bit like me?' I nodded. 'Then you saw me at the train station and followed me because your friend kept asking you to see a photo?'

'Yes.' I was so cold, my legs had started to shake, and I could feel my nose running again. My face was stinging in the wind, and I pulled my hands up inside my jumper sleeves and blew into the ends.

'So why were you at my daughter's school?'

'Because I'm doing some marketing for the radio station at Christmas fairs in the area. I knew the school was having one because—'

'Because you'd followed me there?' I nodded. 'And who is Greg?'

'I had to give you a name.'

'And you made this all up because you wanted your friend to believe you'd been on a date?'

There was a long silence.

'I did it to make my life sound more interesting than it is.' I looked down at my feet. 'I'm sorry. It just got out of hand.'

'If I see you again anywhere, I am going to call the police. Okay?'

'Okay.' I started kicking the wall one foot at a time. 'I've got a free ticket to see *Rainbow Gnomes* tomorrow afternoon if you want it?' I said. 'As a peace offering?'

He didn't reply because he was already on the other side of the road, shaking his head.

I stayed in the office until six p.m. to make up for the time I'd spent that day sorting out my chaotic life, even though Gary had gone home long ago.

When Poppy got up to leave, she topped up her lipstick in a small hand-held mirror and brushed her hair. She wrapped a very long, large, colourful scarf around her neck.

'So, was Greg okay about you giving the police his details?'

'Yeah, he was fine. Just a bit stressed because he doesn't want his ex to find out he's dating again.' I'd had all afternoon to think of this.

'So, I've been thinking,' Poppy twirled a strand of her hair around her finger. 'Why don't you and Greg come over for dinner?' Poppy said, flashing me a smile.

I looked up and forced my cheeks to stretch towards my ears, hoping my eyes didn't deceive me. You can tell a lot from the eyes.

'I'll invite a few friends. People I think he'll get along with. You can meet some of my people. It'll be fun.'

I had longed for a social invite from Poppy for such a long time, but not like this. Not with a plus one who had just accused me of stalking him and given me a self-imposed restraining order.

'That sounds great,' I said.

'Excellent, I'll ping you some dates,' Poppy said, picking up her bag. 'Don't forget to set the alarm. You can't trust anyone these days.'

On the train home, I overheard a mum and daughter talking. They were heading to Regent Street in London's West End to look at the Christmas lights and the Hamley's Toy Shop window.

'It won't be the same this year without Nana.'

'I know, love, but she'd still want us to go.'

'Can we go to a different place for tea and cake after, though? I think we'll feel too sad if we go back to the same place.'

'I've already booked us somewhere that Elaine at work recommended. Cake and Bubbles. They serve cake with champagne, which I thought was right up our street.'

'Ahhh, Nana would have loved that,' her daughter said.

'She would,' her mum agreed, putting her arm around her and pulling her in close for a hug.

Cake had been a rare treat when I was growing up. Birthdays, Christmas, and, occasionally, if Auntie Jean was visiting, which was odd because baking a cake for someone was a nice thing, and my mum didn't do things like that.

'It's your mother being competitive,' Dad said when I asked him why she did this for her sister who she didn't like.

My birthday cake always made me feel special, but then, one day, it didn't.

It was my fifteenth birthday and a school day, so it had been nothing out of the ordinary, but I knew I was getting cake for dinner. The three of us sat at the table and ate our dinner. Mum then got up and moved to the sofa.

'Where's the cake?' I said.

'You're fifteen now, Evelyn. You're not a baby.'

I remember looking at my dad and him looking away, and I remember feeling really sad because I didn't have a cake.

The next day, I told Kai I didn't have a cake, and he feigned shock.

'You are joking me! I hope you called the NSPCC,' he said.

I smacked his arm.

'I'm thinking of divorcing my parents,' I said.

'I agree. That is definitely grounds for divorce. It's emotional abuse.'

I smacked him again, and we laughed, and I forgot all about the cake until later that day when Kai came running up behind me.

'I've put our names down to help in the Year 7 after-school cooking club,' he said, looping his arm through mine and doing an about-turn.

'What? Why?' I said, trying to pull him to a halt.

'Because it's Bake Week, and guess what?' He carried on before I could answer, 'Miss Dubois said we can make a cake.'

'Ahhh, that's why you volunteered. The gorgeous Miss Dubois from Paris?'

'Sadly, she is way out of my league!' Kai said.

'And a teacher,' I added.

The cake had tasted much better than it looked and Kai had even managed to find some small wax candles to stick on the top. Only about three, but still. The Year 7s, Kai, and Miss Dubois all sang happy birthday to me, and from then on, the Year 7s always waved when they saw me. Kai even went on to do Food Tech GCSE, but I think that was more to do with Miss Dubois than his love of cooking.

Even though it had been quite a stressful day, I still needed to keep the stories about Greg coming, especially now that Poppy had invited us for dinner. I hadn't worked out what to do about this yet, but in the meantime, Christmas lights, Hamley's window, and Cake and Bubbles all got written down in my dragonfly notebook when I got home. I also wrote down *Dead Nana* but realised that story could get complicated, so I crossed it out.

For the rest of the week, I kept my head down while preparing for the next couple of school fairs. I made sure I was on time in the morning and the last to leave in the evening. Poppy said I could take a day off in lieu of working at the weekend, but I declined. I was finding my own company more and more miserable. Also, Gary was being even more dismissive than usual, and I felt I needed to convince him I was dedicated and reliable. In the evenings, I watched rubbish TV, ate yellow sticker dinners, wrote and deleted messages to Kai, and wrote notes on conversations I'd overheard on the train. Everyone around me seemed to have their lives all worked out. People everywhere I went seemed to be achieving great things and going to great places. I listened to conversations about people I didn't know, their lives, and their plans for the weekend. What they were going to wear, where they were going to eat, what show they were going to watch, and which country they were travelling to. In the meantime, I got up, went to work, came home, watched TV, and went to bed. Fourteen words summed up my existence. I'd even started fantasising about Transport for London allocating a specific carriage for sad, lonely people, offering them a new way to meet people in a safe and public environment. Or maybe the marketing bug was getting to me.

On Saturday, I headed for Barnes Prep School. A small school I'd contacted when I overheard two mums discussing the 'depressing' waiting list for a place as I queued for the self-service tills in Waitrose. Needless to say, there wasn't a yellow sticker to be seen in either of their baskets.

I already regretted my choice of school because Barnes wasn't that easy to get to and required me to get two tubes and a train, then a ten-minute walk. The forecasters had been warning of strong winds all week, and I lost a load of my flyers as I crossed the common, the wind tossing them around like autumn leaves. When I did eventually arrive, I found I'd been allocated a space in the corridor. It was still very cold and windy, and I had to pin the remaining flyers down with the coffee jar. No one wanted to stop and talk, and every time I managed to get the attention of anyone, they either had to move because they were causing congestion or leave me mid-sentence because their child had run ahead into the main hall where all the action was. The whole thing was a bit of a waste of time, and so was wearing Gary's t-shirt because I kept my coat on the entire time.

The highlight of the afternoon was meeting Sam, the caretaker, who made me a cup of tea. He told me he was meant to retire last summer, but after losing his wife to cancer the year before, he'd decided to carry on working to keep himself distracted. I told him about Thames FM, and he promised to give it a listen. Sam kept me company for most of the afternoon and, after talking about his wife some more, asked me if I had a boyfriend.

'No, Justin Bieber is taken, unfortunately,' I said, trying my best to make a joke. It was a poor one, but Sam indulged me.

'Oh, you can do better than that,' he said. 'My wife had a soft spot for him, too, you know. Far too young for her, but I think she wanted to mother him.'

'Your wife sounds lovely.'

'She was. You remind me of her when she was younger.'

'I'll take that as a compliment,' I said, my heart melting for him.

Before leaving, I helped Sam get the classrooms ready for Monday and discovered there was something very therapeutic about stacking chairs.

'I promise to give your radio station a try,' Sam said again.

'For that, you deserve a sticker,' I said, planting one on his collar.

On Sunday, I went to a school in South Kensington, where the number of Range Rovers pulling up to drop off children, all accompanied by their au pairs, made me realise it was another bad choice. I gave away lots of pencils and stickers and got a free cappuccino from the drinks van that was serving proper coffee in the playground. The stall next to mine also gave me a caramel slice and a ten per cent discount code to use on my first online order. The children's behaviour was terrible, and the noise made it difficult to speak to anyone for more than a couple of seconds. When I got home, I dropped everything in the hallway and went straight to run a bath. I'd made it through another weekend without Kai, but it wasn't getting any easier. I was missing him so much, and it was beginning to consume my thoughts.

CHAPTER 10

The idea that my little project would launch my career died as quickly as my dad's belief that England would win the World Cup again in his lifetime. Each time it came around, he was convinced we were going to 'bring it home.' While he mourned the team getting knocked out at various stages, I mourned the time we spent together watching the matches on TV. I remember one time when a player got seriously injured, and I asked my dad if I was lost in a desert, would he walk a hundred miles to save me.

'I'd walk a million miles to save you,' he said.

His answer had made me happy at the time. Now, the memory only saddened me because I think I had just wanted proof he loved me.

It hadn't been an unhappy childhood, but it had been a quiet one, except for when the Euros or the World Cup was on. It was like Mum gave Dad a bi-annual pass to raise his voice, and he would take full advantage, shouting at the TV that he could do a better job 'than that bloody idiot'—amongst other things.

Since commuting on public transport, I'd realised many men believe their talents were wasted and that they should be managing the national team. These conversations always reminded me of happy times with my dad.

On Monday, as I got ready for work, I started to feel anxious. I couldn't stop my thoughts that were galloping through my mind like a herd of wild horses. I'd told Poppy so many lies that I was beginning to forget what I had and hadn't told her. I was worried I was going to make a mistake and get caught out.

'Good morning,' Poppy sang out. 'How were the fairs at the weekend? Are you sick of Christmas already?' She waved her perfectly manicured nails in my face.

I laughed as I went to the coat stand, calculating the best hook to use to avoid it falling and knocking me out, although, under the circumstances, this might not have been a bad thing.

'If I hear "Jingle Bells" one more time, I might scream,' I said. 'But I think I managed to recruit a few more listeners, so it was worth it.'

'Brilliant,' Poppy beamed. 'And how's the review coming on?'

'The review?' I said.

'We need to demonstrate how successful this little marketing campaign has been.' Poppy tapped the table with her fingers. 'So we can get more money and do more with it. Remember we discussed this?' Poppy sighed loudly.

'Yes, of course. I'm working on it today,' I said, feeling like I'd been told off again.

I created a Word document and stared at the blank white screen. Most people I'd spoken to hadn't even heard of Thames FM, and those who had said they didn't listen. There was no way of monitoring if our listenership figures had gone up over the past few weeks or even knowing what our listening figures were. How was I supposed to demonstrate how effective my little PR campaign had been? All I had was a number of requests in the coffee jar, a record of how much merchandise I'd given away, and the email requests, which were up slightly. But there was always an increase at Christmas and we hardly played any of them because the listeners didn't understand we weren't live.

The national radio stations subscribed to an out-of-date monitoring system that involved random members of the public ticking a box each time they listened to a specific radio station. It cost loads of money, and Gary wouldn't even discuss the possibility of us subscribing.

'It's about as effective as a bucket with a hole in,' Gary said. Which was all well and good, but meant we had no idea if we had one listener or hundreds of thousands.

Warwick complained selling ads to advertisers without listener numbers was like 'selling tickets to a concert without knowing who was performing.'

'Can't you just make it up?' Gary said. 'How would anyone even know?'

'No because I am a professional who works in sales and not a professional fraudster,' Warwick said.

'Maybe the schools can send me some information on how many people attended, etc,' I said, thinking out loud.

'Oh, that reminds me. We got an email from one of the schools. Someone called Caroline. She attached some pictures, but I haven't had a chance to look at them yet. It would be good to include them in the review, though.' My stomach did an Olympic medal-worthy somersault. Poppy yawned. 'I'm so tired,' she said, then started telling me about her weekend, which, as usual, seemed to involve lots of parties, lots of people, and lots of drinking, but I wasn't fully engaged in what she was saying because all I could think about was that I needed to stop Poppy from seeing the photos. The only pictures Caroline 'call me Caz' took, as far as I knew, were of me and 'Greg.' How the hell would I explain what Greg was doing at the school fair with me and a small child?

'Eve, Eve? Did you ask Greg about dinner? Eve—hello, anyone there?'

'Sorry, what? Oh no, sorry, I thought you were going to send me some dates?'

'How about this Friday?'

'Friday? Friday, as in this Friday?' I said, trying to think of something of great importance that I had to do on Friday.

'Yes, Friday?' Poppy said.

'He's away on a shoot for a couple of weeks. Back just before Christmas.' It was quick thinking, but now I'd lied about who he was and where he was, and if Poppy opened the email in her inbox, both these things were going to be very difficult to explain.

'That's a shame.' Poppy sounded genuinely disappointed. 'I was thinking of doing a Christmas do.'

'I could come on my own if that's...'

'No,' Poppy said, quicker than a passing bullet train. 'That won't work. It's a couples thing.'

'Sure. No problem.' Wait, a couples thing? I didn't know Poppy was in a couple. How could I not know that?

'So you have a boyfriend? You kept that quiet,' I said.

'You're not the only one having fun, Eve.' She pulled a kind of smirky face that didn't suit her.

'Why didn't you tell me?' I smiled, not wanting to show how gutted I was that I didn't know this. I thought we were friends!

'When you and Greg come for dinner, you can meet him.' Her phone started ringing. 'Until then, I'm going to keep you in suspense,' Poppy said, beaming as she answered her phone.

'*Dear Eve,*

Thank you so much for joining the school community in celebrating Christmas last weekend. Please find attached a photograph of you with one of our parents and one of our nursery pupils, which we have used in the school newsletter.

With best wishes,

Caroline Mitchell,

PTA Chair'

I clicked on the image. There I was, with Greg and his daughter, who was the only one smiling. Poppy ended her call. I had to act quickly.

'I need a coffee—I've got a headache from hell today,' I said, hoping she might offer. She didn't. However, a hero in the unlikely form of Gary came to my rescue when he called Poppy into the studio to listen to some new trailers. I dived into her chair and clicked on her email icon, scanning her inbox for the email from Western House Primary School. I couldn't see it. I typed 'Western House' into the search bar and pressed search. The studio door opened, and the email appeared on the screen. I clicked the delete button just as Poppy walked over.

'What are you doing?'

I spun around to face her.

'I was just looking for Bob's email address.'

'Why?'

'So I could email him the review.'

'Before you show me?'

'No, of course not. I was just checking his address. It seems silly—me sending it to you and then you sending it to him each time.'

'I'd rather it came from me,' she said, sounding peeved. 'And I need to see it before you send it, okay?'

'Sure,' I said. I could handle her being in a mood as long as she forgot about the email, which was very likely judging by how many emails were in her inbox.

Poppy was quiet for the next few hours, but then Gary came over, and she seemed to snap out of it, acting like everything was fine again. He sat down on the corner of Poppy's desk.

'Girls, are we having a Christmas party?'

'If you enter the twenty-first century and stop calling us "girls,"' Poppy said. 'Also, it won't be much of a party with the three of us, will it? What do you think, Eve?'

'Ummm yeah, it would be nice to do something.' I stumbled on my words. We'd never done anything before. Usually, the chairman sent us a tin of celebrations. Gary ate them all except for the Milky Way and that was as close to an office party as we got.

'What about a drink at the pub? We can invite Bob, and then you can meet him properly,' Poppy said, looking at me. 'You never know; he might even offer to pay for the drinks.'

'If he does that, I'll piss my pants,' Gary said.

'That's nice,' Poppy said, giving him a look.

'Not on a Friday, please, cos that's my lads' night. And a proper pub, please; not one of these places that charge £10 a pint,' Gary said, seemingly unbothered by Poppy's sarcasm.

'I'm happy with whatever,' I said.

'Of course, you are,' Gary said, jumping up off Poppy's desk. 'How about Thursday?'

'It's a date,' Poppy said.

I was about to reply, but my phone lit up with a message from Mad Auntie Jean.

Not around this Christmas. Volunteering at the community centre, serving dinner to the homeless. You're welcome to join if you fancy it.

My only living relative had ditched me for the homeless. Obviously, I admired her philanthropic spirit, but it made me feel like it was me against the rest of the world. Nothing I did seemed good enough for Poppy. Kai had just walked out of my life without a second glance, and now, even my eccentric Auntie Jean didn't want to spend time with me, choosing to spend it with the homeless instead. The only thing I had to look forward to was the office Christmas drinks.

On Thursday, I made sure I dressed up a bit. I'd washed my hair the night before and was wearing my nicest jeans, a velvet top I'd had for years that looked quite party-ish, and my black boots. I packed some make-up in my bag.

Neither Gary nor Poppy had dressed up, and if anything, Poppy looked more casual than usual. For a minute, I thought I'd got the wrong day.

'You look fun,' Poppy said. I wasn't sure if 'fun' was a compliment or not. 'Are you going out somewhere after the pub, or is this especially for us?'

'I might be meeting up with some friends later,' I said. Lying came so easily to me these days.

The pub was pretty soulless when we arrived. Gary went to the bar, and me and Poppy sat down at a table in the far corner. It was cold, and I touched the radiator, which had a hint of heat coming through it. I pushed myself back against it and kept my coat on. This was definitely not a venue that warranted a sleeveless velvet top.

Gary came back with two glasses of wine and two pints of Guinness.

'Bob's on his way, and I know for a fact he's a Guinness man,' he said, taking a swig and licking away a white moustache. 'Ahhhhhh,' he said. 'The taste of Ireland.'

'My nan always pours Guinness on the Christmas turkey,' Poppy said. 'It makes it so moist.'

'Sounds sexy,' Gary said. Poppy ignored him.

'What are you doing for Christmas?' Poppy said, looking at me.

'Just a quiet one in London.'

'You cooking for the rellies or going somewhere for lunch?'

'They're coming to me. Just my aunt and her family.' I paused. 'Only four of us, but it'll be nice.'

This was the first lie I didn't feel guilty about. I'd said it for Poppy's sake as much as mine. What could she have said if I'd told her I was going to be on my own? It would be awkward and embarrassing, and she would think I was a total loser or, worse, feel sorry for me. It was just easier that I made Poppy feel better about my situation.

Bob arrived soon after. He took an excessively long slurp of his Guinness and then introduced himself to me. He exchanged some football banter with Gary, then went to buy a round and returned, saying he'd ordered some fries, onion rings, and breaded chicken. A few more people came into the pub, and the noise level picked up. Gary was soon on his third pint and getting maudlin about his kids spending Christmas with their respective mothers this year. Bob patted him on his back like a dog, and Poppy started scrolling on her phone. I waited for the food to arrive.

As Christmas get-togethers go, it wasn't particularly festive, but it was nice being social with my colleagues. After me and Poppy had finished our second glass of wine, I started to feel much happier and more relaxed. I told Bob about the schools and what people had said about Thames FM, although Poppy kept interrupting and telling Bob the things I'd told her, which was a bit annoying.

'You've both done a great job,' he nodded at Poppy.

'Thanks, Bob. With more money, we could do even more,' Poppy said.

'I'm working on the budget after Christmas, but well done.'

I was disappointed Poppy didn't give me more credit, and Bob definitely seemed under the impression it had been a joint effort. When she moved really close to me and started telling me how much she liked me, I realised she was already quite drunk and probably wasn't thinking straight.

'I used to think you were so dull, Eveeee, but now I really like you,' she said. 'I mean, you've got a boyfriend and everything. I didn't think you'd ever get a boyfriend, but you did it. Well done, Eveee. I'm so proud of you.'

'Thanks,' I said, unsure again if this was an insult or a compliment.

By nine p.m., Gary wasn't making any sense. Bob said he needed to get home, and Poppy said she was going to get an Uber to her friend's house, leaving me to walk on my own to the station. I was pretty hungry as the boys had eaten most of the food, and I was also feeling quite woozy.

When I got to Kings Cross, I went straight to the kebab shop. I tucked the warm foil parcel under my jacket like a kitten, then went home to watch TV with just a kebab to keep me company. I watched a programme on how eating certain foods can make you live longer, and as chilli oil dribbled down my chin, I figured my days were probably numbered. Not long after, I fell asleep on the sofa, then woke around one a.m. and crawled into bed, but I couldn't get back to sleep. I kept thinking about Kai and how, even though we had never spent Christmas Day together, we always FaceTimed when opening our gifts and spent the rest of the day exchanging messages about how bad our day was—trying to outdo each other. With a week to go, I couldn't believe we weren't going to be doing our annual traditions this year. Surely he was going to forgive me during this season of goodwill? I turned on my side light and opened my dragonfly notebook.

Hi Kai

Apologies for the bad handwriting—a side effect of insomnia that I'm blaming you for. Well, you and a slightly dodgy chicken kebab and too much wine. No—you abandoning me hasn't turned me to drink; I've been at my work Christmas party. Well, I say party, but it was only four of us in a pretty grim pub, but still, it was a step up from last year, when we opened a box of chocolates in the office and then went home.

I'm spending Christmas on my own this year as Mad Auntie Jean has volunteered to help at the community centre kitchen. Don't feel bad; I'll be fine, although being on your own at Christmas does feel particularly tragic. It's now been over a month since we spoke, and I'm really missing you. I've messaged you "sorry" a billion times and tried calling you. Please, please, tell me what I have to do to get you to forgive me? I need you. You're my lifesaver and my screensaver.

Eve

PS There'd be no contest if we'd played compare the Christmas game this year anyway.

I curled myself into a foetal position and let the tears slowly roll down my cheek. Maybe Kai had finally realised how different we really were. While he made my life fun and spontaneous, I offered him nothing in return. Without him, I didn't go anywhere or do anything. Without him, my life was just a big fat lie.

Friday morning, Poppy was manic because Gary had called in sick. To make up for the lack of a presenter, we were playing back-to-back Christmas music, with the Thames FM jingle every three songs. So far, we hadn't had a single complaint.

Next week, the Christmas schedule kicked in. The volunteer presenters had all pre-recorded a four-hour show to be aired at various times and on different days. I went out for coffee, emptied the fridge and the bins, and set the 'out of office' email on the station account, which was my latest genius idea to stop the weekend requests. At the end of the day, I asked Poppy if she fancied going for a drink or something to eat, but she turned me down, saying she still had too much to do. I offered to help, but she said it was easier if she just did what needed to be done rather than explain to me what to do. She told me to go home and wished me a happy weekend without looking at me.

I had another long weekend ahead of me, with days filled with nothing but memories. Memories of Kai, memories of me begging Mum to let me decorate the tree, which she never let me put up earlier than a week before Christmas, insisting it was down on Boxing Day. Memories of Auntie Jean arriving, Mum changing personality instantly, and Dad choosing this moment to take me out shopping for Mum's gift. This was my normal, but the older I got and the more I listened to people talking about their Christmas, the more I'd realised just how reclusive as a family we were.

To stop my thoughts, I decided to ride the tube past my stop and listen to voices other than my own. Every platform and every carriage was full of people going out to celebrate. They were dressed up, holding carrier bags of booze and gifts. It was noisy and hard to make out what anyone was saying and the only vaguely interesting story I heard was a guy telling his mate how he'd cracked his tooth while eating at a restaurant called Annabel's. He described the pain to his mate as 'like having your big toe cut off without pain relief.' It made me feel faint, so I got off at the next station, crossed over the platform, and went home. I met my neighbour on the stairs and stopped to stroke his cat. He asked me how my parents were and said he hadn't seen them in a while.

'They're well. Thank you,' I said. I couldn't face talking about them today.

For the first time since I had chicken pox in junior school, I didn't leave the flat all weekend. Even though I knew this would send me into a downward spiral, I couldn't get the energy to get up off the sofa and go out. Also, it was still very cold and windy. This was my least favourite type of weather; every time I looked out the window, all I could see was rubbish blowing around the streets, people hugging their coats tight and pulling their hats down over their ears. There was nothing to go outside for and no one to go outside with, so I didn't. I drew all the curtains, turned off all the lights, and slept intermittently on and off until Sunday night when I got woken up by someone knocking on the door again, which I ignored—again.

On Monday morning, when my alarm woke me up, I found myself lying on the sofa with a crick neck. I didn't feel too good, so I turned off my alarm and went back to sleep. I woke again at midday to three missed calls from Poppy.

'Shit,'

I called her back and got her voicemail.

'Hi Poppy, I'm so sorry. I was at the dentist. I needed an emergency appointment. I've been in agony all night. I'm on my way in now.'

The fear of losing my job and upsetting Poppy got me in the shower and out of the flat in record time. I powdered my face so I looked even paler than usual and bought a bottle of water and some cotton wool balls en route to work. I pushed several balls into one cheek, and when I arrived, I looked half gerbil-half human.

'I'm *mo morry*,' I said, sounding like I was being smothered.

'God, you look awful,' Gary said.

'Are *mou metter?*' I said.

'He's fine,' Poppy said, 'but by the looks of you, you shouldn't be here.'

'I'm *mine, monestly. Morry*, I didn't call. I was in *mo* much pain. I cracked it on *momething* I ate last *might*.' All my words were muffled, but some were harder to say than others.

'Where were you? What did you eat?'

This was such an obvious question. I couldn't believe I'd been so stupid and not prepared an answer. I needed to up my game if I didn't want to get found out.

'Annabel's. Mi mink it was a *mone*.' I smiled inwardly. I had pulled this gem out of of nowhere. Like a dentist pulling out a rotten tooth!

'Bone? I thought Annabel's was an oyster bar?'

'I mean *mell*.'

'Poor you. You must have been so disappointed, especially as you have to book a table so far in advance. I hope you've complained? You definitely should, you know. You'll probably get a free meal or something.'

'Mmm, maybe,' I said, wondering if Poppy knew every single restaurant in London.

'You were lucky to get an appointment. I have to book my dentist six months in advance.'

'He's a *mamily mriend*.'

'But he is a dentist, right? You didn't go to some back alley in the East End and get your tooth extracted with pliers like in Le Miserable?'

I couldn't answer because the cotton wool had moved, and I was worried it would fall out if I opened my mouth. I pushed it back into position with my tongue and nodded like one of those toy dogs in the back of cars.

'Who were you with?'

'Meg. He *mooked* it as a *murprise*.'

'Greg? I thought you said he was away?'

I should have confessed to everything there and then because it was becoming increasingly obvious. I wasn't cut out for this double life. Making up stories, dancing with the law, and following people around London clearly wasn't my forte after all. I'd had a good stab at it, but I was beginning to think that the quiet, boring, dull me was less stressful. The only problem was I wasn't sure I was ready to let go of my interesting life just yet.

'He *mame mack* early as a *murprise*,' I muffled.

'That is so sweet! Why didn't you tell me? We could have had you guys over. Let's do something in January—yes?'

'...*efinitely*.'

CHAPTER 11

It was ten a.m. on Christmas Day, and I was still in my pyjamas. I ate a bowl of Rice Krispies and tuned in to Magic FM, but the non-stop Christmas hits made me feel sad, so I switched to Radio 4. Maybe I needed to connect with God. I quickly realised that wasn't for me either, so I turned it off and sprawled out on the sofa, wishing I'd made an effort to get a tree and maybe a couple of baubles. I channel-flicked between *Kids TV* and old movies. By midday, I felt like going back to bed, but I already knew how that would make me feel, and that knowledge was enough to get me into the shower.

I don't remember washing, getting dressed, putting on my coat and boots, or locking the door behind me. My mind was either in the past or in the future. When I got outside, the cold air seemed to bring me back to the present and the reality of my situation. I wasn't living my best life, but it could be worse. I had a home, a job, and a friend in Poppy. Our friendship wasn't the same as my friendship with Kai had been. But I'd known Kai half my life, and we'd grown up together. Poppy and me had only been friends for a few months.

I decided to leave the sad, miserable me indoors and take the happy me outside. I wanted to enjoy Christmas Day, even if I was on my own.

The streets weren't as empty as I thought they'd be. A few shops were even open. I walked past a man sitting on a large sheet of cardboard. He was squirrelled inside a grubby-looking sleeping bag that was pulled up high to his neck. There was a dog asleep at his feet.

'Happy Christmas.'

'Happy Christmas.'

'Can you spare any change, love?'

'No, I'm sorry,' I said, walking past. I stopped and turned back. 'I don't have any cash on me, but I can get you something from the shop.' I smiled at him. 'If you tell me what you want?'

£30 poorer after buying a tin of dog biscuits, a packet of cigarettes, a bottle of whisky, and a cheese sandwich, I felt like a modern-day urban Father Christmas.

'Bless you, love. You're a proper Christmas angel,' the man said when I handed him his gifts in a plastic carrier bag. I walked away and could almost feel the halo burning brightly above my head.

I went to the square, sat on a bench, and sent Kai a message.

Eve: *Happy Christmas. I hope you're having a good day. Let me know if you want to play 'compare the Christmas Day game'–telling you now though, that I've won.*

No reply.

There were no trains or buses, so I was pretty limited as to where I could go until serendipity intervened. Just as I was considering going back home, the sun came out from behind a cloud and temporarily blinded me. I walked straight into one of those bloody e-bikes that had been left abandoned in the middle of the pavement. I bent down to pick it up and had a flashback of the last time I'd seen Kai. That day in Battersea Park, before we bumped into Poppy and before I said what I said. I scrolled through my phone and found the app that Kai had downloaded and scanned the QR code. The bike released, and suddenly, I was free. Free to go wherever I wanted to go. No passengers to distract me, no listening to other people's conversations, just me and my thoughts on Christmas Day in glorious London town.

As I powered my way through London, I thought about Thames FM. The listeners had no idea that the Christmas songs, festive dedications, and references to the king's speech had all been pre-recorded weeks ago. Nor did they know that Gary, our Christmas Day host and voice of the station, was spending the day at his local pub while his two daughters spent their day with their respective mothers. But if we provided company for our listeners, what did it matter if we were live or recorded? We were offering a friendly voice and company on a day many people found difficult. Maybe I should listen with a new perspective. Radio could become my friend and help make my life less lonely.

Without much thought or planning, I cycled along the empty roads of the city. I headed first for the river, then down towards Holborn and The Strand. I cycled past a family group walking their dogs, a couple of runners (who runs on Christmas Day?), and a few Christmas solos like me. I was used to listening to other people talking about their lives, but today, I was only seeing them. It made me want to know what their story was. Were they heading somewhere for lunch, had they argued with a loved one, or maybe they were spending Christmas day alone? It gave me comfort knowing I wasn't the only one.

I reached Waterloo Bridge. There were people on both sides, taking pictures at one of the most photographed sites in London. Tourists taking a festive vacation, grinning against the backdrop of the London Eye and the Southbank Centre. These photographs would become memories of a special Christmas Day for years to come, and I felt both nostalgic and envious.

On the other side of the bridge, a young couple took a selfie. Tower Bridge and The National Theatre dominated the skyline. At night, this was one of my favourite views of the city. Panels on the sides of tall buildings lit up in bright green and purple. Fairy lights looping from tree to tree along the Southbank. It made me happy every time I saw it.

When I reached the other side, I turned right onto Lambeth Walk and cycled past The Covid Wall—hundreds of red hearts dedicated to loved ones who lost their lives in the pandemic. A stark reminder of how insignificant my problems really were. This strange time in history that had impacted the whole world. The repercussions were still being felt today.

In theory, bikes weren't allowed on the path that ran alongside the embankment, but it was so much nicer cycling alongside the Thames than on the road. It was quiet compared to normal, and I figured I could break the rules this once. The chances of seeing a police officer patrolling the streets on a Saturday night in Kings Cross were rare—seeing one in broad daylight on Christmas Day was nigh on impossible.

It wasn't until I reached Vauxhall that I decided to go and surprise Auntie Jean. I'd found myself in the right part of town and had already wished several times I'd said yes to her invitation. This thought kept coming into my head like a weed that wouldn't stop growing, but once I let it in, it bloomed like a flower. I might be too late to carve the turkey, but I could clear plates or wash up. I got off the bike and sat on one of the benches facing the Houses of Parliament. It was a big, imposing, beautiful building. All those powerful people working in one place, yet just down the road, people like my Auntie Jean were cooking Christmas dinner for people with nowhere to go. I googled the address of the community centre, telling myself if it was nearby, I'd go, and if it was too far, I'd go home. It was a twenty-five-minute walk or an eight-minute bike ride away. Google had spoken.

I left the bike at a docking station and walked around the back of a modern red brick building. I could hear Christmas music and the hum of people talking. There were several people outside, smoking.

'Is this where the Christmas lunch is?' I said.

'Too late love. It's all gone.'

'I'm here to—' I trailed off, realising he thought I was homeless. I'm not judging anyone for how they dress or live, but 'living on the streets' wasn't the look I was going for. I actually blamed Kai for this. Despite his slightly alternative tastes, he was my fashion guru, and since he'd abandoned me, I'd clearly lost all dress sense. 'I'm here to help,' I said.

'Good on you.'

'Thanks.' I smiled to hide my battered ego. 'Happy Christmas,' I said.

I scoured the room. It was a happy scene. Several long tables were decorated in paper tablecloths and there were remnants of Christmas crackers and festive wrapping strewn on the tables. Two ladies were walking up and down in between the tables; one scraping plates into a bucket, another collecting plates and cutlery in a plastic washing-up bowl. There were jugs of water on the tables, and at the far end of the room, slices of Christmas cake were laid out on large serving platters. Cups and saucers were stacked on top of each other like Jenga, and two large silver teapots sat on large, thick, cork placemats. A lady carrying a four-pint carton of milk and a bag of sugar with a spoon sticking out of the top backed out through a door. She placed them on the table.

'Anyone for tea and cake?' A chorus of cheers filled the room. 'Form an orderly queue. No pushing in, or you'll be sent to the back.'

'Hi, Auntie Jean,' I said, smiling.

'Ah, if it isn't my lovely niece.' She pulled me into her with more warmth than I remember her ever showing me before. 'You came!'

'Sorry, I'm late.'

'Perfect timing.' She handed me a knife. 'You can help with the cake, then there's plenty of washing up. Oh, and do not let that knife out of your sight! It's blunt as a duvet, but still.'

Two middle-aged men came over to where we were standing.

'Tea? Cake?' Jean said.

'Has the cake got booze in it? I'm in recovery,' one of them said.

'Same here,' the other one said.

'Don't you worry, my loves. There's no booze in the cake, but there is plenty of butter, sugar, and fruit. So you can count it towards your five a day.'

I dived behind the table, keeping the knife firmly in my grip.

'Go wash your hands and ask Dave for an apron. Tell him you're my niece.'

'Dave?'

'Reverend Dave—can't miss him. White collar around his neck. Looks like he can't breathe.'

'Right.'

By the time I was back, the queue for tea and cake was snaking around the room. I started handing out the cake.

'I don't think there's enough slices,' I said to Jean, worried she was going to make me be the one to break the news.

'There's at least another four out there. In the chocolate tins stacked by the oven. Slice them into squares—the same size; otherwise, you'll start World War Three.'

'Got it,' I said, heading for the door. Reverend Dave came to help me, and soon, two of the cakes were ready to go out. I carried one to the table, and Dave carried the other. He then went to join a group sitting at one of the tables and started talking with them. The more cake I handed out, the more people went over and joined in, and whilst it wasn't enough to convert me from definite atheist to possible Christian, it was enough to make me understand what this meant to the people who were here. People who, like me, would have otherwise spent Christmas alone and who were dealing with challenges a lot harder than mine.

The buzz of chat competed with the music as I handed out the last few slices, then Reverend Dave wheeled a TV in and set it up in front of where we'd been serving. Soon, King Charles' face filled the screen. The music was turned off, and the room fell silent.

I'd never watched the queen's or king's speech before. It wasn't something my parents showed any interest in, and so by default, I wasn't interested either.

The king talked about universal values between religions and communities and asked that people 'seek the good of others, not least the friend we do not yet know.'

When it finished, the room clapped and cheered. I looked around at the smiling faces of these people who had so little possessions, yet they had each other, and today, at least, this had brought them the gift of joy.

It was six o'clock by the time the washing up was done, the tables were cleared, and the floor was swept. Several bags of rubbish were tied neatly and stacked outside. Reverend Dave stood by the door, wishing all the guests a happy Christmas and thanking them for coming. Many shook his hand, some hugged him, and he handed everyone a flyer with information on the community groups that were run by the church volunteers. When the last guest left, he shut the door and came over to shake the hand of all the volunteers, taking each hand in both of his, thanking them for their time and kindness.

'I hope to see you again, Eve,' he said when he reached me. 'Your aunt is a very special person. You are very lucky to have her, and so are we.' I nodded, feeling strangely proud.

I waited for Jean to say her goodbyes, then walked with her to her car.

'How did you get here?'

'I cycled on an e-bike.'

'A what bike?'

'An electric bike.'

'Those green things abandoned all over London? Horrible hazards,' Auntie Jean said.

Jean had always been opinionated, which was the reason she and Mum clashed. Mum was secretive and reserved, kept herself to herself, and didn't even let her only daughter get close to her. Jean was loud, carefree, and not at all sensitive to how she made others feel. She often used to leave, saying, 'If I've upset your mum, that's her problem, not mine.' Maybe it was time I channelled my inner Auntie Jean.

'Thank you for your help today,' she said. 'To be honest, I didn't think you'd come. Thought you'd be with that friend of yours from school.'

'I didn't have any plans. It was fun,' I said, smiling at her.

'Oh, love. You were going to spend Christmas Day on your own?' She looked genuinely upset. 'I'm sorry. Why didn't you say?'

'It's fine. I'm not a big Christmas person. As you know.'

'Well, I blame your mum for that. She was very antisocial, and it made you a wallflower.'

'I'm just not a fan of crowds.'

'You could've fooled me, the way you were chatting to the guests today. You were in your element. Oozing confidence you were. There's a quote, what is it?' I shrugged. 'I can't remember now, but I don't believe you for a second, and I blame your mum for that, too. Telling everyone you were shy before you even had a chance to find your voice.' She raised her eyebrows. 'I used to say to her, "Let your daughter define herself."' Jean looked away. 'But she didn't listen. Thought she knew best.' She sighed. 'And now, look at you.'

'What do you mean?' I whispered, fighting a desire to crawl into a dark cave and not hear her answer.

'I mean, look at you. Young, beautiful, the world at your feet, and you're spending Christmas Day with me and a load of men who haven't showered in weeks.'

We reached Jean's car. An old white two-seater SEAT. I recognised it from her rare visits, but I'd never been in it.

'Jump in. I'll run you home.'

I climbed in and sat amongst empty coffee cups and Marks and Spencer sandwich packets.

Jean talked all the way, telling me the sad stories about some of the people at the lunch today. I looked out of the window at the bridges lit up in the night sky and wondered what made these people get up in the morning. Each day harder than the one before. Maybe it was hope that the new day would be better.

Jean pulled up around the back of the flats.

'Do you want to come in?' I said, surprising myself with how much I wanted her to say yes. 'I haven't got any wine, though. Sorry.'

'I couldn't anyway,' she said, dangling the car keys in my face.

'I have tea and coffee?'

'Hot chocolate?'

'Maybe, but it might be out of date. I think Mum bought it.'

'What's a few years amongst family, eh?'

We sat in the lounge, two mugs of hot chocolate cooling on the coffee table in front of us.

'So how is your friend from school? What's his name again?'

'Kai?'

'Yes, that's right, well done,' she said like I'd got a really hard question right.

'We fell out.'

'Surely you can sort it out. You've been friends for a long time.'

'It was my fault. I've tried to apologise, but he's not interested.'

'Maybe he's in love with you.'

I laughed.

'No, he definitely isn't. We're just friends, honestly.'

Jean shrugged. 'Okay, if you say so,' she said.

I reached down for my mug and let the warm, sweet drink warm my body.

'Are you lonely living here on your own?' Jean said.

'I like my own company.'

'That's not an answer,' Jean said. 'I'm sorry I haven't visited you more since your mum and dad died. I assumed you were doing okay.'

'I am okay.'

'You always were a bit of a loner.' I didn't reply. 'Your mum was complicated, but she loved you.'

'Yeah, I know,' I said quietly.

'But she also made some mistakes, and she didn't like it when I told her.'

'Like what?'

'Like stopping your dad from visiting his family in Malta.'

This was news to me.

'Did she? Why?'

'She was worried he'd want to go back there.' She raised her eyebrows. 'Paranoid he'd reconnect with his old girlfriend.'

I looked at my aunt. 'What?'

'He never would have. He loved your mum too much.'

'Dad had a girlfriend?'

'Your parents did have lives before they met each other, you know. But your mum and me.' She paused. 'We were very different. All she wanted was to settle down, get married, and have children.'

'And you?'

135

'I wanted the total opposite. Independence and freedom. That's why, we,' she paused again, 'I don't want to say fell out, cos that's not what it was, but we tolerated each other. If we weren't sisters, we wouldn't have been friends.'

'Oh.'

'I told her she was stopping you from knowing your family. Your dad's family wanted to see you and get to know you. I told her you needed more people in your life.'

'But I had them and you,' I said, feeling I should at least try and defend my mum.

'I was hopeless. I wasn't able to be the doting auntie you deserved. I've never been maternal, and the thought of zoos and funfairs made me shiver. It still does.'

I laughed. 'Don't fancy a trip on the Southbank Merry-Go-Round, then?'

She shrugged. 'Sounds fun, but can I watch from a bar?' I laughed. 'I loved you; of course, I did and still do. But I didn't know you, and I still don't really.'

'Mad Auntie Jean. That's what she called you.'

Jean threw her head back and laughed. 'She was a cow,' she said.

We sat in comfortable silence for a few moments.

'You should go find them. Your relatives.

'I don't need to,' I said. 'One mad auntie is enough.'

Jean laughed again.

'And I'm not brave enough.'

'Nonsense. You don't need to be brave.'

We sat in silence, finishing our drink.

'What made you find God?' I said, keen to change the subject away from me and the relatives I didn't know—or have any desire to get to know.

'I'm not religious! Not in the slightest,' Jean snorted. 'Don't worry, Reverend Dave knows how I feel. In fact, the only real shame is that there's no chance for us. He's rather dishy, don't you think?'

I didn't agree. He was overweight, with a full head of hair that looked like it had been cut under a pudding basin, and he had porky fingers.

'He's not my type,' I said, and Jean laughed.

'I help out at the church community centre because I like the people and I like to feel useful. Those people who came today to celebrate Christmas. Most of them still have families, but they made mistakes. Took the wrong path in life. Made a bad choice.'

'That's sad,' I said, stating the obvious.

We sat in comfortable silence.

'You should make up with your friend,' Jean said. 'Good friends are hard to come by.'

'I've tried. Like loads of times,' I said, my voice getting higher.

'He'll come back. Be patient.'

When Jean was leaving, she hugged me again.

'Maybe we can go out for dinner sometime or go for a walk in Regents Park? What do you think? I could be a real aunt and take you to London Zoo?'

I laughed.

'I'd really like that,' I said. 'The walk or the dinner, but not the zoo.'

Just as she was about to go, Jean slapped herself on the head.

'I've remembered the quote—*You're braver than you believe, stronger than you seem, and smarter than you think.* Guess who said that?'

I chewed the inside of my cheek. 'Mother Theresa?'

Jean shook her head.

'Nelson Mandela?'

She shook her head again. 'You're close,' she laughed. 'Christopher Robin to Winnie the Pooh.'

I smiled.

'And they were the best of friends.'

CHAPTER 12

On Boxing Day, it rained. Horrible, hair-spoiling, pathetic rain, not proper pounding rain that washes away the grime on the streets and makes the world look shiny and new. I stayed in all day and let the clouds back in as I counted down the hours until the next day when I could go back to work. I needed something to get up for, something to stop me from getting swallowed up in my misery. Not even *It's A Wonderful Life* or *The Snowman* brought me back to the surface. I was sinking, and I needed something or someone to stop me from drowning. Yesterday, it had taken a herculean effort to get out of the house, which had paid off. Today was a new day, and it all felt too much.

The next morning, I dragged myself into the shower, wishing I could take my head off instead of fighting the voices telling me to stay in bed. I needed my job to keep me sane; I needed to stay connected to the real world, even though I was living in a made-up world. I stood outside the flat and breathed in new air. London was still quiet; routines weren't back to normal. On the underground, I sat next to a couple heading to the sales and listened to everything on their wishlist. An air fryer was at the top.

'I'd been relying on Mum to get us one for Christmas. I dropped enough bloody hints,' she said.

'Why don't we just take back the bird table and swap it for the air fryer? It's not as if we have room on our postage-stamp patio for it anyway,' he said.

'We can't. You know what she's like. She'll definitely notice, and I'll have to confess, then she'll be upset.'

'But we're going to have to lose one of the outside chairs because the table—ours and the birds—won't fit otherwise.' He pulled a face. 'But obviously, nature takes priority over us being able to sit outside together at the same time,' he said.

'I reckon she did it on purpose to make us move nearer to her and have a—'

'Proper garden,' they said in unison.

'I could do with a new pair of boots,' he said.

'I need a new black coat because this one doesn't look nice when I'm dressed up,' she said, picking at the sleeve of her black coat.

'Does it matter what your coat looks like? Surely you take it off as soon as you get to wherever you're going?'

'Of course, it matters,' she said.

'But we don't have room for all this stuff you keep buying.'

'You can talk. Your golf clubs take up the entire cupboard downstairs.'

'It's there, or our bedroom. What would you prefer?'

'My exercise bike is going to go in the bedroom. Can't you put your golf clubs in the boot of the car?'

'No, because your gym stuff is always in the boot and—'

I zoned out. This couple had far too much stuff and should probably move to a bigger place.

The lights were on and Poppy and Gary were already in when I arrived. Poppy gave me an enthusiastic welcome hug.

'How was your Christmas? God, I can't believe how quickly it went, can you?'

She was wearing a jumper I hadn't seen before. It was silky soft, silver grey. A long, arty-looking cotton scarf was hanging around her neck, and she had a pair of baby pink trainers on.

'Great, thanks. I like your jumper. And your trainers,' I said, keen to deflect away from her questioning, 'and your scarf!'

I didn't feel like sharing the community kitchen experience with Poppy. I didn't think she would get it, plus I'd already told her I was spending the day with my made-up relatives.

'Ahhh, thank you. Christmas prezzies. The jumper is Angora. What about you? Did you get anything nice?'

I hadn't wrapped or opened a single present. Usually, I got something small from Auntie Jean, but I'd turned up unannounced at the community centre. Besides, she'd given me something money can't buy. She might not know it, but Christmas Day had been one of the nicest days of my life—which was kind of sad but true. Apart from meeting some great people, I'd learnt that even an introvert needs to be around people sometimes, and I also felt me and Aunt Jean had connected in a way we hadn't done before.

'I got an airfryer.' I shrugged. 'Haven't got a clue how to use it though.'

'Oh, they're life changing! Trust me,' she smiled, 'and it's air fryer. Two words. Not airfryer.'

I hung my coat up on the wobbly coat stand, put the kettle on, and sat down at my desk. As I worked my way through the Christmas request emails, Poppy told me about the goose they'd had instead of turkey, the three desserts, her cute nieces and nephews, and the games they'd played. She described a Tesco Finest Christmas. Everything was premium, everything was delicious, everything was perfect. In fact, it was the most Poppy had ever told me about herself. She rarely told me about her life outside of work; usually, she just dropped names of people into our chats as if I should know them and talked about places I'd never heard of.

There were several emails from listeners complaining about the Christmas playlist, saying it was too repetitive. I forwarded it to Gary for feedback purposes, which was a mistake because moments later, he stormed out of the studio.

'I can't invent more Christmas hits, can I?' he shouted across the office.

'Apparently, we played "Last Christmas" three times in one hour,' I said quietly.

'I love that song,' Poppy said.

'Bloody idiots, the lot of them,' Gary said, slamming a pile of copying on my desk.

'Don't shoot the messenger,' I said under my breath.

'He's in a bad mood today,' Poppy said.

'That makes a change,' I said, picking up the copying. 'We also had one email from a listener saying we'd kept her company all day.'

'Ahhh, that is so sad,' Poppy said.

'Maybe I should've told Gary about that one first?'

'He's not that sentimental,' Poppy confirmed.

'Imagine spending Christmas on your own.' She pulled a sad face. 'So, did you see Greg? Did he get you anything nice?'

'Errr no, not yet. He was with his family.'

'I haven't forgotten about dinner,' Poppy said. 'How about the first Friday of February? That way, all the annoying people doing Dry January can drink. What do you think?'

'Great. I'll ask him.'

Poppy lowered her voice.

'I'm also going to invite Gary, but not until nearer the time. Then, hopefully, he won't be able to make it.'

I nodded, wondering how it must feel to have so many people to invite to dinner that you have to hope some can't come.

I made the tea and took one into the studio for Gary.

'So, how was your Christmas?' I placed the tea on the studio desk, and he moved it to the floor with a dramatic sigh.

'Bloody expensive and not good for my liver.'

I left him to it.

'I need to talk to you about arranging a meeting with Bob,' Poppy said as I sat back down. 'So you remember before Christmas when we went to the pub?' I nodded. 'Me, Bob, and Gary ended up going for a Chinese after and, oh, don't look like that!' Poppy reached out and stroked my arm, 'We didn't plan it or anything. You went out with some friends, remember?'

I nodded, annoyed I'd let Poppy see my disappointment. I could feel tears prick in my eyes; I couldn't help it. They'd all gone out together that night after the drinks. The night Poppy said she was getting a taxi to a friend's house.

'Yeah, yeah, course, it's fine.'

'Anyway, he wants to have a meeting to discuss marketing next year, and I really want you to be involved.'

'Great,' I said, trying to sound cool, but the news of the Chinese meal had delivered me a real stomach blow.

'I'll send Bob some date options and let you know, but get thinking up some new ideas, yeah?' Poppy said, oblivious to the pain she'd inflicted.

The rest of the week felt disjointed. It was those weird days after Christmas and before New Year, where you don't know what day it is, and getting to work late and leaving early is acceptable for no reason other than it's the weird Christmas week. Poppy was excited about her New Year's Eve plans.

'I'm being whisked away for an all-inclusive mini break that includes a five-course dinner with a live band.'

'Wow,' I said.

'I know. I am so lucky.' She smiled.

'Spoilt more like,' Gary said, walking out for a fag break.

I tried again to find out more about her mystery partner, but she stayed tight-lipped, telling me I'd meet them at her dinner party.

'What are you up to, Gary?' Poppy said, winking at me.

'Drinking,' he said.

New Year's Eve had never been a big deal for me, but this year was looking like it might be an all-time low. In the past, Kai and me had gone out for some fast food and sat on a bench in the park with a couple of ready mix cocktail cans but parted ways before midnight because neither of us could afford New Year's Eve Uber prices. As he got drunker, Kai became more melancholy. Rambling on about how he hated his stepdad, hated living at home, but couldn't afford to move out, and was wasting his life. He wanted to travel the world and pleaded with me to quit my job and go with him. It was the one time when we had a role reversal and I would be the one trying to cheer him up.

'You can't just run away from your life,' I said. 'You're a grown-up now.'

'Come on, Eve, please. We'd have so much fun.'

'How would I survive without my TV shows?'

'I'd be really entertaining the whole time,' Kai said. 'I can't live at home anymore. You don't know what it's like.'

'That's because you never invite me over,' I said.

'Trust me, it's hell.'

'Move out then.'

'To a rabbit hutch?'

'How about a day trip to Brighton instead?' I said, but not until the summer.

'And rent a beach hut?'

I ended up going to bed at ten p.m. and sleeping through the whole thing. This was a good decision and helped me to forget all about this significant yet very insignificant end to the year.

New Year's Day was like Boxing Day on repeat. Same unremarkable nothingy weather and a cloud of gloom following me around the flat. As far as the first days of the year go, this one was down there with the barnacles at the bottom of the sea bed. By the evening, I'd managed to lift myself a little, inspired by the bombardment of uplifting posts on Instagram, the only social media I looked at. 'It starts by loving yourself.' 'Make this your year.' 'Don't change for your friends; change your friends.'

I made a decision that day. I needed to get Greg out of my life. Obviously, there was no actual Greg, but I needed to get out of the situation I was in. Even if that meant Poppy finding me boring again. This whole thing had happened by accident and had gotten out of control. The only question was, *how should I break up with him and why?* Poppy's dinner was just a few weeks away, and I really wanted to see where she lived and meet her friends and her 'secret partner.' I also wanted to show her how fun I could be and make her proud to be my friend. I had two options:

1. Tell Poppy me and Greg split up and risk being uninvited.

2. Go to the dinner solo and tell Poppy Greg was coming later. (Then halfway through, pretend to get a message saying he couldn't make it.)

I circled option two. Surely, she wouldn't throw me out if I was already there, and by then, I'd be the life and soul of the party, and she wouldn't care that I was there on my own.

I laughed out loud. Who was I kidding? Who was I even talking about? *Life and Soul of the party* wouldn't be me in a million years, no matter how much I pretended.

The first proper week back of the new year started off okay. The weather had turned unseasonably mild, and Poppy was upbeat and chatty. Even Gary had become almost human in his interactions, which, according to Poppy, was his New Year's resolution.

'I'm Gary's New Year's resolution?'

'No, not just you. He said he's working on being more "personable."'

'Wow, I mean, I'll believe it when I see it, but that's unbelievable. Literally unbelievable,' I said.

'He is also trying to cut down on smoking. He said he was going to give up completely, but I told him not to. Can you imagine his mood?'

'You're not interested in extending his life then?'

'No. Our sanity is more important.'

'I didn't think Gary listened to anyone but himself?'

'Trust me, he's a mouse in a lion's body. You need to stand up for yourself a bit more.' I nodded, not convinced. 'And I,' Poppy said, resting her hand on her chest in preparation for a big announcement, 'am giving up lattes from over the road. What about you, any New Year resolutions?'

'I haven't really got any, but I think I'll join you in no coffee from over the road. My bank balance will thank me.'

Poppy sighed.

'I know you're underpaid. I promise you I am working on it. If we can get this marketing budget from Bob and bring in some new listeners, then maybe I can bring it up with Bob again?'

'I wasn't saying that, I just meant— '

'Yes, you were, and you're right. You are underpaid.' She flicked her silky hair, then went back to her laptop and started typing with her perfectly manicured nails, painted in just the right shade of pink. 'Don't apologise for asking for what you deserve.'

I was confused. When I was telling the truth, Poppy didn't believe me, and when I was lying through my teeth, she did. My New Year's resolution should really be to stop lying about my life, but until Poppy's party, I had to keep my fake life going if I wanted to keep my invite. Another resolution: accept that Kai was no longer in my life. He hadn't replied to my message on Christmas Day or any of my messages before that, but I just couldn't believe we weren't going to be friends anymore.

Over the next few weeks, Poppy talked about her dinner party almost every day. She hinted at the food she would be serving, although she kept changing her mind because the weather kept changing, and this was key to the menu apparently. She confirmed there would be twelve of us, including Gary and his girlfriend. (Assuming he could make it after he received his last-minute invite.)

I asked Poppy about the dress code.

'There's no dress code.' Poppy laughed. 'Just wear what you would usually wear to a dinner party.' Needless to say, this wasn't at all helpful.

'What are you wearing?' I tried a different tact.

'You'll have to wait and see,' she said. 'But I am so looking forward to meeting Greg properly. I've told my friends he's a top photographer, so warn him he might get asked to take some snaps.'

I'd managed to keep the stories of me and Greg coming, keeping them as simple as possible. Listening to other people's conversations provided me with just enough to keep up the pretence. The other day, two guys had got on the tube dressed in sports gear and carrying tennis bags. They were heading to Holland Park, which gave me a perfect answer when Poppy next asked me about my weekend.

'You play tennis? I never had you down as a sporty type.'

'Greg is much better than me, but it was fun, especially as it's so mild at the moment.'

Another time, I told her he'd taken me to a pottery cafe.

'That is sooo romantic. What did you paint?'

'Me? I painted,' I paused for a moment too long, 'a mug with a heart on the side.'

My mug story was inspired by a woman and her girlfriend proudly admiring their craftwork on the train journey home the week before. One of them had painted her mug a deep sky blue, with a large pink heart on each side. The bag carrying their masterpieces was printed with the name of the pottery cafe on the side. A quick Google when I got home told me everything I needed to know. I then convinced Poppy I'd spent a happy and creative Sunday afternoon with my boyfriend. Kai would have loved a creative activity like this, but instead of going with him, I had to pretend I'd been with a boyfriend who didn't even exist.

'I hope it comes out okay. I got an A in my art GCSE, so I'm feeling hopeful,' I said.

'Well done.' Poppy said, making me feel five years old.

To make sure Poppy believed all my stories, I'd started throwing in a few about things I'd done solo. I couldn't expect her to believe I spent all of my spare time with Greg. Taking a leaf out of Poppy's book, I invested in some gym wear; only mine was from Oxfam. Hers from Lululemon. I even braved Gary's mocking by wearing it to the office.

'What's with the Lycra?' Gary said. 'That new man of yours isn't a twat on a bike, is he?'

To be honest, I was surprised he even noticed what I was wearing.

'No, I've just come from an early morning yoga class. I've got a change of clothes in my bag,' I said confidently.

'Have you started doing yoga?' Poppy enthused. 'Vinyasa or Hatha?'

'Ummm, Hatha,' I said, my plan already backfiring.

'Really? I find Hatha too slow. Where do you practice?'

'Just at home,' I said.

'I mean the class,' Poppy said. 'Which studios?'

'Oh, Yoga World, near where I live,' I said, thanks to a super cool twenty-something I'd seen wearing a branded hoodie a week before. 'It's a beginners' class.'

'But yoga is all about the individual, not their expertise,' Poppy said.

'No perfecting your downward dog in the office, please,' Gary said.

'Yes, that would be inappropriate.' Poppy laughed, and I laughed with them, changing in the toilets soon after.

I often got it wrong. Like the time I'd tried to impress her with my night out at the Royal Festival Hall listening to classical music.

'It was Greg's idea. It's not my thing, but it was a really special night.'

'Classical music? God, I think I'd rather watch paint dry,' Poppy said.

'I kept applauding at the wrong moment,' I said, a direct quote from the man I'd heard this from. Poppy practically yawned in my face. Repeating this story had obviously been a mistake. 'I think Greg booked it because Nicola Benedetti was playing,' I said, referencing the conversation I'd overheard and attempting to sound cultured.

'Never heard of her,' Poppy said, turning to her laptop and starting to type.

Her enthusiasm for Greg seemed to wane a little after that. Maybe I'd be enough on my own, after all.

CHAPTER 13

It was the day before Poppy's dinner party and I was starting to lose my nerve. The charity shops had nothing that made me feel good enough, so against all my usual principles, I ordered a black dress and a pair of black knee-length boots with small heels in the January sales. When I tried them on, I almost didn't recognise myself—and not in a good way. I felt like a child playing dress up. At nursery school, I'd always picked the superhero cape—not because I was a tomboy, but because it was the easiest outfit to put on and didn't require undressing.

I never wore dresses. I felt uncomfortable, both literally and in my mind. The dress was made of a fabric that didn't stretch, and I felt restricted. The boots pinched my toes. If looking this good felt like this, I was happy looking bad. I attempted to take a selfie like the influencers on Instagram did. I could send it to Kai, maybe. But I couldn't work out how to do it. When I took the picture of my reflection in the mirror, there was a flash on the screen. If I lifted my arm, aimed and clicked, I cut off half my face. I gave up. If Kai saw a picture of me in a black party dress, he would potentially have a heart attack, although if this were to happen, he would only have himself to blame. I wrote him a letter in my dragonfly notebook instead.

Hi,

I've decided to stop messaging you. I don't know if you've noticed, but it's kind of a New Year's resolution. I still think of you all the time, and I'm still sad and sorry about what happened, but I can't mourn your loss forever.

Guess what? I bought a black dress from a shop (in the sale.). And a pair of boots with small heels (very low because I don't think I can walk in proper heels). I copied 'the look' from one of those Instagram accounts you made me follow. The next time you see me (if you see me), you might not even recognise me.

In case you're wondering, the reason for the outfit is that tomorrow night, I'm going to a dinner party at Poppy's house (the lady with the fluffy ginger dog who we saw in the park). It's actually very complicated, because I'm meant to be going with someone, but I haven't got that someone to go with, so I'm going on my own (which is against the rules of the invite.). I'm hoping to pull it off. You always said I didn't take life's opportunities, so I'm proving you wrong, which would be a lot more satisfying if you actually knew about it.

Love, Eve

PS I don't know how to do my hair and make-up, so I am sending you a telepathic message to come over and help. If it works, I promise not to talk to you.

I hung the black dress on a hanger on the back of the wardrobe door and went to bed. I slept badly, and every time I woke up, the dress stared at me like a ghoul. Eventually, I got up and hung the dress inside the wardrobe because it was really giving me the heebie jeebies. I went to the bathroom and gulped water directly from the tap, then lay awake for the next hour to try and still my racing mind.

The next morning, I had a splitting headache and huge bags under both eyes. I downed some painkillers and had as cold a shower as I could bear to try and reduce the puffiness.

'Good morning,' Poppy sang. 'Are you excited about tonight?'

'Can't wait,' I said, using every ounce of enthusiasm I could find.

'Everything is under control; all I need now is to transform myself into a *Hostess with the Mostest* and get the party started.' She did a little dance and I attempted a smile, willing my facial muscles to cooperate. 'I hope you don't think this is cheeky, but if you're bringing chocolates and wine, can you not buy Ferrero Rocher? I really don't like those. And red, not white. I have so much white wine, but everyone always drinks red in the winter. Also, we're having venison and that is a red wine meat. A nice Merlot or a Shiraz, if that's okay? Or a Pinot Noir, if that's not too cheeky an ask.'

Gary walked past and mimicked Poppy.

'A nice Merlot or Shiraz or a Pinot Noir. Got that, Eve?' he sniggered, pointing at me. 'Polly doesn't drink the cheap stuff, but don't worry, I'll drink anything.'

'I'm not going to apologise for being sophisticated,' Poppy said. 'You can bring whatever you like, but not Pinot Grigio. Pretty please.'

'Got it,' I said, feeling the heat rising in my cheeks and an ice-like sensation layering my stomach. So, Gary was coming. That was disappointing news.

This whole charade was nearly over. Once I'd successfully infiltrated myself into Poppy's social group, I could tell her Greg and me were over and by then, I'd have a whole new circle of friends. The lying could stop, using other people's stories as my own could stop, and sitting on a train to pass the time could stop. I would get invited to things all the time and have a host of people to call on if ever I was at a loose end. I felt sick, but I had to go through with this. My life was empty and if I pulled out now, I didn't have a plan b.

As the hours passed, my anxiety increased. I was finding it hard to focus on my tasks. I'd already sent the copier into meltdown by pressing one thousand copies instead of 10, and thank goodness for the lovely man working at our suppliers, who called to check I really did want five-hundred reams of copier paper, instead of the usual fifty. As we reached the final hour of the working day, Poppy came over to my desk looking flustered.

'Eve, I need you to literally save my life. It's an emergency!'

'What's happened?'

'My air fryer broke. I dropped it. Long story. Anyway, I was promised the replacement would be delivered today. They've just called to say they're out of stock. All the food for tonight is being cooked in the air fryer, except the appetisers and dessert, but the menu won't work with the oven. I need you to come early and bring yours. I promise not to drop it.' She put her hands together in prayer.

Oh God.

'The problem is it's quite heavy; I'm not sure how I would get it to you?' I said. I had no idea how heavy an air fryer was, but in the adverts, it looked quite cumbersome.

'Taxi, of course? How else were you and Greg going to get to mine?'

'Train?'

'Train?' Poppy laughed. 'I'm sure Greg can treat you to an Uber?'

I left the office bang on five, and ten minutes later, I'd bought a Russell & Hobbs air fryer from Argos for £88, which I needed to collect from Islington before eight o'clock. I got there in under an hour, checked in on the digital screen, and waited for my item to appear on the magic shelf. As I handed over my receipt, the sales assistant handed over a huge box, and I was now the proud owner of an air fryer.

By the time I got home, my arms were killing me. I could feel the sweat running down my back. I put the box on the table and stared at it, hating everything it represented. I slid down onto the floor, my back against the kitchen cabinet. I put my head between my knees, and my tears fell on the floor in front of me. I couldn't do it. I couldn't get dressed up in clothes that made me feel like an alien and make small talk with glamorous people who I didn't know. Also, I couldn't turn up with an air fryer I didn't know how to use. Me and Poppy discussed our mutual love of air fry cooking regularly, and we'd even shared recipes. How would I explain my brand new, unused machine that I had no idea how to operate?

Once I'd made the decision not to go, I actually started to feel better. My heart stopped racing, and I felt strangely calm. I knew I was jeopardising my friendship with Poppy and that I probably wouldn't ever get to meet her cool friends, but I was exhausted with pretending. I felt like I'd become two people, one an imposter and the other the real me. The imposter was taking over my life, but the real me needed to take back control. I sent Poppy a text.

Eve: *So sorry, can't make it tonight x*

Poppy: *WTF!!!!!!*

I turned my phone off and stared out the window while regulating my breathing. The same window, with the same view that I'd stared out of when sitting at the table with my parents. No one speaking, the sound of cutlery on the plate, the hum of the fridge and passing sirens outside.

I don't know how long I sat there, but it was after nine p.m. when I opened the air fryer box and read the instructions.

What is the first thing I should cook in my air fryer?

The answer:

155

Brussel Sprouts.

I quite liked brussels sprouts despite their stench. Fortunately, it was the right time of year for this hugely unpopular vegetable, so I grabbed my coat and went to the local late-night Sainsbury's and bought a bag of sprouts, a small bag of potatoes and some spray oil, which was essential according to the complimentary recipe book. I went straight back home, feeling a tad excited about trying an air-fried sprout.

An hour later, I was sitting on the sofa in my pyjamas, eating a bowl of crispy sprouts and chips—both of which were pretty good, although the flat didn't smell so good. I opened the windows and shivered under a blanket, watching TV until I couldn't keep my eyes open any longer. Then I went to bed and slept like a baby.

In the morning, I showered, cleaned the flat, did some washing, sorted through my wardrobe, tidied the bathroom cabinet, sorted the spice shelf, disinfected the fridge and cleaned the oven. I didn't turn my phone on because I wasn't ready for the messages from Poppy. I was like a whirling dervish; as soon as I finished one job, I looked around for another, and I kept going until I was so hungry that I had to stop or I'd faint. All day, the crying came in waves between my more proactive moments, and I didn't fully stop until it was dark outside and I could draw the curtains again.

On Sunday, I turned my phone on.

Poppy: *Are you joking?*

Poppy: *What about the AF? I NEED IT.*

Poppy: *Pick up!*

I spent Sunday perfecting the air-fried chip and arguing with customer services on the phone, who wouldn't let me return the black dress and boots because it was past the fourteen-day return policy for sale items.

I sent Auntie Jean a message wishing her a happy new year and thanked her for inviting me to help out at the community centre. She replied immediately, telling me it had been the best Christmas she'd ever had, which, considering she'd spent every Christmas until this one with me, was hard not to take personally, but then she sent a follow-up message.

Jean: *Everyone loved you and I am a very proud auntie.*

I wasn't expecting that or the tears that followed. Surely I don't have an endless supply of tears, and they must run out at some point? This was the sort of fact Kai would know the answer to. In the meantime, I was going to dehydrate at this rate.

The sofa was fast becoming my day bed, but every time I lay down and closed my eyes, Kai's voice would wake me up.

'*Get your arse off the sofa and get yourself outside. Those ducks need feeding.*'

Even turning the TV on didn't drown out his voice in my head.

'Fine,' I said out loud.

I walked forty minutes to Regent's Park, then headed to the perimeter fence of London Zoo, where Kai and I used to sit and listen to the animal noises coming from within. I walked to the pond to do some duck spotting. Kai had taught me the names of the different breeds, and that bread was bad for their guts. He'd taught me so much useful and useless information, which was what I missed the most. Kai made my life fun. I threw handfuls of porridge oats into the water and then sat down on a bench to watch the mandarin ducks and red-crested pochards as they pecked the floating oats off the surface. Two women sat down on the bench next to mine. One was crying, the other looked sad. They were both clutching take-out coffee cups. One put their arm around the other and pulled her in close.

'C'mon, he wouldn't want us to be sad. I know it's hard, but we need to be strong and remember the good times. We have so many happy memories.' She paused. 'We're lucky,' she added.

They sat in silence, staring at the pond, their sadness new and raw. No matter how my life was panning out, there was always someone in the world going through something worse than me. This was a life lesson Aunt Jean had taught me, and right now, it did me well to remember it.

'I just can't believe that one day he was here and the next he was gone. I knew he'd have an accident one day,' one of them said.

'I told him his luck would run out. The way he cycled that bloody bike around town. I think he knew it too. I mean, who writes their own bloody eulogy?'

'That was Dad, though, wasn't it? He always did want the last word.'

'It was funny though. I mean, people were laughing—at a funeral!'

'That's what he wanted.'

I was too scared to move. I didn't want to distract them or stop them from talking. Although they were sad, it was nice listening to them talk about their dad like this. They were so consumed with their grief that I wasn't sure they'd even noticed me. I could feel a single tear trickling down my face. I let it fall.

'You know I was supposed to be seeing him on that day. I called him to see where he was,' she stumbled on her words, 'and the police answered.'

'I know.' She squeezed her sister's hand.

'We did the right thing. He would have hated being kept alive by a machine.'

'We didn't have a choice.'

Both of them seemed heartbroken. They left soon after, still holding hands. United in their grief.

That night, I tried to write the first sentence of my own eulogy. Just for fun, I told myself.

If you are listening to this, you are most likely one of only a few people...

I couldn't carry on. There was nothing else I could think of to say.

'Thirty years on earth, and what have you achieved?' I said out loud. 'You haven't made the most of your time, seen the world, been to enough places, got to know enough people.' I sighed a huge sigh, deflating like a balloon. 'You need to start making changes and living a better life.' I choked up when I said this, and as big as this little pep talk to myself was, I had a more pressing problem. What was I going to say to Poppy tomorrow?

I searched up the symptoms of heartache.

Quiet

Withdrawn

Subdued

Loss of appetite

Insomnia

I could do this. I was going to tell Poppy that Greg had gone back to his wife and that I had been too upset to come. Hopefully, she'd be understanding, and after a few weeks, everything would return to normal. If it meant Poppy stopped being my friend and we went back to being colleagues, then so be it. That would be better than living in a world full of lies and other people's stories.

I couldn't face breakfast. I'd let Poppy down, and now I had to face her. *Should I buy her some flowers as a peace offering?* No, that wasn't the sort of thing someone who had just had their heart broken would do. Would it be the other way around? Friends bought flowers for friends who were sad. I needed to stay one step ahead and remember that I was the one who needed consoling, not Poppy.

'Oh my God, Eve. What the hell happened to you? You missed such a fun night.'

'I'm sorry.'

'God, I thought something awful must have happened when you didn't call back.'

My mind was racing already. Poppy didn't seem too pissed off, and it sounded like the night had gone well, despite the lack of air fryer. Maybe things were going to be okay. I carefully hung my coat up and returned to my desk.

'Well? You'd better have a bloody good excuse.'

'It's Greg. He—'

'What? What's happened?'

'He had an accident. Got knocked off his bike.' Poppy gasped. 'He went to the hospital and was put on life support, but his family, they—' I started sobbing. Big, huge, snotty sobs that I couldn't stop. Poppy and Gary stared at me in horror while I mourned the loss of my boyfriend. I couldn't stop crying. Crying for my big, stupid, idiotic self, for Kai and my parents, my life and the ridiculous situation I had now put myself in. Just at the point when I was about to be free. Why had I just not stuck to my plan? What was so wrong with me that I had to use other people's heartaches and steal them as my own? My heart was aching enough already.

CHAPTER 14

'Oh my God, Eve,' Poppy rushed to comfort me. I could smell lavender in her hair as she embraced me. 'You poor thing. What are you doing coming to work? Go home, you shouldn't be here.'

I wiped my face with my sleeve.

'I didn't want to be on my own,' I whispered. 'I'm sorry.' My chest was heaving up and down.

'Gary, go and get Eve a coffee from over the road,' Poppy ordered.

'Why me?' Gary responded.

'Okay, you comfort her, I'll go,' Poppy said, glaring at Gary.

'Fine. I'll go.'

'Get me one, too, please, and a small bottle of whisky from the shop?'

'I've got some in my desk,' Gary said.

I extracted myself from Poppy's arms.

'What about our New Year's Resolution?' I said, wiping my nose with a scrunched-up tissue I'd pulled from my pocket.

'Fuck that.'

I went to the bathroom and washed my face with cold water. What the hell was wrong with me? Why had I just dug myself a hole I couldn't get out of? Why did I not just stick to my plan? Why was I such a bloody idiot?

A coffee was on my desk when I returned, and Eve was waving a small bottle of whisky around.

'Do you want some?' she said. I shook my head as she poured a capful into both cups. 'Here, you need it,' she said, thrusting one of them into my hand. 'What an awful thing to happen. Was it on the news?'

'I don't think so,' I said, shaking my head.

'Whereabouts did it happen? Was it in London?'

'I don't know the details. I was in too much shock to take in what the police were saying.'

'Oh God, it's so awful,' Poppy said, rubbing my arm.

'Have you got anyone who can stay with you for a few days?' Poppy said. 'You really shouldn't be on your own.'

I shook my head. 'I'll be fine, honestly; just being at work is a good distraction.'

As the day went on, I saw Poppy and Gary whispering in the kitchen and later again in the studio. I'd been offered copious amounts of tea, and Gary had generously told me there was no rush for his copying. Five o'clock couldn't come soon enough, and I guessed there'd be no sarky comments from Gary today under the circumstances.

'I'm going to go if that's okay?' I said to Poppy, so desperate to leave the office that I'd already opened the door and had one foot out on the street.

'Absolutely not. You are coming home with me,' Poppy said, pulling me gently back in. 'And I am not taking no for an answer.'

Poppy's home was straight out of *Exclusively Mayfair* magazine, and if I wasn't meant to be grieving, I would be asking her how the hell could she afford to live here? The door to the apartment block was opened by a security guard who greeted her by name and called the lift to take us to the tenth floor. The first thing I saw when I walked in was a wall of glass offering a panoramic view of Battersea Park and other London landmarks. The London Eye, BT Tower, and The Shard all stood tall against the landscape. It was an incredible sight. Everything inside the apartment was white. White walls, white curtains, white sofas, white kitchen, and white bathroom.

'Make yourself at home,' Poppy said, heading to the kitchen and returning with a bottle of red wine. I had never felt less at home in all my life as I perched on the end of a white chaise lounge. She handed me a glass. 'Don't look so nervous,' she said, slipping her shoes off and curling her dainty little feet with perfectly painted toenails underneath her cute bottom. I gripped the wine glass for dear life. 'I'm going to run you a bath, order us some food and then we can talk or watch rubbish TV, or you can go and rest in the spare room. Whatever you want, okay?'

'Thank you,' I said. 'I really appreciate it.'

Thirty minutes later, I was trying to relax in Poppy's huge bath. She'd dimmed the lights and lit a candle, and soft instrumental music was playing from somewhere nearby. There was evidence of a man. Aftershave, shaving foam, and a pair of large black Adidas sliders. She knocked on the door.

'Take your time, I've left the guest robe for you on the back of the door and some loungewear.'

Guest Robe? Loungewear? If I wasn't grieving my fake boyfriend's fake death, this would be heaven. I was in a five-star apartment with the coolest person I knew, who was going out of her way to make me feel pampered. It was such a shame I had to pretend to be miserable.

Poppy ordered a Chinese takeaway. It was some of the best food I'd ever tasted, but I held back, picking slowly as part of my grieving act. Poppy kept topping me up with wine, which was increasing my stress levels instead of reducing them. I couldn't take my drink at the best of times, and I needed to stay focused. No matter how much I regretted what I'd done, I had to stick to my story and see it through. Just a few more weeks, a couple of months at most and this would all be over. Securing this overnight stay at Poppy's was almost going to be worth it.

'You don't need to come to work until you feel ready,' Poppy said. 'I understand what you meant about being on your own, but you can just stay here. It's different surroundings and you can go to the park, clear your head. Take as much time as you need.'

'Thank you. You're being so kind.' We sat in silence for a while. 'By the way, how did your party go? I'm so sorry about the air fryer.'

'Oh, don't be so silly—I'm sorry you couldn't make it...' Poppy trailed off.

'Yeah, me too. Another time.' God, I'm such an idiot. *Another time when my boyfriend hasn't just been in a fatal accident.* 'I mean, maybe I can meet your friends another time.'

'Sure.'

'Your place is really nice.'

'Thanks.'

'Do you own it?'

'Oh my God, no. I don't own any of this, not even the furniture. It's rented.'

'Oh.'

'My ex-husband pays the rent. It's the least he can do.'

This was news to me. Big news. Poppy had been married? Like, when had she got married and divorced? Considering I'd seen her practically every day for the past five years, how could I not know this?

'It was a long time ago. I don't like to dwell on that chapter in my life. It's certainly not something we should be talking about tonight,' she said. I gave her a half-hearted smile. 'Are you okay?' Poppy said, reaching out and resting her hand on my shoulder.

'Yeah, I'm fine. I hadn't known him for long, but it's just a shock, you know,' I said, hating myself.

'Do you want to talk about it?'

I shrugged.

'How did you find out?' Poppy said.

'I was waiting for him to pick me up for your dinner and he was late. I called him to see where he was, and the police answered.'

'Oh my God,' Poppy said. 'What did they say?'

'They said he was being taken to Guys Hospital by ambulance. I called the hospital, and they said his family was already there.'

'Did you go?'

'No. I didn't feel I could. I mean, I've never even met them,' I reeled off my rehearsed story with confidence.

I looked away, feeling sick to my stomach.

'Have you thought what you're going to do about the funeral? Sorry, is it too soon to be asking this?' Poppy bit her lip.

I shook my head. I didn't know what to say to that because I hadn't worked that part of my story out yet.

'I'm in touch with the Liaison Officer,' I said and left it at that.

The spare room was the nicest room I'd ever slept in, which, until then, had only been my own, my nan's spare room, a tent, and a dormitory on the school trip. The pillows were soft and plump, the bed enormous, and there was a cute little velvet armchair in the corner. I stripped off to my underwear and climbed in. The last thing I remember thinking was, how was I ever going to get to sleep?

The next morning, the sunlight came streaming in through the window. I rolled over and looked at my phone; it was nine o'clock. I couldn't believe I'd slept so late. A combination of red wine and mental exhaustion had given me the best night's sleep I'd had in a long time.

I pulled on the bathrobe and went to the kitchen. There was a note on the table along with a set of keys.

I hope you slept okay. Make yourself at home.

P x

I was on my own in Poppy's apartment, which felt like the perfect opportunity to have a look around. Everyone would do this, right? Every drawer was tidy, every cupboard organised. The tea bags were in a white china jar labelled TEA, coffee the same. Even the muesli was in a container. Every soap dispenser was full, and the fridge was clean and coordinated. Poppy either had severe OCD or, as I already suspected, was simply perfect.

I made myself a coffee, opened the curtains, and got back into bed, propping myself up on the pillows and letting myself sink back into them as I stared out across the city.

What I had done was unforgivable. I knew that, and the fact that I was now taking advantage of Poppy's generosity made it even worse. If I was looking in on this situation from the outside, I would consider myself a very screwed-up individual and suggest some kind of psychological help. However, I was confident I was still sane despite what I'd done. This was a situation that had got totally out of hand, and once I'd got through this, everything could go back to normal, and I would never again make up any stories. I wouldn't lie about what I did at the weekend, in my free time, or who I spent time with. Just a few weeks of acting appropriately sad and then I was done. No one would ever know the truth, and this time, I really meant it.

I allowed myself time to enjoy the coffee and the view, then had a power shower, using all Poppy's expensive toiletries. I got dressed, made the bed, and washed up my mug. I wrote a note on the bottom of Poppy's note to me.

Thank you so much for last night. You are a true friend.

I've gone back home and will be back at work in a few days.

Thank you again.

E x

On my way to the station, I walked past a florist. I bought a bouquet for £30—the most I'd ever spent on flowers, then returned to the apartment and asked the concierge to give them to Poppy later. They were guilt flowers that didn't make me feel any better, but they were a gesture of genuine appreciation. Poppy had taken care of me when she believed

I was heartbroken and had no one else in the world to turn to.

The next day, it rained like the sky was crying for a broken heart, and I cried with it, hiding under my duvet in the dark. I had never had many people in my life—which suited me. But to have no one at all made me feel really sad. At some point, I forced myself to get up and make some tea, only to collapse on the sofa again soon after. I looked around me at the four walls. I was sure this room was getting smaller. There was no food in the fridge, and I had nothing to do despite being in one of the best cities in the world. There was a disconnect somewhere, and I couldn't work out where it had broken. When had my life become this insignificant, this small, and this lonely? I needed to fill it with something worthwhile, something exciting that would lift my heart, but I didn't want to do it alone. I wanted to do it with Kai. My best friend and my soul mate. He was the connection I needed. I pulled out my dragonfly notebook.

Kai,

I'm a mess without you in my life, and I don't know what to do.

No one makes me laugh like you do.

No one knows me like you do.

No one makes me a better person like you do.

Please come back into my life.

Eve

I shut the notebook and stroked the cover. Either I let this life I had made for myself swallow me up, or I changed it. I found my dad's golf umbrella, went outside, and walked until it got dark. I passed a lady pushing a small pram with a dog inside. Is this what lonely people did? Was I going to have to get a dog? I went to the supermarket to buy some food. A pizza and a chocolate yoghurt—both yellow stickers. Things were looking up. Everything was going to be okay.

The next few weeks weren't as difficult as I thought they were going to be. I acted subdued and took full advantage of arriving late to work and leaving early. I was claiming 'emotional overload,' like it was a bug I'd picked up and needed to recover from.

To begin with, Gary was kind, but I soon realised this was only when Poppy was around. Things went back to normal pretty quickly. Poppy continued to be sweet and caring, but most of the time, she got on with her work, and I got on with mine. She hadn't invited me back to stay, and other than occasionally asking me if I was okay, we didn't talk about what had happened that often, although she did ask me again about the funeral.

'Do you know when Greg's funeral is yet?' Poppy said one lunchtime.

'No, not yet,' I looked away.

'You've made contact with his family, though, right?'

'The hospital put me in touch. It's a bit awkward cos of his ex-wife, but they said they'd let me know.'

'I can come with you if you want. You shouldn't go on your own.'

'I think it's just close friends and family, but thanks, that's really kind of you.'

As I was answering Poppy's questions, the answers were coming to me naturally. It was as if I really was grieving for a boyfriend who'd had a fatal accident and a tricky ex-wife. Sometimes, I even forgot what I was saying wasn't true. But when I was at home alone, my thoughts got the better of me, and I felt a blanket of guilt laying so heavy on my shoulders that I couldn't shrug it off. I tried walking for hours on end, distracting myself with chores, and sitting in cafes until I was asked to leave, but sometimes, I gave in and let reality fill my head until it felt like it was going to burst, all the lies gushing out into the street for everyone to see. My only escape was writing to Kai.

Hi

It's been nearly three months now since I saw you, and things haven't been that great with me. Although I am the cause of all my problems, I really need a friend, and as you are/were my only real friend, I could really do with you. I know you wouldn't have let me get myself into the mess I'm in, and even though blaming you is unfair, that is what I'm doing. I've done something really stupid, and I feel bad about it. It's a mess and if it wasn't so awful, it would actually be quite funny, although I'm not sure even you would laugh at my current predicament.

I pretended I had a boyfriend and made up stories about him. Then, the Perfect Poppy invited him and me for dinner. Obviously, I had to make an excuse, so I decided to tell her that I had broken up with him, but then something in my stupid brain took over, and I told her he'd died in an accident. Now I'm having to mourn him, and it's exhausting.

Please don't laugh. I'm a terrible person, and I really miss you telling me I'm not.

Eve x

One Wednesday, a few weeks after Greg had 'died,' I woke feeling relaxed and rested. I never knew from day to day which me I was going to wake up with. Either way, I was beginning to wean myself off my grieving girlfriend act. Obviously, if this were a real-life situation, three weeks would be nowhere near enough to get over such a tragic loss, but to be honest, Poppy seemed to have lost interest, and I was getting a bit bored with the whole 'poor me' thing.

I arrived at the office and smiled at Poppy.

'Good morning,' I said.

Poppy stared at me, unsmiling. Her eyes fixed in a steely blue stare.

'Everything okay?' I said.

Poppy shook her head slowly.

'What's happened?' I said. I could feel the heat rising, and my cheeks were beginning to burn. 'Poppy?' I tried again, but she just stared at me, shaking her head slowly from side to side. 'What? What is it? Is it Gary? Please, tell me; you're making me nervous.'

'Did you think we wouldn't find out?' Poppy said. 'Or did you think we wouldn't care that we'd be lied to for months?'

'I don't know what you're—'

'STOP!' Poppy shouted. 'I know everything. Everything, okay?' I stopped walking towards her and stood still. 'For your own sake, just stop.'

My heart was beating fast. My instinct was telling me to turn around and run away. I knew the situation was unsalvageable and if I wasn't so scared of Poppy's reaction, I might have felt relieved that it was over. However, the vibe I was getting was that this was going to get a lot worse before it got better.

'Do you want tea?' I said, trying to buy myself time. I wasn't sure what she knew or how she knew whatever it was she knew, but maybe I could somehow justify what I'd done. I knew she wouldn't want me as a friend anymore, but that was okay. I would accept this, and we could go back to how it was before and just be colleagues.

'You need to leave. We'll pay you until we can access some legal advice. You should get some, too. We'll be in touch.'

'No, wait, please, let me explain. If you could just tell me what it is that I've supposedly done, I'm sure I can explain.'

'YOU KNOW WHAT YOU'VE DONE!' Poppy shouted very loudly at me. 'I saw him. I saw Greg.'

'What? You can't have. He died. It must have been someone that looked like him.' I started to cry, and I could feel my chest rising and falling as I tried to get some air back into my body, clinging on to some hope that somehow, I could save this.

'I spoke to him,' Poppy said, and that's when I knew that all of it was finally and definitely over.

My legs were shaking so much that I had to sit down.

'How?'

'How did I speak to him?' Poppy snapped. 'How did I speak to a dead man?'

I couldn't look at her, so instead, I stared at a large water mark stain on the floor, praying it would open up and swallow me whole. 'I saw him at the station. I didn't believe it was him at first. I didn't want to believe it. I COULDN'T BELIEVE IT,' she shouted. She stopped to catch her breath. 'So I went up to him and asked him if his name was Greg?'

I swallowed a mouthful of bile.

'Obviously, he said no, but I recognised him. Do I need to go on?' Poppy was still shouting.

'I can—'

'Save it. I don't believe a single thing that comes out of your mouth. You're a stalker and a psychopathic liar. I should report you to the police.'

'It isn't like that,' I whispered, tears rolling down my cheeks.

'What is it like then? When someone follows a stranger to their home, takes photos of them, follows them to their work, turns up at their child's school—what is that then? Because it sounds like a textbook example of stalking to me. She shook her head and had a strange smirk on her face. 'Did you think because you're a woman, you'd get away with it?'

'I can explain. Please, at least let me try and explain?' I was sobbing now, but Poppy was showing me no mercy.

'I can't even look at you. Get your things and leave.'

CHAPTER 15

I stumbled to the door, bashing my hand as I yanked the handle. Once outside, I stood in the middle of the pavement and took some deep breaths. I felt dizzy and thought I might faint. I slid down onto the floor.

'You alright, love?' A lady with a shopping trolley stopped. 'Do you want me to get you some help?'

I shook my head.

'I'm fine. Thank you.'

'You don't look fine to me,' she said.

'I am, honestly. Please just leave me alone.'

I don't remember much about my train journey home, but I do remember closing all the curtains in the flat, double-locking the front door, and climbing into bed. Other than using the bathroom and shoving my head under the bathroom tap to gulp water, that's where I stayed for the next forty-eight hours.

Sleep came and went. Sometimes, deep and long. I'd wake with a heavy head, my legs feeling like they were made of stone, my clothes sticking to me. Other times, I tossed and turned, unable to escape my thoughts, punching my pillow, then forcing it into my mouth while I screamed. I pulled the covers up tight and curled myself into a ball, wanting the world to go on without me and leave me behind.

The next time I woke, it was still dark outside, and I could hear the wind raging against the windows. I went to the bathroom and looked in the mirror, not recognising the person staring back at me. My skin was grey, my eyes puffy, and my hair plastered to my head. My mouth was dry and when I ran my tongue around my teeth, they felt gritty. I was disgusting. It took every ounce of effort just to turn the shower on, climb in, and wash my hair. The water pounded onto my head and down onto my body. I finally felt some sensation return to my fingers and toes, like a warm liquid slowly filling my veins. It gave me enough energy to brush my teeth, strip the sheets, and put them in the wash. When I'd finished, I sat on my bed, out of breath. I felt nauseous. I hadn't eaten since Wednesday, and my appetite seemed to have deserted me, but my stomach was starting to protest.

I held the wall for balance. The oven clock told me it was four-thirty-four a.m. I filled the kettle and stared inside the fridge. A half tin of baked beans and an egg looked back at me. My stomach was aching to have something put inside it. I made toast, heated the beans, and fried the egg. I forced it down but left the egg. The grease glistening under the spotlights made my stomach turn.

When I next woke, I was on the sofa. I lay there longing for more sleep to come again, but it didn't. Instead, it slowly dawned on me that I might need some professional help. I was behaving irrationally, and it was having consequences on my life.

I tidied up and then went outside. The cold air hit me instantly, making me feel alive for the first time since my confrontation with Poppy. I bought a coffee and made my way to the underground. I got on the circle line and pulled my coat tight around me, one hand hugging the thick cardboard take-out cup. I slunk down into my seat and that is where I stayed for the next two hours, relaxing into the motion of the train, barely noticing the stops. I fixated on the thick black tar-like dirt stains on the seats, then an empty can of Red Bull, then a scrunched-up crisp packet. I stared for too long at 'Donna love heart Teddy' keyed onto the train window and attempted to read *The Metro* newspaper, which was upside down on the floor. Passengers got on and off, along with dogs, suitcases, musical instruments, pushchairs, school groups, tourists, families, couples, commuters, shoppers, diners, and night workers. All this time, I sat there in the corner and breathed, letting the conversations wash over me. There was no need to concentrate, make notes, or think about how I could use their stories. Those days were over, and I was truly and honestly really relieved.

There was an advert on the opposite side of the train carriage for holidays to the Mediterranean. It looked nice. A blue sea, delicious food, happy, smiley people, and sunny weather. A mum and her young son sat opposite me, and I thought she looked tired. She was attractive and fashionably dressed. Her hair was in a high, scruffy knot on top of her head. She wore well-loved white trainers, jeans, and a branded bottle-green puffer jacket. Her son had dirty blond hair that hung over his face. He was holding a red toy car in one hand and a yellow toy car in the other.

'I'm hungry,' he said in a whiney voice.

'We'll be home soon,' his mum replied.

'I'm hungry now.'

She sighed. 'Not long now, okay?'

'Noooooo, I can't wait.'

'Don't be silly, of course, you can.'

'You're silly.'

'Don't be rude.'

'You're rude.'

'Stop it now.'

'You're a mean mummy.'

She paused and looked at him. 'I'm a good mummy.'

'No, you're not.'

Some passengers were laughing, and others were smiling. The mum seemed oblivious. She picked her son up off his seat and sat him on her lap, hugging him tight.

'I love you,' she said, kissing the top of his head.

'I'm hungry,' he said.

'I know you are, and when we get home, I am going to make you some food, but until then, I'm going to fill you up with love.' She started tickling him, and he started squealing. The other passengers smiled. I wiped away a tear, then got off at the next stop.

I went home via the supermarket and bought some yellow sticker vegetables, a box of cereal, milk, chicken breast, and a pot of natural yoghurt.

I needed to survive, and for that, I needed money. For the next few days, I tried to embrace my new unemployed, single, and friendless status and developed a new daily routine. Get up, shower, cereal. Travel around London on the train, listening to people talk, then home via Sainsbury's to check out the yellow stickers. The conversations I heard made me feel less alone and helped me get some perspective. I heard people talk of being evicted, getting divorced, dealing with sick relatives, challenging teenagers, money pressures, being victims of crime, dealing with controlling colleagues and overbearing family members, and conversations that made me feel lucky to be single. The list went on and on. Sometimes, I closed my eyes because I realised there was only so much you could see with your eyes. You could find out so much more if you just listened. I overheard happy stories, too. Much-wanted pregnancies, engagements, reunions, dream job offers, promotions, and holidays to exotic locations. People getting on with their lives while mine stood still, going nowhere and with nowhere to go.

On the Picadilly Line, a young couple with a huge suitcase got on. She sat down, and he stood in front of her, one hand on the rail above, one hand on the suitcase. She looked at him.

'How many stops to Heathrow?'

'Twenty-five stops to happiness, baby.'

I hadn't had much holiday experience. A camping trip in Wales that I don't remember much about, other than it was very cold and windy, and I'd stayed with my mum's family in Kent a few times, which I found boring, other than the horse in the field at the bottom of the garden that I liked to talk to. Kai holidayed abroad with his parents every year. He told me he hated it and only went for the sun tan and the fashion. He always joked about us going away together to Ibiza, but I think we both knew this would never happen.

'You gonna miss England?' she said, looking up at him.

'Not the weather, or the traffic, or the cost of everything.' She smiled.

'Me neither.'

'It's time.'

'Yep. Time for a new adventure.'

'We can always come back if—'

'We won't. Italy is going to be home.'

'Italy is in your blood.'

'And yours, all that pizza and pasta you eat.'

They laughed, and he bent down and kissed the top of her head.

I stood on the escalator, wishing I'd stayed on the train and listened to them for a bit longer. They seemed like a nice couple who had put their trust in each other to start something new. I needed some of that. I needed to take a leap of faith. I passed posters for the latest West End shows, new book releases, vitamins to make you glow, and winter sun getaways. All of them telling me to do more with my life, to be someone different.

When I got home, I turned on my laptop. It came to life, and I stared at that day's screensaver. A stone arch from land to sea, with the setting sun captured perfectly inside. I clicked on the icon.

'Azure Window in Gozo, a small island off Malta. Unfortunately, the Azure Window fell into the sea during a storm in March 2017, but it is still a popular and beautiful place to visit.'

Malta. Was this a sign? My moment? Was this my dad's homeland calling me? I had no job, no friends, and nothing to keep me here. I Googled flights to Malta in February, and £149 later, I'd made the biggest, most impulsive decision of my life. I needed to take a risk and commit to changing my life. Having spectacularly wrecked my career and my social life, why not go the whole hog and risk making myself skint as well?

The one thing I had was a home. I'd probably always be confused why my parents hadn't left me the flat in perpetuity, but right now, it felt like the biggest gesture of love they could have shown me because I was free to pack up and go. No landlord to negotiate with, no mortgage payments to make.

I reserved an Airbnb. I was running away, burying my head in the sand and all on the pretence that I was going in search of my ancestral roots.

As soon as the plane took off, I discovered something new about myself: I hated flying. I'd been more anxious about getting to the airport on time and getting on the right plane than the actual flying itself, but within minutes, I felt claustrophobic and queasy. I asked one of the cabin crew for some water and he returned with a paper bag and told me to place it over my mouth and breathe in and out slowly. This worked as a distraction for my dark thoughts about crashing but didn't help much with the heart palpitations. When the same cabin crew member told me to think happy thoughts and picture myself on a beach somewhere, I thought of Kai and imagined he was sitting next to me, on our way to Ibiza with me, saying, 'I told you I'd do it one day.' Hopefully, Kai was hungry because it was time for him to eat his hat.

I'd booked one night's accommodation in Malta and a couple of nights' accommodation in Gozo, which was as far as I'd got with planning the rest of my life. I didn't know where in Malta my relatives lived or anything about them, and I didn't want to know either. I'd used this to justify getting on a plane and escape from my messed up life. I hoped to feel free of all the lies and empowered to start again, but right now, I was feeling way out of my comfort zone and already starting to have regrets.

When the plane touched down, I looked outside at bright blue skies and finally released the paper bag scrunched so tight that it had started to disintegrate. I was the last to leave the aircraft because, despite desperately wanting to disembark, I needed my heartbeat to return to normal to avoid fainting and causing a scene.

Once on firm ground, I started to relax. Relieved I wasn't in the ocean and hadn't had to top up my life jacket with air, blow my whistle for attention, or fit my oxygen mask before helping others. I'd survived.

The taxi driver spoke good English and gave me a brief history lesson before dropping me off at a white-washed hotel. All the rooms had balconies overlooking an oval-shaped swimming pool, and a few of them had laundry flapping gently in the wind. A young girl showed me to my room, gave me my key, then left me alone. I wanted to call her back and tell her I needed a friend, I didn't know anyone, and didn't know why I was here. But I didn't. Instead, I shut the door and looked around me, trying not to cry.

There was a basket of fresh fruit on the table and a welcome pack containing a coffee sachet, a selection of tea bags, and a local Maltese biscuit called an *Ottijiet*. It tasted like a spicy shortbread, and my stomach received it gratefully after I'd spent two hours blowing air into it. A jug of milk and a carton of juice were in the fridge. I welcomed these small gestures that made me feel at home. I went out onto the balcony, and I could see the sea in the distance. I felt a huge sense of achievement. I'd done it; I'd escaped England and left the past behind. I felt calmer. Maybe I'd found my happy place.

I changed into a pair of wide-legged navy linen trousers and a pale pink shirt I'd bought from a charity shop before I left. I unpacked my sunglasses, a bargain from my local Barnardo's store, and headed towards the town square, where I found a small cafe with tables inside and out. I ordered a coffee and sat at a table outside, which was shaded by a pretty trellis and covered in vine. So far, I was smashing this new life. If Kai was here now, he wouldn't recognise the girl who liked nothing more than watching re-runs of *Friends* and had an aversion to leaving London, let alone the country. That girl had managed to get herself on a plane, out of the country, and even managed to dress quite well.

'You are on 'oliday?' a local man on the next table said between drags of a cigarette.

'Yes,' I nodded.

'Why you come in winter? Summer much better, no?' I didn't know what to reply to this, especially as the sun was shining. Compared to London, this weather was perfect. I just shrugged and smiled again. 'Marius, nice to meet you.'

'Eve,' I said and lifted my hand in a wave, even though he was sitting right next to me.

'So you are waiting for your boyfriend?'

I shook my head and laughed.

'No boyfriend.'

'So you come to Malta to find a boyfriend?'

I laughed again. 'Maybe,' I said, feeling bolder than usual.

'You must go to Gozo, where I am from. It is better for love in Gozo.'

In London, this conversation wouldn't have happened. I would have got up and walked away by now. Fearful of his motives, I would have escaped at the earliest opportunity, but sitting here, I felt calm and under no pressure to run away. My coffee arrived, and Marius and the waiter spoke to each other in Maltese. They spoke quickly and laughed together. I suspected they were laughing at my expense, but I didn't care. I was feeling positively carefree.

'I'm actually going to Gozo to see the Azure Window,' I said once the waiter had left.

'Ahhh, but it fell into the sea.' He shook his head. 'Everyone was very sad,'

'I read about that.' I nodded.

'But still, you can go and watch the sunset. It is very beautiful.' His phone rang. 'Good luck with your 'oliday,' he said before answering. Then he left and didn't look back.

On the way back to the apartment, I went to a supermarket and bought some bread and cheese, which I enjoyed on the balcony. I spent the rest of the day reading in the sun, then took a long shower and got an early night. I lay in bed feeling free and empowered. This was my chance to start over, and I needed to take it.

To get to Gozo, I had to catch a thirty-minute ferry. I got a taxi to the port, bought a foot passenger ticket, and dragging my parent's old suitcase behind me, I made my way towards a small kiosk selling ice cream. I sat on a large rock to wait for the ferry to arrive, enjoying frozen strawberries and white chocolate in a dark chocolate-dipped cone. It was another nice day, but there was a strong breeze, and the boat was crashing into the sides of the harbour, bouncing off a wall of tyres.

On board, there was a large cafeteria and seating area. I found a seat in the corner and immediately wished I hadn't had the ice cream, which was already trying to re-enter the world. Two women sat down at a table next to me. They were dressed in trouser suits and spoke to each other in Maltese, which was frustrating, but reminded me this was a new beginning and I didn't need to listen to other people's conversations to create a life for myself.

Once we had left the harbour, one of the ladies opened her bag and took out a wad of flyers. She started handing them out to passengers and left some on empty tables. She handed one to me, and I shoved it into my pocket as a wave of nausea washed over me. I stumbled outside just in time to wretch over the side of the boat, not entirely missing my shoes. I stayed outside until I could see land, then managed to stumble into the ladies' toilets to wash my hands and face. I looked in the mirror at my ghost-white skin and pushed my hair off my face with my wet hands. I looked and felt awful. This was the second worst I'd ever felt in my life. The first being the forty-eight hours I spent in bed following my sacking from Thames FM. Both self-inflicted, but for very different reasons. I made it to the corridor, then slid down the wall and sat on the floor, my head between my knees. And this is where I stayed until a tannoy told foot passengers to make their way below deck and get ready to leave the vessel. I was discovering I was not a very good traveller.

I had never been so relieved to stand on land as I was when I got off that ferry. My legs felt like they were going to give way, and it took every last bit of energy I had left to make my way towards the taxi rank. When I got there, I took one look at the row of saloon cars queuing up, and another wave of nausea hit me. I wasn't ready to face a car journey yet. I stumbled away and sat on a stone bench overlooking the harbour. Clutching my water bottle like my life depended on it, I breathed deeply in through my nose and out through my mouth. In and out, in and out, until slowly, the dizziness started to pass. The bench was under two large palm trees, and the shade meant the stone was cool. I lay down and rested my cheek against it, letting it seep into my skin. I closed my eyes and listened to the sound of the waves crashing against the harbour wall. I think I may have fallen asleep because I jolted when a car pulled alongside me and beeped.

'Hay Lady. You need taxi?'

I sat up, then stood up, steadied myself, and pulled my suitcase towards the car.

'Yes, please. I am going to Victoria.'

'Okay. You have an address, because Victoria is a big place with lots of houses and hotels and streets. I cannot take you just to Victoria.'

I scrolled through my phone and found the address. I showed him.

'Ahhh, yes. I know, I know. Get in. I take you okay.'

CHAPTER 16

Victoria in Gozo, didn't bear any similarities to Victoria in London. Victoria, Gozo, was a small town with shops and restaurants on either side of the high street and an all-day market which sold everything from beach towels to saucepans. There were several jewellery stalls, and almost every trader sold sunglasses. Victoria, London, was known for being close to Buckingham Palace and Hyde Park and the very busy train and coach station.

The driver stopped at the top of a one-way street.

'You must get out and walk now, lady. Okay?'

I pulled my case along the uneven stones and came to a double wooden door with a large black iron knocker. I banged it hard twice and waited. A buzzer let me in and I found myself in a dark hallway with a terracotta tiled floor. A large-chested woman wearing a knee-length apron with a large pouch and open-toed shoes appeared, wiping her hands.

'You are English lady, yes?'

I nodded. She had a friendly face, weathered by the sun. Her hair was espresso-brown, with grey strands.

'Welcome to my home. Follow me this way, please.'

I carried my case up two flights of wooden stairs and waited while she unlocked the door.

'The key is on the table. If you have any questions, you can call the number on the keyring, or come and find me, okay? Anytime is fine.'

This apartment was smaller, darker, and less welcoming than the one in Malta, but it was also a lot cheaper. I'd only booked it for four nights, but as there was absolutely no way I was going to get back on the ferry any time soon, I was already thinking I might need to extend my stay. The bedroom was just about big enough for the double bed which was in the middle of a stone wall. There was a clothes rail which had two large wicker baskets underneath and a shelf above. The bathroom had a bath with a hand-held shower attachment and a small circular sink. The toilet was separate in a cupboard room next door. The kitchen wasn't really a kitchen, just a microwave, a kettle, a fridge, and a small shelf. It reminded me of the Thames FM office, but I didn't want to think about that. That was behind me now, and I wanted to forget all about Poppy, Gary, Greg, and everything I'd done.

The living space in the apartment was small but cosy, comprising two non-identical armchairs and a coffee table. There wasn't any outdoor space, but there was a floor-to-ceiling window covered by white linen curtains hanging on a black iron pole. The window opened onto a Juliette balcony that looked down onto the street. For now, this was perfect.

That evening, I stocked up on a few provisions and even managed to make myself a salad by slicing a tomato, crumbling some feta, and scattering a tub of olives in oil on top. (When in Rome and all that.) There was no TV in the room and still drained from my ferry crossing ordeal, I got another early night.

For the first few days, I felt like I was on holiday. I got up late, ate breakfast, wandered around the town, sat at small cafes drinking coffee or eating ice cream, and did a lot of thinking and reflecting, which was exactly what I needed. But this wasn't a holiday. This was my new life, and I needed a plan and, more importantly, I needed money.

I had no skills, no useful work experience, and didn't even know what I wanted to do. I was as lost here as I had been in London, and I felt foolish. I hadn't come to Malta to start a new life; I'd run away. Ran away from my problems, away from my life, and away from the sadness of losing my best friend. Now that I'd stopped running, I was still lonely. But I couldn't go back yet. I needed to at least try and make a new life for myself. I might fail, but quitting before I'd given it a chance was just going to drag me down deeper into the pit I'd just pulled myself out of.

Every day for the next week, I walked in and out of all the cafes and all the shops, asking if they were looking for staff. They all said no, except for two of the restaurants who said to come back in the summer. I went to the tourist office to ask there, but they were closed until April. I even went to the McDonald's in the shopping complex, but even they said no. I ordered a McFlurry and sat staring at the wall. I felt like I was losing my mind. I'd messed up again.

Auntie Jean had done a great job encouraging me to step outside my comfort zone and come here, but she didn't know me. I wasn't one of those people who just landed on their feet wherever they were in the world. The type who would head off to Bali, and the next thing you knew, they were working in a hostel bar, getting free accommodation, and had fallen madly in love. This was actually a conversation I'd overheard at the airport, but this sort of thing didn't happen to everyday people. Only special people who had some magical scent or something that just made other humans like them. Auntie Jean herself had told me she'd spent a summer in France working on a farm picking crops.

Maybe I needed to roll my sleeves up and try working as a farmhand. Me and farming weren't an automatic pairing. In fact, me and the great outdoors weren't the best of friends, but it was warmer here and maybe I could do it for a few months. It might even toughen me up and make me more resilient. It was the type of work that people sent their wayward teenagers to do, to find themselves and learn about being an adult in an adult world. Maybe it would do me good.

It took me a day of research to find a farm that employed fruit pickers and who could speak English, and eventually, after several missed telephone calls, I spoke to a lady who told me she was the farmer's wife and that they didn't usually take girls because it involved 'very strong work.' I asked if there were any jobs at all I could do, and she said they needed tomato pickers. I told her I loved tomatoes and that I could definitely be a picker.

'You call me in May, and I will tell you yes or no. Okay?'

I had no choice but to book a return flight. I was in my third week and had already extended my stay once.

I started to make a mental list of the things I needed to do. First of all, find a doctor who could knock me out for the ferry trip back to the mainland. I also needed to book a flight, let my landlady know I was leaving, and start packing. My dream was well and truly over. I had failed.

I slipped off my trousers and climbed into bed. Something fell from my pocket and floated to the floor. It was the flyer I'd been handed on the ferry.

URGENT

English-speaking teachers wanted.

Gozo Language School

Good rates.

Maltese not essential.

No experience necessary.

Early night on hold, I opened my laptop and saw I had a new email notification.

To Eve

It is with regret that we are writing to inform you that your contract has been terminated with immediate effect.

We hope you will agree with the settlement terms in the attached. Please sign and return the document at your earliest convenience.

Yours sincerely,

Poppy Wilson

Even though I had been expecting this, I still felt strange seeing it in black and white on the screen in front of me. I could never face Poppy again after what I had done. I felt guilty and stupid and sad all over again. I had nothing to go back for and nothing to stay for, but one thing was for certain: I was currently marooned on an island, and I needed a job. A renewed sense of determination came over me. I wasn't going to give up yet. I needed to prove to myself I could turn things around.

I sent my application to the Maltese Language School, embellishing my work experience and adding that I'd recently worked with schools in the UK, where I'd communicated with students, parents, and staff. A bit of creativity never hurt anyone.

When I woke the next morning, I felt rested after another good night's sleep. I climbed into the bath and held the shower above my head, letting the water spill over my body. I wrapped myself in a towel, made a coffee, and heated a croissant in the microwave. I sat in one of the armchairs, watching the sun rise over the town. It was blissful, and I felt happy. My emotions were literally yo-yoing by the minute. I didn't know how long I could stay here or if I could pull off the job at the language school, but I had enough money for a couple of months and still had the tomato-picking job to fall back on. It had taken a lot to get to this point. I'd done something I never thought I'd do, and I owed it to myself to give it a proper try.

I went downstairs and knocked on the door. A mouthwatering smell of just-baked bread hit me.

'Ahh, hello, madam, how are you?' My landlady's apron was coated in flour.

'I was wondering,' I paused, 'and hoping I could stay for a little while longer?'

'Yes, madam. You pay me when you leave. No problem.' She had a smile as big as her face. 'Would you like some bread?'

We were interrupted by several loud explosions that made me jump. I looked behind me and then back at my new landlady, who seemed unphased.

'What's that noise?' I said.

'Fireworks. All the time, there is fireworks,' she laughed. 'In the morning, during the day, night time, all the time.'

'Is there a party?' I said.

'Probably a party, yes. Maybe not. In Malta, we celebrate everything with fireworks.' She shook her head and laughed. 'You can read about it. The Order of the Knights of St John. It is his fault we have all the fireworks.' I nodded. 'Fiestas, beer, and fireworks.' She raised her eyes. 'This is Gozo.'

It was the best bread I'd ever eaten—no butter, no spread, just warm, bouncy, freshly baked deliciousness. Finally, I felt like I might be making progress.

I hadn't yet replied to Poppy's email. I didn't want to think about her or what had happened or Thames FM. I had chosen to think about that later, and even that felt empowering. In the meantime, today's plan was to watch the sunset at the Azure Window. There was a bus that would get me there at around five o'clock, and until then, I was going to visit the town and try to find the tourist information centre and start getting my bearings. Poppy could wait.

Just after midday, I had a call from Lydia at the Maltese Language School asking me if I was available for an interview this afternoon. There was only one benefit to this being such short notice—I didn't have too long to feel this anxious.

The school was easy to find. When I arrived, I climbed some large, old stone stairs and found myself staring at a modern office building. The two didn't go together and as I took a step forward, I had one foot in the new and one the old. This exact moment represented my life.

I immediately felt like I was back at secondary school. Groups of young adults wearing lanyards were hanging about. Some were sitting on the stairs, and I had to step over them to pass. Once inside, there was a corridor of rooms, all with matching doors. Notices were stuck on the walls, and music was playing from one of the rooms. A sign directed me to the main office, and I knocked on the door.

The two ladies I had seen on the ferry greeted me. Lydia and her colleague, Mansweta. If they recognised me as the lady slumped on the ferry floor, shoes splattered in vomit, they didn't let on. Lydia led the conversation.

'It is very nice to meet you, Eve. Where are you staying?'

'I'm renting an apartment near the market.'

'So you walked here?'

I nodded.

'That is good. We have students from all over the island, and parking can be difficult.'

I nodded again.

'First we need to ask you, do you have a visa to work?'

'No,' I said, about to stand up and leave.

'That's not a problem; we can help you with that.'

'Oh.'

'How long are you planning on staying in Malta?'

'I'm not sure. A few months, maybe longer.'

'The course we run for the students is twelve weeks. Would you be able to stay this long? It's important for the students to continue with the same teacher.'

'Yes,' I nodded. 'Of course.'

'What brings you here to Malta?'

Because I faked my entire life in England—my boss found out and I got fired. Then, I heard some people talking about Malta, and I remembered I had a distant Maltese relative who I'd never met and knew nothing about and thought, why not?

'A couple of reasons,' I said before engaging my brain with what came out of my mouth. 'My grandmother was from Malta. I didn't know her, but I wanted to see where she was from.'

'You have family here?' Lydia exchanged a look with her colleague.

'No, not anymore, but I want to find out more about the country my family came from.'

'But this will help you with your visa I think. If you can prove your grandmother was from Malta, this will help.'

'Really? I didn't know that,' I said.

'You can become European again,' Lydia said, smiling.

Now, that would make Kai jealous.

'And?' Lydia said.

'And?'

'And the second reason?'

'Oh. I broke up with my fiancé.'

'Oh, I am sorry,' Lydia said.

Mansweta patted my knee like I was a puppy. 'He break your heart, yes?'

'We'd been together since school.' I looked away. 'I haven't heard from him since he told me he didn't want to get married and I,' I took a breath, 'I needed to get away. Make a fresh start.'

Lydia shook her head.

'Men, they can be—' she paused. 'How do you say in England?' Lydia looked at Mansweta.

'Pigs?' I offered.

They laughed, and I smiled. I needed to stop talking. I was being unprofessional and I didn't want a sympathy job offer. I was here to start a new life. But saying all this out loud made me acknowledge that falling out with Kai had been heartbreaking, and it did feel like a break-up.

'I am so sorry for you,' Lydia said, reaching out and touching my arm gently.

'Thank you.'

'You fall in love with our country,' Lydia said. 'Forget about him.'

The rest of the interview went well, until the end, when I started to lose my nerve and realised I might actually get the job.

'All successful candidates need to come in and take a class so we can see them teaching—it's very relaxed. Nothing to worry about.'

I clenched my fists and swallowed loudly.

She smiled at me. 'It sounds scary, doesn't it? It's just to introduce yourself, tell them why you want to teach, maybe give them a short exercise. That sort of thing.'

I nodded and forced a smile.

'There is some training and safeguarding procedures; plus, we will need a reference from a previous employer.'

I nodded again.

I could speak English and was pretty good at grammar, so it wasn't like I couldn't do the job. But the speaking out loud to a group bit? That was making me feel sick, and I hadn't even got the job yet. I'd applied on impulse, which was how I seemed to be running my life right now, and I was more worried about getting the job than not getting it. The fact that I'd lied about a break-up with my fiancé and needed a reference was making my already busy mind overflow again. When would I learn to stop making my life so complicated?

'We provide all the resources. The students are not beginners and can all speak basic English. It's a nice job.'

I nodded again.

'I am afraid I don't speak any Maltese,' I said, hoping this might rule me out for consideration.

They stood up, and Lydia offered me her hand.

'That is no problem. Thank you for coming in; we will be in touch, but I want you to know we like you very much.'

We like you. Those three words made me feel warm and fuzzy.

When I got back outside, I sat down on a bench and tried to calm myself down. I'd been an idiot for telling them I'd broken up with my fiancé, but it wasn't a lie like before, just an exaggeration of the truth. I needed to explain why I'd come to Malta because people didn't just leave their lives without a reason. I should have just told them about my nan, and that was it, but I didn't know anything about her. Not even her name or where she'd lived. Maybe I'd actually come to escape the heartbreak of losing Kai. So what if he wasn't my boyfriend, never had been, and, most definitely, was not my fiancé? He'd been my best friend for over fifteen years, and his friendship had been the most important relationship in my life. I was in mourning.

I spent the rest of the afternoon in the library, getting information on how to apply for a visa and researching the Maltese adult education system. At four-thirty, I left to get the bus to the Azure Window, which the bus driver told me was still called the Azure Window even though there was no longer a window.

I arrived in plenty of time and walked along the cliff top, looking out at the ocean. It was beautiful and made me feel happy, and a feeling that everything was going to be okay washed over me. There were lots of couples stopping to take selfies. I walked on until it became less busy and found a large, smooth stone to sit on. I hugged my knees in close and looked out to sea. Several boats were in the water, their sails blowing, the hull bobbing. People were on deck holding drinks, waiting to toast the end of another day. I thought of Kai and wished he was here with me. He was on my mind wherever I went, reminding me that my life wasn't as good without him in it. In fact, it had taken a serious turn for the worse. I didn't blame Kai for my mistakes, or for losing my job, but the consequences of him not being in my life hadn't been good.

The sky turned a hazy pink, then purple, and then a deep orange. People appeared from every direction, sitting and standing on the rocks, some taking pictures, some sitting solo and pensive, and others with arms entwined. *Damn it, Kai, I so want to send you a picture of this. Tell you I'm travelling solo and that I might even stay out here for a while. Tell you I miss you.*

I stayed until the little orange ball disappeared into a new day, leaving me with a new sense of peace. *Everyone is special, but we are all so insignificant,* and if I could remember that, maybe I would stop trying to pretend my life was something it wasn't.

On the way back, I stopped to watch a large group of scouts, all wearing the recognisable green uniform, cap, and neckerchief. They were sitting cross-legged on plastic sheets, listening to their scoutmaster.

'Each and every one of you is here because you want to invest in yourself and learn new skills that will stay with you for the rest of your lives. Think of this trip as a gift. By the end of this week, you will have the ability to survive in a variety of situations. Among you are future leaders. People will look to you for help, and most importantly, you will not need to rely on anyone for your happiness and success.'

The group was silent, all of them looking up at their leader.

'Congratulations for being here. You have made a very wise decision.'

The boys clapped and cheered and slapped each other on the back. They were inspired.

On the bus back, I wrote down as much of the scout master's speech as I could remember. I stared out of the window at the moon, the stars, and the fireworks. This was a magical place. Before going back to my little apartment, I stopped at a pizza van that had taken up residency in the market. I ordered a Margherita and ate it overlooking the street in my little room with the balcony doors wide open. Not a single person in my very small world knew I was here.

Not Kai, Auntie Jean, Poppy, Gary, or my neighbours, or the staff at Waitrose, my local 24/7 Sainsbury's, and the people I saw every day but knew nothing about.

On Sunday morning I opened up my emails again. I had an email from the Maltese Language School asking me if I could go in at ten a.m. on Wednesday and take a copy of my passport, my visa application reference, and either a reference from a previous employer or their contact details. I'd been offered a trial.

I had a shower, made a coffee, and opened the email from Poppy again. This time, I read through the attached 'termination of employment notice.' It was cold and impersonal and read like it had been written by a robot. There was a space for me to sign. I scrolled down to the next page.

If you would prefer to write us a letter of resignation, no further action will be taken. Your salary will be stopped with immediate effect.

I didn't know much about employment law, but I knew enough to know that it wasn't easy to sack someone after five years of employment. I also knew I could never go back to work at Thames FM. I didn't want what had happened to become public, and I wanted it all to go away as quickly as possible.

Dear Poppy

Thank you for your email. I would like to do what is best for you and Thames FM. If you could please send me a positive employment reference, I will write my resignation letter by return and accept the immediate end of my contract.

I look forward to hearing from you.

Eve

CHAPTER 17

To Whom It May Concern,

Evelyn Robertson was employed by Thames Radio for a period of five years. During that time, blah, blah, blah... I would have no hesitation in recommending her for employment. We will miss Eve greatly and wish her every success in the future.

Regards,

Poppy Wilson,

General Manager

It was the day of my teaching trial, and all I could stomach was a strong black coffee. I hadn't slept well, and when I had drifted off, I'd dreamt I was standing naked in a classroom of students, exposed and alone. Now I was awake, but I still felt like that and right now, jumping into the sea and swimming back to England felt like a better option than going through with this trial. Who was I kidding that I could do this? Listening to strangers was easy, but speaking to them was not my personality type. It was bad enough having to do it in my sleep, and now I was about to do it consciously. The only difference was that I would have clothes on. As for teaching, I'd never taught anyone anything in my life except for teaching Kai how to make the perfect omelette. I'd mastered this by mistake when I forgot how many eggs I'd used and accidentally used one too many, producing the best omelette ever. Ever since then, Kai's favourite saying was, *'Life is better when you add an extra egg.'*

I showered and dressed in straight-leg jeans, a white shirt, and a pair of navy All-Star trainers I'd bought in the market. I wasn't wholly convinced they were genuine, but my aim was to look cool but also professional. This look did both. However, I would have liked Kai's opinion on this.

The market stalls were being set up for the day, and street cafes were setting out their tables and chairs. Elderly ladies dressed all in black carried baskets full of provisions; others swept their steps. I felt I'd gone back in time and, not for the first time, wondered if I was really here. Had I really got myself on a plane, made my way to a small Maltese island, found somewhere to live, and potentially managed to convince two total strangers I was capable of teaching English to a group of young adults? Things like this didn't happen to me, and if someone had told me a few months ago that this would be my life, I would have laughed, opened a sharing bag of nachos, and put the telly on.

'Good morning, beautiful lady,' a man carrying trays of freshly baked bread into his restaurant started whistling. Was it me, or were people happier here than in London?

'Good morning.' I smiled.

'Come here for your dinner tonight; it is very good.'

I smiled again. 'Today is a good day,' I said, more to myself than to him.

'Every day is a good day,' he said.

'I hope so,' I said as I carried on walking.

'Good luck, beautiful lady.' He started singing in Maltese, and I felt a little bit lighter as I walked.

When I arrived, the lady at the reception asked for my passport and told me how she and her husband hoped to visit London one day and hopefully see The King.

'You meet The King?' She asked me.

'No, I've never met the king.' I laughed. 'I saw The Queen in her car once, but that's all, I'm afraid.'

She seemed excited by this. 'Thank you for sending us your reference. It was very good. Your boss was sad you leave your job at the radio station. No?'

I nodded but said nothing.

'I know your boyfriend, he leave you. I am sorry when I hear this. We live in a beautiful country. It will help heal your heart.'

I nodded; the guilt in my stomach mixed with the black coffee gave me a sour taste in my mouth.

'And Lydia, she tells me you have family here?'

'No, no, I don't,' I said, wishing I hadn't told Lydia about my heartbreak or my distant relatives. 'My grandmother was from Malta, but I never met her.'

'Like The King?' She laughed. 'So we have good news regarding your visa. I have spoken with the office and they are going to try and fast-track your application. But while we wait, we can get all the checks done and enrol you on the training programme.'

I nodded and swallowed loudly, then sat on my hands so she wouldn't see them shaking.

'But first, you need to meet the students. They are a new class, and this is the beginner group. Their English is already very good. You ready?'

'I'm ready,' I said, my stomach somersaulting.

I did regret telling Lydia about my broken heart because although it was true, in a way, it now seemed that I was the talk of the town. I felt annoyed with myself, but I wasn't going to let it spoil my plan. I was going to change my life and be a better person.

I followed her into a room of twelve students, all talking and laughing. Some were sitting on the desks with their backs to the door.

'Students, sit down, please. You have a new teacher today,' the lady from the reception said. She was so full of confidence that I wished she'd just take the class instead, and I watch. The students scraped their chairs as they moved back to their desks. The music and talking stopped. 'Students, please say hello to Eve. She's from England, so, of course, her English is excellent.'

'Hello, everyone,' I said, lifting my hand for a half-hearted wave. Several students greeted me back. 'I understand you can already speak some English, so please raise your hand if you understood what I just said?' A sea of arms went up in the air. 'That's very good news because I do not speak any Maltese.' A ripple of laughter came and went just as quickly. 'Hopefully, you can teach me, and I will do my best to teach you English. Is that okay?'

'Yes,' the class chorused as I swallowed down the bile stinging my throat.

I took out my notebook. My speech had been inspired by the scout leader at the beach. The notes were my security blanket.

'Each and every one of you is here because you have chosen to invest in yourself and learn a skill that will help you as you move forward in your life.' I paused. 'I would like you to think of this course as a gift,' I paused again, 'because soon you will be able to live, work, and communicate confidently in many countries around the world. Congratulations on being here; you have made a very good decision.'

The class started clapping and so too did the lady from the office. I started to breathe normally and even managed to go around the class asking everyone's name, writing it down on my hand-drawn map of the classroom. The remainder of the class required the students to read a paragraph in Maltese and then translate it into English while I supervised. Then it was over.

'Thank you for your time, everyone. I hope I see you again soon, and please, when I do, sit in the same seats because this will help me learn your names,' I said. A tip I'd picked up when I'd Googled *how to be a good teacher*.

The students filed out of the classroom, several saying 'thank you' as they left. I started to tidy away my things.

'Well done, Eve. You did very well,' the lady from the reception said.

'Thank you.'

'We would very much like to offer you a job. I will speak with Lydia.'

'Really?' I said, my excitement bubbling, and sounding like I was five years old and just been told I was going to Disneyland. I'd done it. It had gone well, and I felt amazing. Like I'd just won a huge prize for the first time in my life.

'I hope you will accept?'

'I do. Thank you.'

'Fantastico! Tonight we go for a drink to celebrate at Rosa's Bar. We will be there from seven o'clock, okay?'

I couldn't believe it had been that easy. I'd got myself a job, had somewhere to stay, and been invited out for drinks all in the space of a few weeks. Not bad for an introvert who liked nothing more than watching TV alone in my pyjamas.

Damn you, Kai, for not letting me share this with you, cos I know you'd be proud of me.

On the way back to the apartment, I walked past a newsagent. It had a rotating postcard holder outside. I bought two, one a picture of Gozo surrounded by crystal blue sea on the front and the other showing a cocktail on a table with the sunset in the background. I chose the cocktail one for Kai and sent it to his office. At least he would know where I was, even if he wasn't in my life anymore.

Time to eat your hat. x

The second postcard was for Poppy, but I couldn't decide what to write. Pen poised, options popped into my head:

Gone to live on an island

Living the dream

Sorry x

She didn't care where I was living or what I was doing with my life, and why should she? My behaviour was unforgivable.

I didn't send it, deciding it would make a good bookmark instead.

When I got back to my room, I made myself some toast and a cup of tea. All I wanted to do was change into my joggers, wipe off my make-up, and get an early night. The adrenaline had left my body and been replaced with fear. I wasn't cut out for drinks in bars in European cities with people I didn't know. Just the thought of it was making me anxious. I'd come here without a plan and very quickly found myself a new life, but now that I had it, I wasn't sure if I was ready. I felt overwhelmed and the only place I wanted to be was back in my dark, damp flat in Kings Cross on my own. I distracted myself by doing some washing, my favourite domestic chore. A piece of twine on the balcony had been tied from one side to the other, and a few wooden clothes pegs had been pushed to one end. I pegged my underwear onto the string, hung my tee shirts on a clothes horse, and started thinking of possible excuses to get out of going for drinks.

At seven o'clock, I was still curled up in one of the chairs when there was a knock on the door. It was the lady from downstairs. She was holding several pairs of my knickers in her hand.

'I am sorry to disturb you, but I find these on my cactus. Are they yours?'

I grabbed them back off her, muttering my apologies. She chuckled.

'Also I have a call from the English school to confirm you live here?'

'Oh. Yes. Sorry,' I said again. 'I applied for a job, and I needed to give an address. Sorry. Is that okay?'

'Yes, yes, it is okay. I tell them: yes, you are here. But madam, you want to live here?'

'For a few months, if that's possible? I won't hang my underwear on the balcony again. I promise,' I said, hoping she would find this funny.

'Yes, this is okay,' she laughed. A lovely, warm, hearty laugh. 'You can stay, but I give you cheaper rent. I give you half the price for three months, but you can pay me tomorrow, yes?'

'Thank you very much,' I said, waiting for the catch.

'The lady, she tells me you go out to celebrate tonight?'

'Yes, yes, I am just going to get ready.'

'You have a good time and do not worry about being late. I sleep like a bear.' She turned to leave. 'Madam, I am very sorry when I hear that your wedding, it not happen. I give you good rent to say I am sorry for you, and I do this, too, for your nanna.'

'That's very kind, but really...' I trailed off.

'Your heart will mend in Gozo.'

I smiled and said goodbye. I wouldn't be surprised if my life story was front page of the local paper tomorrow.

Thanks to my new landlady, I went for the drinks. I needed the job and I couldn't think of a good enough excuse not to.

The bar was dark, the music was loud, and I couldn't understand a lot of what was being said, even though everyone was speaking in a mix of English and Maltese.

'I'm sorry we are talking about people and things you don't know,' Lydia said.

'It's fine.' I smiled. 'I need to learn,' I said, perfectly happy people-watching. At least it made me feel at home.

'The Principal, she was very impressed with you today.'

'The Principal?'

'The lady who supervised your class; she is very good, but very,' she paused, 'difficult to please. She will be here soon. She likes to work late hours.'

So the lady I thought worked in the reception was the *principal* of the school and knew about my broken heart. How had I done this again?

Throughout the night, I was introduced to my new colleagues; I answered the same questions again and again about London. I got bought drinks, and I bought drinks. The crowd got bigger, and everyone seemed to know each other. I began to feel out of my comfort zone and started planning my escape, Lydia squeezed in next to me.

'We are going to get pizza now; it's the best pizza in Gozo.'

I wasn't hungry, I'd drunk too much, and I couldn't afford to spend any more than I had already, but this was my welcome party, and I needed to make a good impression. I followed her through alleyways and across a square with a large ornate water fountain in the middle. We passed several statues lit up with spotlights in the night sky.

Lydia was right about the pizza and the local beer, but I was fading fast. I felt hazy and slightly out of control. Like I was watching myself from a distance, and although I wasn't hating this experience, I wasn't loving it either.

'How much do I owe for the food?' I said, placing my phone on the table to look for my wallet.

Lydia picked up my phone and looked at my screensaver.

'Is this your fiancé?'

I grabbed it back.

'Yes—my ex-fiancé.'

'What's his name?'

'Kai.'

'Kai, he looks nice. You must miss him.'

'Not anymore,' I said, staring at Kai's face.

'He has cool hair,' Lydia said, peering over my shoulder.

I looked at the picture. He did have cool hair and nice eyes, nice skin, and a gorgeous smile. But he had shown his true colours, and he was no longer in my life.

I got up to leave and pushed my phone into my back pocket, making a mental note to change the picture.

'The night is young. We are going dancing. Eve, you must come. Dance away your troubles.'

I protested and placed thirty euros on the table.

'I'm tired,' I said. It was a pathetic excuse, but better than creating some elaborate story that would be front-page news within hours.

'I upset you talking about your boyfriend?'

'No, honestly, you haven't. I had a really nice time, but I promised my mum I would call her when I got back.

'Ahhhh, I see. You must miss your mum and your family a lot.'

By the time I got back to my apartment, I wasn't feeling good. Not only had I drank too much and eaten too much, I'd used my dead mum as an excuse not to go dancing. For someone who was attempting to make a fresh start, I wasn't doing very well. There was obviously something wrong with me. I Googled *pathological liar.' Lies continuously without obvious gain.* I didn't want to be that. I needed to stop doing this. I was going to stop.

I woke up feeling more positive. I had to give this new life a proper go. I had nothing to go back to, so nothing to lose. I knocked on my landlady's door to let her know I'd transferred the money. A man, who happened to be very good-looking and in his thirties, answered the door.

'Hello, you must be English lady from upstairs with the flying knickers?'

I laughed. 'Sorry about that.'

'My mama, she is not here, but she told me I must show you Gozo. I am Mario.' He thrust his hand towards me.

'Hi, Mario. Eve,' I said, shaking his hand. 'Nice to meet you. Can you tell her I have sent her the money for the rent?'

'I will.'

'Thank you. Have a nice day,' I said, 'and sorry again about my washing.'

'No problema!'

I started to walk away, but he shouted out after me. 'Have you been to Ramla? Do you want to go to the beach?'

'Ramla?'

'The beach?' I shook my head. 'We leave in one hour. Okay?'

'Great,' I said, already trying to think of a reason why I couldn't. He seemed nice and funny, but going to the beach on a whim with a man I didn't know was the sort of thing that happened in novels, not in real life. Not in my real life, anyway.

'I will see you outside, okay?' he said.

An hour later, I found myself in a white Suzuki jeep, driving through tomato fields, down a long, winding dusty road, towards the sea with a man who kept calling me Eva.

Mario told me he lived on the mainland. He was a mature student at the university studying International Relations. He had come back for a few days as it was the end of the first semester, and he liked to visit his mum. He was easy to talk to and asked a lot of questions about England and especially London, telling me he wanted to live in London when he graduated.

'It is expensive, though, no?'

'Yes, it's expensive,' I confirmed.

'But a beautiful place to live?'

'I'm not sure beautiful is the word I'd use,' I said, picturing my flat, the homeless, and the rubbish that falls from overflowing bins, blowing into every nook and cranny in the streets. 'It depends where in London you live.'

'But there are lots of museums, theatres, and historic buildings?'

'Yes, yes, there are.'

'In Gozo, we have the oldest standing building in the world.'

I nodded, wishing I could recall some knowledge about any of the old buildings in London to impress him.

'I like old buildings,' I said, which was another lie and sounded a bit weird when I said out loud.

'Really?' Mario said. 'Then I must show you. There is a temple here on the island which was built between 3600 and 3200 BCE.'

'BCE?'

'Before Common Era. I am sorry, I am a nerdy.' He laughed, and I found myself admiring his teeth, his jawline, and his olive skin.

'You mean nerd,' I said, laughing with him.

We walked along the seafront, then went to a cafe on the beach. Everyone there seemed to know him, and he introduced me as 'Eva, his English friend.' The time passed quickly, and when we got back to the apartment, I almost invited him upstairs for coffee, but I lost my nerve when his mother came to greet us.

Maybe I was a pathological liar with a split personality disorder. Was it possible to be an introvert and an extrovert? Or was it just this magical island making me think I should invite a man I'd known for a few hours into an apartment I'd lived in for a few days? I decided to stop self-analysing. It wasn't good for me.

The next day, Mario greeted me with a kiss on both cheeks and took me to Xlendi, a fishing port where you could hire pedalos and kayaks in the summer and go scuba diving all year round. The harbour was surrounded by restaurants, many of which were closed for the winter, but a few were open and benefitting from the unseasonally warm weather. Mario asked me questions about my life, my childhood, England, and my Maltese nana. I told him I used to work for a radio station in London, which made me sound pretty cool, and I told him I lived in Central London, in my own flat. While this was also true, I suspected the image in his mind wasn't the reality. I asked him about his family, and he told me his dad had died in the army when he was young, and his mum had brought him up alone.

'I'm sorry about your father,' I said. 'Your mum has been very kind to me.'

'She tell me you came to Malta to heal your heart, so I am sorry for you, too.'

'Thank you,' I said, not trusting myself to say any more. Did everyone on this island know my heartbreak story?

CHAPTER 18

Induction complete—now, I was just waiting for my start date to be confirmed, but then, there was a problem.

'Hello, is that Eva?'

'Yes. Hello, who is this please?'

'I am calling from the Language School office. It is regarding your visa. Please, we need a police clearance certificate.'

'I don't know what that is, I'm sorry. Where can I get that from?'

'From your country, just to say you have not been arrested or been to prison.' The person on the other end of the phone laughed. 'All these rules and hoops we have to jump through. Please, if you can do this, then we have everything we need.'

My dream was over. How could I get a police clearance certificate when just weeks before, I'd been in a police station and been interviewed in relation to a crime? Even though I had nothing to do with it, my name was still going to be on some computer system in London with a big red flag attached. Even if I could get a form, it might say I was a criminal liar or something; whilst this obviously wasn't the worst crime in the world, it wouldn't exactly instil confidence in me.

I spent the rest of the day going over my options. I could contact Michaela and beg her to take my name off the system, but I don't think the police are allowed to do that sort of thing, so I decided against that idea. I could tell the Language School the truth and hope they saw the funny side. But it made me sound pretty crazy and alarm bells would definitely start ringing if someone came to me with a story of following strangers around and pretending to be places they weren't.

I went from being annoyed to upset to angry to sad, and in the end, I just put some music on and hoped it would drown out my thoughts because they were really beginning to get on my nerves.

In the morning, I had a better perspective. I Googled how to get a police clearance certificate. I found myself on a website where I completed an online form. It said I would receive my certificate within fourteen working days. I emailed the Language School to tell them, and they replied with a smiley face emoji, saying no problem.

Three days later, the certificate arrived in my inbox. I really must stop catastrophising.

While I was waiting to start, I discovered more places around town and bought a few things in the market to make my room feel more homely. A blue cracked porcelain vase from a second-hand store was my favourite purchase, followed by a brass lamp from a DIY shop that only cost ten euros. I also bought some flip-flops and a baseball cap with a daisy on the front and discovered a lovely deli about a ten-minute walk away. They even did end-of-the-day markdowns on their fresh food, which was a welcome discovery and reminded me of home. The only other reminder was the picture of Kai and me at our prom. At first, I'd put it next to my bed, but then I moved it to a small pine table near the window in the living space. Waking up in the night and staring at my old best friend wasn't good for me.

Mario had gone back to the mainland. We had messaged a few times and he'd offered to help me trace my family tree.

He'd also invited me to the mainland, and if it wasn't for the ferry journey, I might have said yes. But there was no way in a million years I was getting back on that ferry. Plus, while my new job wasn't full-time, I taught at least one class every day, so I had a ready-made excuse that didn't involve me having to reveal my lack of sea legs, or involve me lying, which made a nice change. As for my family tree, I told him I'd think about it, but I didn't need to. The thought of finding relatives I knew nothing about and had nothing in common with didn't appeal to me at all.

I spent my evenings reading, which was quickly becoming my new obsession. I was already on my third book, and even though Mario's mum said she would organise a television for me, I was in no rush. I enjoyed losing myself in the lives and stories of the characters. It filled the void my eavesdropping had left.

My visa was fast-tracked and just over three weeks after arriving in Malta, I was settled into my new apartment and teaching five English classes a week. The students were nice and wanted to learn, and the school seemed happy with me. The fact that I could speak English and turned up on time seemed to be enough. Lydia had let slip that they had students on the waitlist and not enough teachers to teach the ones already enrolled, which explained why I'd been given the job so readily.

I was enjoying planning the lessons, but still dreaded the actual teaching, which was always better than I'd feared. It was like booking a keep fit class, hating it, managing to get through it, then afterwards, feeling great and booking another one. But unlike exercise, I was motivated to keep teaching because I needed the money, and the job gave me something to get up for each day and took me further away from the life I'd left behind.

Sometimes, I went for a drink with Lydia and the students. I always said yes reluctantly, then like my lessons, always enjoyed it more than I thought I would. However, I was always the first to leave. I had learnt more about myself in these past few weeks than I had in my entire adult life. I was beginning to feel enlightened. I'd even given myself some self-inflicted rules, including not speaking about Kai, my ex-fiancé who broke my heart, causing me to flee, or my 'alive' mum, as much as possible.

In my spare time, I visited the library, which had a good selection of English books, wandered around the market, and went to my favourite cafes. I ordered coffee and made it last while I listened to other people's conversations—for entertainment purposes only. Not all the customers spoke in English, though, which was frustrating.

It was Friday night, and I hadn't checked my emails since Poppy had sent me my reference. She had gone totally overboard, clearly happy to say anything so long as she didn't have to see me. Reading it again made me feel nauseous.

Eve is efficient and organised and responds well to instruction. She engages well with the listeners and is kind and considerate to the callers. Eve has a cheerful disposition and always carries out her duties with a smile. She is creative, funny, and lovely to have around...blah, blah, blah.

I'd been putting off contacting Auntie Jean, not because I didn't want her to know where I was, but because I knew she'd pressure me to see my dad's family. She might even tell them I'm here. That wasn't why I'd come, and it wasn't something I wanted to do. I wasn't interested. They were strangers, and a few shared genes didn't change that. But I did feel I should at least let her know I was temporarily living abroad, especially after our Christmas Day experience. There were very few people in my life that actually cared about me and Jean was one of them, possibly the only one.

The emails loaded one by one, popping up in the inbox in date order. My heart stopped and I did a double take. It stood out like the moon in the night sky. *Kai Jenkins.* I clicked on the message and waited for it to load, my impatience already at boiling point.

Hi

Thank you for your postcard.

Having just eaten my hat, I thought I would email you while I wait for it to digest.

So, how are you? As you appear to have left grotty England and moved to sunnier climes, I assume you are very well indeed. Have you gone to Malta to eat Maltesers and track down your sultana relatives?

I know I've been a total idiot. I have so many questions, so please, please reply:

What the hell are you doing in Gozo?

How long are you there for?

What about your job—did you resign?

If yes, please tell me you told that slimeball Gary where to go?

How was Christmas? (Mine was dire)

Are we still friends?

Did my mum really ask you to hang out with me?

Reply quickly cos I'm dying to know everything.

Lova ya

Kai x

PS I have a new mobile number—long, weird story.

The email was dated over a week ago.

My phone buzzed.

Mario: *Eva, I am coming home this weekend. Beach?*

Mario x

I opened the windows to let in some air, then paced around the room. The cicadas were chirping loudly, the curtains billowed in the breeze, and fireworks lit up the sky. I wanted to reply to Kai straight away but needed to think first. If there was one thing I'd learnt these past few months, it's to wait before I do or say something I would regret later. I stared down at the street and wondered again if I was really here. I pinched myself on the flappy bit of skin bit between the thumb and first finger, then, for added measure, dug my nails in. It hurt. My instincts were to reply to Kai, telling him how much I'd missed him and how sorry I was, but I was angry. He'd been the worst friend on the planet, having literally abandoned me in my hour of need, and I wanted to tell him that. How dare he just email me casually like this? How did he even know my email address? We'd never emailed each other ever before.

I opened a Cisk beer, which I'd become quite partial to, thanks to Lydia and my students. I took a sip and sighed out loud. A knock on the door interrupted my thoughts. Mario's mother was holding a small wooden crate of strawberries. She pushed them towards me.

'Strawberries in February?' I said, looking down at them.

'Of course,' she said. 'You are in Gozo, not England.' She laughed. 'Tomorrow Mario, he comes to see me, and I think he comes to see you. He is a lovely boy, and you are a lovely lady, and these,' she forced them into my arms, 'are lovely strawberries.' I smiled, I had a feeling she might be trying to set us up.

I sat down, my computer on my lap. My Cisk and the strawberries on the table in front of me.

Hi

So I could pretend I was making you sweat and got your email last week, but I have only just opened my emails, so apologies for not replying before now.

In answer to your questions:

I am in Gozo because you told me you would eat your hat if I ever went to an island on my own, and I really wanted you to get painful indigestion.

I am here for the rest of my life because to get here, I had to get a ferry, and it made me so sick, I now have PTSD about ever getting on a ferry again, and it is too far to swim, so I am marooned— literally.

I left my job by mutual agreement—sort of. It's a long story that I can't really explain in an email.

No, I didn't tell Gary what an arsehole he is. I decided to rise above it—get me!

I spent my Christmas with Reverend Dave and my Mad Auntie Jean, who invited me to volunteer at the community food hall. It was a surprisingly nice experience, although I was mistaken as homeless, and so you'll be happy to know I have decided to smarten up my appearance—a little bit.

I'm ignoring the next question.

No, of course your mum didn't ask me to hang out with you. That would have been so lame if she had, and I definitely wouldn't have done it. I'm not that nice!

Don't leave me hanging.

E x

PS—New number, please, so I can message you in the middle of the night when I can't sleep.

Kai's email had thrown me off my new and happy path, like a sudden bump in an otherwise smooth road. I replied to Mario with a thumbs up, then went to bed and tossed and turned all night, trying to still my troubled mind.

Mario knocked on my door. It was nine o'clock, and I was still in my pyjamas.

'Mario, you are here already?'

'I get the first ferry. How are you?' he said, walking in.

'I am good. Thank you, but I am not dressed.'

'Only in my imagination are you not dressed, Eve.' He laughed, and I blushed. 'I will go and see my mother and meet you downstairs in one hour. Is that okay?'

I nodded.

'I see my mother bring you strawberries.' He picked one up and offered it to me. I shook my head and pointed to my coffee.

'Bit early for strawberries.'

Then Mario picked up the framed photo of Kai and me. 'Is this your boyfriend?'

'Ex.'

'He has good hair.'

I nodded.

'Why do you have this photo? He treat you very badly, no? We must not live in the past. Okay? I see you in one hour.'

I shut the door and leaned against it, making a mental note not to share ANYTHING personal with Lydia ever again unless I wanted the entire island to know about it.

An hour later, I was sat alongside Mario in his jeep again.

'Eve, you are distracted today. Am I right?'

'I'm tired. Sorry.'

'Why do English always says sorry when you have not done anything?'

'Sorry.' I laughed.

'You are sorry for saying sorry?'

'Guilty.'

We walked along the cliffs, and Mario told me how he used to go fishing and somersault off the rocks into the sea.

'Tell me about when you were little,' he said.

'Umm, there's not too much to say,' I said, fighting the voice in my head, telling me to make up a fantasy childhood full of holidays, laughter, and huge family outings.

'Okay, tell me about your parents.'

'Well, my dad was—' my mind went blank. 'He was a businessman and—'

Mario interrupted me, 'What sort of businessman? Come on, Eve, why are you being secretive? Is he a famous billionaire?'

'No, definitely not that. I don't really know what business. Financial, I think.'

'All business is financial. No?'

'I guess,' I said.

'How do you not know about your father's job? Did you not talk to your father?'

'Yes, of course, I did, just not about his work,' I said, sounding more irritated than I meant to.

'And your mother, did she work?'

'Sometimes, in a shop. Why so many questions?'

'I am just wanting to get to know you.' There was an awkward silence. Mario was waiting for me to tell him more, but I didn't want to discuss my parents. 'I am sorry if I have upset you. We can talk about something else if you like?'

'Sorry. I mean, I'm not sorry...' I trailed off, not sure why I felt so heavy-hearted.

Later, Mario invited me to have dinner with him and his mother downstairs. I declined, saying I was tired and had a headache, but we agreed to go for coffee on Sunday morning before he went back to the mainland.

I'd resisted checking my emails all day, but when I was alone again, I opened up my inbox.

OMG, you took a week to reply. You absolute cow!

So, obviously, I have 101 questions and, ideally, with answers that are longer than 5 words. If you are staying there forever, maybe I could come visit you sometime?

K x

I replied straight away.

Ha Ha, obviously, I'm not staying forever. I'm just waiting for someone to build a bridge or an airport in Gozo so I can fly back. I am currently working in a language school, practically full-time, and living in a room/small apartment belonging to a local woman who lives downstairs and gives me strawberries and freshly baked bread and retrieves my underwear from her front garden. No guests allowed.

On Sunday, I woke early to wash my hair. I put on a long lemon-coloured linen skirt I'd bought in the market and a pale blue tee shirt. I liked Mario, and I liked having a friend here. I felt bad for not accepting his invitation last night, but I also felt unsettled by Kai's email and Mario's questions. I sprayed on some perfume, brushed some mascara onto my lashes, and dabbed on some lipstick. When I looked in the mirror, I noticed my skin had already picked up some colour.

'Not bad,' I said to my reflection.

'I'm sorry about last night,' I said as we walked towards St George's Square. The square was overlooked by St George's Basilica which, according to Mario, dated back to 1672. It was surrounded by narrow streets and dark stone alleyways. It was always busy, especially on a Sunday, with large family groups gathering around outside.

Children ran around playing, and locals were dressed for Sunday service. Everywhere I looked people were smiling, laughing, and talking.

'You are good today, yes?' Mario said.

I nodded. 'I like it here,' I said.

We took a corner table outside, overlooking the square facing the sun. I put my sunglasses on.

'You look very pretty today,' Mario said.

And you look quite handsome, I thought.

'*Grazzi,*' I said

We ordered coffee and croissants, and I listened to Mario talking to someone at the next table.

'Do you know everyone in Gozo?' I said.

He laughed, translating what I'd said to the man he'd been talking to. The man laughed back and said something in Maltese.

'I bet when I come to London, it is the same with you?' Mario said.

Now, it was my time to laugh.

'I don't know hardly anyone in London,' I said. 'It is not that easy to meet people there.'

We sat in silence. Behind my sunglasses, I could see he was looking at me.

'Eva. I know you are still healing from your broken heart, but I like you very much.' The waiter came over with the coffee and pastries, giving me plenty of time to panic about what to do or say next. We sat in silence for probably a minute, but it felt like an hour. 'I'm sorry if I say the wrong thing.'

'Now you're saying sorry.'

'Must be catching, no?' Then, I replied to his confession, 'I like you, too, Mario, but I don't know how long I am going to be here in Gozo.' I shrugged, my heart beating fast. 'I'm actually not very good at relationships. I have a habit of messing things up—'

Mario tried to interrupt me. 'You mustn't blame yourself for—'

'Please let me finish because I'll forget what I want to say.' He nodded. 'I've forgotten what else I was going to say,' I said, and we both laughed. Then I took a bite from my croissant, which saved me from having to say anything else.

CHAPTER 19

Lydia was laid back—not at all like Poppy. She trusted me and seemed happy to let me get on with the job and do it my way. If I had a question, I never had to wait until she had time to speak with me, and she praised me often. My students were making progress, and I was proud of them. Lydia visited the class sometimes just to say 'hi' and see how we were all getting on. I was like a proud mother duck showing off her ducklings. I'd been given an extra class on Saturdays, too, so now, I worked every day except Sundays. Against all the odds and my unintentional attempts at self-sabotage, I was living a brand new life, and I was happy—most of the time, especially on Sundays, which were spent on the beach. Sometimes with Mario, but mostly on my own.

The days were already getting warmer and longer, and by mid-morning on Sunday, I was already on the bus to Malsaforn Beach. I found a cafe overlooking the sea and watched groups of divers enter the water, fully clad in wetsuits, masks, and breathing apparatus. They reappeared thirty minutes later, excited about what they'd seen in the ocean world. Afterwards, I walked along the shore, letting my feet touch the cold sand, then headed to the rocks and sat alone, watching the waves. When the sun shone on the water, it looked like a thousand diamonds were dancing on the surface. I found it mesmerising and calming, and even though I always took my latest book, I never read it.

Sometimes, Lydia invited me to the bar she was going to with her friends that evening. I wasn't sure if she did this because she liked me or if she was just a really kind person. Maybe she felt sorry for me, or maybe it was just the way Maltese people were. When I didn't want to be on my own, I'd go, but I never drank as much as the others and never stayed as late. One time, I overheard Lydia tell another tutor my boyfriend had broken my heart.

'That's why she's a bit quiet sometimes. They were going to get married,' I heard her say.

He put his hand on his chest.

'That's terrible. Poor Eve. Is that why she looks sad?'

I started using the fact that I 'looked sad' to my full advantage. It helped me get out of going clubbing, made leaving the bar early acceptable, and if I didn't feel like going out at all, all I had to do was play my trump card.

'Sorry, I'm struggling a bit today.'

'Of course, we understand. If you need a shoulder for crying, please, you must tell us,' Lydia said.

'No, really, I'm fine. I just need to be on my own tonight.' I'd smile. Sometimes, reach out and touch her arm or squeeze her hand in gratitude.

It worked every time. I used my heartbreak to get out of doing anything I didn't want to do or go anywhere I didn't want to go. Then I'd go home to my little room, and Kai and me would message back and forth while my colleagues thought I was crying into my pillow. I didn't feel good about it, but it was effective.

I told Kai all about my job, and he seemed pretty impressed. He started all his messages now with 'Dear Miss' and ended them with 'How are the bridge plans coming on? Are you still stranded?'

I wasn't homesick at all. In fact, Kai was the only thing I missed about England. My old life felt light years away. What was there to miss anyway? A dark, tired flat with nothing but memories of the family life I'd never had, plus a job I didn't have anymore. But I couldn't forget about my life in London completely, because although I didn't want to think about it, I knew I couldn't just leave the flat in London empty. My parents had made sure of that. At some point, I needed to address my long-term future, but for now, it was in the back of my mind, along with any thoughts of Poppy, Thames FM, and everything I'd done that had led to me being here.

During the day, I looked forward to Kai's emails and thought about things to tell him. The ice cream flavour I'd had that day, my new-found love of linen clothes, or the latest gift from Mario's mum. When I told him about my impromptu horse-riding experience, I could hear him laughing in my mind, and I'd laughed with him (out loud on my own).

Would you believe me if I told you I went horse-riding at the weekend? No, me neither and I would have run a mile if I had known that was where my landlady's son was taking me. Poor guy has been forced to show me the island like he's some kind of tourist guide. When he told me to wear trousers and closed shoes, I assumed we were going on some kind of hike. We arrived at a farm—a field in the middle of nowhere—and this farmer asked me could I ride? (No rude jokes, please). I said no, thinking that we would just turn around and go home, but he brought out this donkey and ordered me to 'get on her.' Honestly, if the guy smiled, his face would crack. Next thing I know, he brings out this huge white stallion for my landlady's son, who it turns out is practically a professional rider and off we go.

The upshot is: I get why being rescued by a prince and taken to his castle to live happily ever after is appealing, but I'm not convinced about the horse thing. Don't get me wrong, I like horses, but I think of them more as spiritual animals, not things to be sat on. I prefer

225

travelling by train. Simple to get on and off, and you don't have to take it with you or return it.

Eve x

PS I still can't sit down properly!

The horse ride along the beach had been a surprise last weekend, but now Mario was preparing for his exams, so he wasn't coming home for a few weeks. Neither of us had mentioned the awkward conversation we'd had at the cafe on the beach, and I hadn't let myself think about any feelings I might have for him. I knew nothing could come of it. I'd let him believe that I had an ex-fiancé called Kai who'd broken my heart. I'd dug myself into yet another hole that felt too big to climb out of. I couldn't tell him the truth without jeopardising our relationship, whatever that was, but I also couldn't pretend forever. I was already nervous every time I saw him that I'd say the wrong thing. This was just another problem I didn't want to think about. All the friends I'd made since I arrived believed a story that wasn't true. But apart from this little hiccup, I was enjoying living in this little corner of paradise, miles away from my old life, and although it had been an extreme way to get Kai to respond to me, it had at least worked.

On Wednesday, I walked to work via the best freshly squeezed orange juice cafe that had replaced my latte habit. A much healthier option, and I was drinking pure goodness. I was enjoying the last dregs when Lydia greeted me at the door.

'Eva, I am pleased you are here. I need your help with a student. Do you know Paulo?'

'The one who carries all his work in a briefcase?' I said. 'He is one of my favourite students.'

'Mine, too,' Lydia said. 'But I am sorry to tell you something very bad has happened.' She ran her hand through her hair several times. 'His uncle has had an accident. Paulo is here, but he is very upset.'

'Is his uncle okay?'

'No, not at all. He has died in the accident, and Paulo says his mum is very, very sad. He said she has been wailing, and he cannot console her.'

'Why is he here? He should go home and be with her.'

'I tell him, but he says no, he wants to be here. He doesn't want to think about what has happened.'

'Poor Paulo. What can I do?' I said.

'Please, Eva, can you talk to him? Talk to Paulo. I know you have been through heartache, too, and I think you will be very good with him. You know how he is feeling. Please, Eva, I will cover your class. He is in the office, waiting for you.'

'But, this is very different.' I said, beginning to panic. 'I am sad, but heartache is not the same as grief.'

'But it's a loss, Eva.' She put her hand on my shoulder. 'A loss I know you struggle with. But you are so strong, and you carry on. You can help him; I know you will say the right thing.'

'I can try,' I said, feeling like I'd swallowed a rock made of guilt.

'You are very kind.' She pushed me gently in the direction of the office. 'Thank you, Eve; you are an angel.'

I walked slowly towards the door. Voices in my head were screaming at me. *Just be kind. Don't go in. Tell Lydia you're too upset. You can't fake empathy; that's a very, very bad thing to do.* I knocked on the door.

'Hi Paulo, can I come in?'

Paulo nodded. His eyes were red, and he was clutching a tissue in both his fists.

'Lydia told me what happened, and I am truly very sorry.'

He sniffed loudly, and we sat together in silence for a while. He was tall and slim, his hair dark and curly. He had rock-pool blue eyes and a square jaw.

'Can I get you anything?'

Paulo shook his head.

'Do you want to be left alone?'

He shook his head again. 'Please stay with me, miss.'

'I don't know how you feel,' I said quietly, 'but I do know that losing someone suddenly is very difficult to understand.'

'Thank you, miss.' He paused. 'I know your boyfriend; he leave you before your wedding?'

I nodded, then looked away.

'I am sorry, miss. God is very cruel sometimes.'

'Do you want to tell me about your uncle?' I said, keen to avoid any discussion about religion.

'He was like my brother. He has been with me all my life.'

'Tell me—what did you do together?'

He told me how they went fishing and spent their summers jumping off the rocks at Xlendi. It seemed this was a rite of passage for the locals here. I took his hand in both of mine.

'You must focus on remembering the good times. It will take time, but you will be okay.'

He sniffed loudly.

'He would not want you to feel this sad. He would want you to live your life and to be happy.'

'I know you are right, miss.'

'He is smiling down on you right now, saying, "*Paulo, you are brilliant at English,*"' I said.

Paulo smiled. 'Thank you, miss. It is true; I am getting good at English.'

'You really are, and I know it is a shock when someone goes from your life without warning.' I thought of Kai and how much I'd missed him. 'But it is better than watching them suffer. Remember, he is not in pain; you and your family and his friends are the ones who are hurting. You must remember that and use it to live your best life.'

He looked up and smiled at me. 'You are a very good teacher, miss. Of life as well as English.'

I went to the ladies and splashed some cold water on my face. I looked in the mirror and saw the face of a liar and a fraud. How could I comfort someone in their grief by lying about my own experience of grief? What kind of person did that?

I went back to the classroom and saw that Paulo was there, sitting at the back of the class.

Lydia whispered in my ear, 'Well done, Eva. Thank you. You are an angel from Heaven.'

I couldn't shift my guilt, no matter how much I tried to justify what I'd done. I'd maybe helped Paulo in some small way, but I'd lied to him about my grief, and that was morally wrong and not okay on any level. My conscience was unsettled for a long time after that, especially when I received a gift of a cake a few days later. It was wrapped in greaseproof paper and on my desk with a note.

Miss Eva,

Thank you.

From Paulo and familia

A few days later, I was teaching, and it was a good lesson. I was telling the students about the names of different sports and asking them for associated words.

'Your country has better ladies' football team than men. Is this true?' one of the students asked me.

I didn't follow English football; as far as I could tell, it was a sport that involved obscene amounts of money and fans abusing each other.

'Of course, the ladies' team is better,' I said.

The class laughed and booed, and then Max invited me to go and watch their team play.

'You will see real football, miss, and you will be impressive.'

'ImpressED,' I said.

'Sorry, miss. Please forgiven me.'

'ForgivE,' I said.

'I am better at football than English,' Max said.

The class laughed, and so did Paulo.

The pupils were beginning to feel like friends. Losing my job at Thames FM had been the best thing that had ever happened to me. If I ever saw Poppy again, I would thank her. Without her, none of this would have happened.

Paulo waited behind after class.

'Miss, my mother, she asks that you come to the funeral.'

'That is very kind, Paulo, but I did not know your uncle, and I would not want to intrude. Please thank her very much for the cake; there was no need to give me a gift.'

'You will not be intruding, miss. My mother, she be very happy if you come. She says thank you for sharing your sadness with me. You are a special teacher.'

'I will try.' My jaw tensed as I forced a smile.

'Thank you, miss. The cake, it is blood orange cake. My mother, she is a very good cook.'

That evening, I messaged Mario for advice.

Eve: *'One of my students has invited me to his uncle's funeral. I didn't know him, so it feels wrong, but he wants me to come?'*

Mario: *Paulo?*

Eve: *Yes, do you know him?*

Mario: *I know his family. My mother and me are going to the funeral. There will be lots of people there. You should come, too. You can come with us. He was a nice man.*

Eve: *Okay, thank you.*

Mario: *I have one more exam, then I will be home for a few weeks and can show you more of the island.*

Eve: *Sounds good x.*

At the weekend, Mario's mum brought me some potatoes and beans from her garden and a black dress.

'Mario says you coming to the funeral. You will need to wear black, so I have brought you a dress and some potatoes and beans.'

I took them from her and, without thinking, kissed her on both cheeks. It seemed I was slowly becoming Maltese. 'We can go together. I want to get a good view at the church, so we will need to get there early.'

I nodded. No words would come.

I tried on the dress. It looked like a nightie. When packing to come to Malta, I had only envisaged staying a few weeks and hadn't banked on going to any funerals. Either I wore Mario's mum's dress, or I invested in something new, which felt extravagant, especially as I was going to the funeral under false pretences, but Mario was going to be there, and I wanted to look nice. *Not that a funeral was the place to flirt.*

I bought a pair of black wide-leg, loose-fitting cotton trousers, a black short-sleeved shirt, and a black silk neck scarf. I returned the dress to Mario's mum, telling her it was too long. I also bought a pair of black shoes, which I didn't like, but they were cheap and would be handy for any funerals I might find myself at in the future.

When I asked Lydia for the day off, she hugged me, telling me it was a beautiful thing that I was going and said that she, too, would be there, along with several of the students. My parents had less than twenty people at their funeral, and it had all been over very quickly. It seemed the whole island was going to this one, including me and my fake empathy.

In the days before the funeral, flyers with details of the funeral and a photo of Paulo's uncle started to appear around Victoria. Pinned on fences, wooden posts, and notice boards. I wasn't looking forward to it. I didn't want to go, and I knew it was wrong, but blaming my heartbreak wasn't going to work on this occasion.

The service was at the same church in the square where I'd had coffee with Mario just a few weeks ago. When we arrived, the square was packed with mourners. We made our way inside, and Mario's mum bustled her way in straight to the front, pulling me along behind her. People kept coming up to me and saying '*thank you*' and squeezing my hand.

'Why are they doing that?' I whispered to Mario.

'For being kind to Paulo and his family,' his mum said. 'The family are very grateful.'

'I spoke to him for ten minutes,' I said, feeling irritated. 'How do they even know who I am?'

'Everyone knows who you are.' Mario smiled at me.

When the casket was carried down the aisle, people started weeping. There was a group of very attractive women who looked a similar age to me. They were sitting together, taking up an entire pew. They were solemn-faced, and all of them were wearing large Victoria Beckham-style sunglasses that covered almost half of their face. Mario whispered in my ear.

'He had lots of girlfriends and broke a lot of hearts.'

'Mario, you must not say these things,' his mum said.

'It is true, Mama,' he said, winking at me.

The service was in Maltese. I watched the priest, bowed my head for the prayers, and listened to the eulogies. When Paulo read, he repeated his tribute in both Maltese and English. I felt like a proud auntie.

'Someone said to me, remember he is not in pain, and it is us who is hurting. The people who loved him must carry on and live our best lives in his memory.'

The applause was still going long after I'd wiped my tears.

The organ played as the body was carried out to the waiting hearse. Everyone filed out one by one. The surrounding roads had been closed off to cars, and the congregation proceeded to follow the hearse to the burial site. The crowd was silent other than those who were weeping— some very loudly and, dare I say it, a bit dramatically.

Lydia made her way over to us. She started talking in Maltese to Mario and his mum. I felt claustrophobic being with this many people. I needed air. I lifted my face to the midday sun. I could hear the murmuring of whispered conversations around me, birds squawking as they flew up above our heads. A police siren sounded in the distance, a baby crying, and several dogs barking excitedly. Life was carrying on.

'Eve, Eve.' I looked up, and in the distance, I could just about make out a man who was slightly taller than the rest. His long, dirty-blond hair and brightly coloured clothes stood out amongst the mourners. 'Eve, Eve, I'm over here,' Kai shouted.

CHAPTER 20

I was boxed in, caught in a crowd of mourners, all saying goodbye to a man I'd never met. I wanted to run to Kai, but also away from him, as far as possible. What the hell was he doing here? Was it even him? Was I imagining it? Maybe I was hallucinating. Was I being punished by God?

I looked at Mario, who was in deep conversation with Lydia. Mario's mum was talking with a large group of mourners; many were still weeping.

'Eve, over here.'

I looked up again. It was definitely Kai. Kai was here at the funeral of Paulo's uncle, along with Paulo, Lydia, Mario, and Mario's mum, who all believed Kai had practically stood me up at the aisle. In fact, Kai breaking my heart was the only reason I was even here at this funeral, embraced by the family for sharing my grief. My grief for a man who was standing just a few metres away from me right now, excitedly shouting my name and anticipating a warm welcome from his best friend. Not a cold shoulder from a spurned fiancé. I was a professional fraud, and I was about to be found out—again.

I started to walk backwards, blending myself into the crowd and disappearing into a sea of black. I squeezed into gaps and pushed past people until I could no longer see Mario, his mum, or Lydia. I kept going, pushing my way backwards until it felt safe enough to turn around and run against the direction of the procession. As the dense crowds started to dissipate, I nearly collided with a woman pushing a man in a wheelchair painfully slowly behind the group of mourners. He was fanning his face with the order of service. He looked at me as I dodged out of the way, and I looked away, guilt oozing out of every pore. The sun was beating down, and I could feel sweat running down my back. I was desperate for some water.

I kept going until the funeral crowd were black dots in the distance, and then I collapsed onto the pavement, my head between my knees, heaving great breaths in and out, in and out. My phone started ringing, and I scrambled in my bag, getting a paper cut from the order of service in the process. Or was it divine intervention?

It was Mario. I killed the call and tried Kai's number, which went straight to voice mail, so I hung up. I needed to get out of here. I couldn't go back to my apartment because Mario would go there looking for me. I couldn't think straight. How had Kai found me? How did he know I was going to be at a funeral today? And why was he here?

I stumbled down a side alley and sat outside the first cafe I found. I ordered some water and a black coffee, then called Kai again. This time, he answered.

'Eve, is that you? I'm here, I'm in Gozo. Where are you?'

I wanted to burst into tears. I had wanted to see him and hear his voice for so long, but not today, not now, and definitely not like this.

'I'm in a cafe. I don't know where.'

'I need a few more clues?'

I wanted to laugh, but I felt sick. I tried to grip the phone to stop my hand from shaking.

'I'll send you my location.'

'Order me a beer.'

Kai stood in front of me. I stared up at him. The sun framed his face, and I had to use my hand as a shield. He was wearing pale pink chino shorts and a navy blue short-sleeved casual-look shirt. He looked good.

'Hello.'

'Do I get a hug? I've travelled two thousand miles, risked life and death on the ocean waves, and battled a crowd of mourners to find you.'

I stood up and embraced him, wishing I never had to let go. I inhaled the smell of him, his hair, his clothes, his cologne.

'I mean, who was in that coffin, cos he was one hell of a popular guy?'

'What are you doing here?' I said, pulling myself away.

'Surprise,' he said, giving me jazz hands. 'I must admit I wasn't expecting to find you dressed in black at a funeral parade.' He laughed. 'I mean, that is the weirdest tourist attraction I've ever heard of.'

The waiter brought over our drinks. Kai was now sitting opposite me, his legs dancing about under the table. He picked up his beer, white foam spilling over the top.

'Cheers. To us,' he said, 'and the poor guy whose funeral you gatecrashed.'

'I didn't gatecrash. I was invited by one of my pupils. He was his uncle.'

'Oh, of course, you're a teacher now.' He stared at me, 'I'm proud of you, and I've missed you. A lot.'

'That's nice, but doesn't explain why you're here?'

'I'm here to meet a senorita,' Kai said as three pretty ladies walked past us, arm in arm.

'Wrong country,' I said. 'You're in Malta, not Spain.'

'Damn it,' Kai said, smiling. *How did I manage that?* 'Actually, I'm here because you owe me £8.90 for a Lime Bike ride on Christmas Day.'

'How do you know about that?'

'I linked the app on your phone to my bank account, remember?'

'Okayyyy, no, I don't remember that.' I paused. 'If I had, I would have been flying around town like Elphaba from *Wicked*.'

Kai laughed.

'Christmas Day was kind of weird,' I said.

'Weirder than this?' I looked away.

God, I'd missed him. It was so nice to be with him, and for a moment, I forgot about where we were, why I was dressed in a black trouser suit, and the very complicated situation him being here had put me in.

'So, can I stay with you?' Kai said. 'I left my case at your work.'

'You went to my work?' I said, turning to face him.

'How else was I going to find you?'

'Did you tell them who you were? Who did you speak to?' My stress levels were starting to rise. How was this happening again?

'I have no idea. I saw someone with a hangy neck ID thing and asked them if they knew you. They said you were at the funeral and told me where to go. Is there a problem?'

I closed my eyes. This was going to become messy very quickly, and a familiar feeling came over me. I needed to run away and leave. How could I face Lydia or Paulo once they found out the truth? Let alone Mario and his mum.

'So, can I stay? We can top and tail, or I can take a sofa if you have one?'

'You can't stay with me. I'm sorry.' I searched my mind for a believable excuse. 'My landlady is very traditional.'

'It's not like we're going to be having sex before marriage.' He winked at me. He thought he was so funny. 'Oh wait, this is a Catholic country, isn't it? Just tell her I'm a friend, not a luver!'

'It's not funny. How long are you even staying for?' I said.

'I've booked a flight home in a couple of days. I wasn't sure how long it would take me to find you. Is that okay?

'It's a bit complicated.'

A shadow fell across our table, and Kai and I both looked up.

'Hi, I'm Mario,' Mario said offering his hand towards Kai.

'Kai,' Kai said before I could stop him.

Mario's eyes met mine, and I wanted the earth to swallow me whole.

'I can explain,' I whispered, fighting back the tears that were pricking my eyes.

'No need. You disappeared and I just wanted to check you were okay. My friend, he tell me he saw you come this way. I see you are okay, so I will go now. Nice to meet you, Kai. I hope Eve forgive you for what you did.' He walked away and didn't look back.

I put my head in my hands.

'Okay, so he doesn't like me very much. What did I do?' Kai said turning to face me.

'Mario is nice,' I said, not lifting my head.

You didn't mention Mario in your emails?'

'I did. He's my landlady's son.'

'Ohhhh, Prince Charming on the white stallion?'

I didn't respond.

'And?'

'There's nothing to say,' I said, not looking at him.

'I don't think Mario agrees with you, judging by the way he just looked at you.'

'Don't be stupid.'

'So there's nothing going on with you two?'

'He's been showing me around the island.'

'Is that what they call it over here?' He winked.

'Stop it. It's not funny. I've really messed up.'

'Come on. I'll go and pay, then we can go and collect my bag and find somewhere for me to stay.'

I nodded.

'Don't run away, will you?'

Kai followed me in silence as I led the way back to the High Street and down through the main town. I wanted to point things out to him, like the market, my favourite restaurant, where I bought my groceries, and even where I'd had my haircut, but my head felt like a ball of wool that I needed to untangle. I needed to work everything out. I sat on the wall outside the school while Kai went to get his bag, and then I took him to a street where I knew there were a couple of budget hotels. He booked a room in the first one we came to, and together, we trapsed up the stairs and opened the door to a very basic but clean room consisting of a bed, a chair, and a bedside cabinet. The en-suite had a shower, toilet, and a small round mirror above a small sink. The window was open, and a roller blind was banging softly against the frame. There was a nice view over a small garden square. Kai sat on the bed and took his shoes off. I stood and looked out of the window.

'Do you want to talk?' he said.

I shrugged my shoulders like an insolent child. 'I told everyone you'd broken my heart and done a runner,' I said.

Kai nodded.

'Because?'

'Because you disappeared out of my life, and I needed a reason to be here, so I used you.' I paused. It didn't sound that bad when I said it out loud. 'It was that or say you'd died.'

'Why would you kill me?' Kai said, laughing. Did nothing faze him?

'Because it made my story more believable. I was heartbroken, needed a fresh start, etc, etc.' I paused. 'It would have been an accident.'

'So you really did consider killing me off?'

'I wasn't going to kill you, but yes, I did briefly consider telling people you were' I paused, 'deceased.'

Kai smirked. 'May I ask how I was going to meet my demise?'

'An accident, maybe.'

'Killed instantly?'

'Yes.'

'No suffering?'

'None at all.'

'That's good to know.'

I joined Kai on the bed, where we both sat in silence. Then I started talking, and he listened without attempting to interrupt me, which, for Kai, was a challenge. He just let me talk and talk, and I barely stopped for breath. I told him about the night at the East Hotel, my live interview on Thames FM, the police interview and Greg, my fake boyfriend who was invited to dinner by Poppy. I told him how it had all come crashing down and that I had really needed a friend because I'd messed everything up so spectacularly, and then I told him I'd really missed him and had been very lonely without him. Then I threw a cushion at him.

He got me some toilet paper for my nose and held my hand while I told him how Poppy had found out the truth and how I'd travelled around London for days afterwards. He hugged me and said sorry.

'Then I decided to leave and come to Malta.'

'To find your Sultana relatives?'

'No.' I laughed through my tears. 'I heard two people on a train talking about moving abroad, and my Aunt Jean said I should go, and it was like I'd been given a sign.'

'A sign from who? One of your dead ancestors?'

I slapped his leg.

'When I got here, people kept asking me why I'd come, and so I told them my gran was Maltese, then, stupidly, I said my boyfriend had broken my heart, and I needed to get away. It just snowballed from there. Everyone found out, then my pupil's uncle died, and I was asked to comfort him because I was grieving, too.' I paused. 'Sort of and...'

'Oh, so I was your boyfriend?' Kai raised his eyebrows. 'You didn't tell me that bit.'

'Fiancé, actually.'

'Wow!'

'You basically stood me up at the aisle. You absolute bastard.'

'I didn't! Oh my God, that's awful.'

My head was spinning, but more than anything, I was relieved that Kai seemed to be okay with what I'd done. If anything, he seemed quite amused by the whole thing.

'I think you're being hard on yourself,' he said as we walked through the park later that afternoon. 'At the end of the day, you didn't murder anyone. Well, you thought about killing me off, and poor Greg from Chiswick had a sticky end, but hey, we're both actually alive, so that's good news, right?'

I smiled. 'Stop it. It's not funny. I think there's something wrong with me.'

'Okay, look. I'm not going to pretend that going around inventing boyfriends and killing them off is normal behaviour, but I do think you're catastrophising.'

'It's pretty messed up.'

'It depends what way you look at it. Yes, you lost your job. But look at what you've done since then. The Eve I used to know wouldn't have booked a train to Greenwich, let alone booked a one-way ticket to Malta, found somewhere to live, and managed to get a job. Seriously, that's brave. Lots of people wouldn't have the courage to do any of that? I'm genuinely impressed.'

'Really?'

'And you're looking good. Really good. Black suits you. But maybe better for winter, not spring in the Med. Spring needs colour.'

I didn't want to say goodnight to Kai; I didn't want to leave him. I wanted to stay in his little room and not have to face Mario or his mum ever again, but Lydia was expecting me at work the next day, and just the thought of it made me feel nauseous.

243

'I'll see you tomorrow. Unless you decide to escape while you can,' I said, putting my shoes on.

'I'll be waiting, and Eve...'

'Yes?'

'I'm sorry. Sorry about what happened and sorry I wasn't there for you. I will explain.' I shrugged. 'But please stop stealing other people's dramas. You have enough drama in your own life. Don't be greedy.'

I grabbed a pillow off the bed and threw it at him. This time, getting him on the side of his head. He went down and lay motionless on the floor.

'Idiot,' I said and left.

I'd been in the apartment less than five minutes when there was a knock on the door. Mario's mum stood on the doorstep holding some tomatoes still on the vine.

'Can I come in?'

I nodded.

'I know your mama is not here, so can I be your mama and give you a hug?' She didn't wait for a reply. When I pulled away, I wiped my tears with the back of my hand. 'You must not cry,' she said.

'I'm sorry,' I said.

'You do not need to be sorry. It is your friend who must say sorry.'

I shook my head.

'He wasn't my boyfriend, and we weren't going to be married.' I sighed. 'He is just my friend. He has done nothing wrong. I made it all up.'

'But why you say this?'

I walked into my little room, my haven, and sat down. She followed.

'I don't know.' It was the truth. 'When the school asked me why I had left England, I just said it. I wanted the job.' I shrugged. 'Then everyone found out, and I should have said something then, but I didn't.'

'We have all done things that we regret. Said things that we should not say. We are human beings. and we are not perfect. I am sure you had your reasons to tell the story you did.'

'He's just my friend, but we'd had a fight and,' I could feel my voice start to break. I stopped until the emotion passed. 'I didn't mean to lie; it was a mistake. You and Mario have been so kind and so nice and—'

'Let me tell you something. You know Mario's father. Did Mario tell you he die in the army?'

I nodded.

'He not die in the army. He leave us for a younger woman,' she said, shrugging her shoulders. 'I tell people he die because it was easier.'

'Oh,' I said. A million thoughts went through my mind, which was running out of thinking space. Did this mean my behaviour was normal? Did other people do idiotic things and speak without thinking—get themselves into situations they couldn't get out of? This was such a relief. 'You shouldn't be ashamed,' I said, surprised at how quickly the tables had turned in this conversation.

'I know, but I was. Mario and my sister, they know the truth, but they too told people he had died. To us, he had died. He was gone. He was dead to us.'

'Do people know now?' I said.

Mario's mum gave me a tissue from her large apron pouch. 'Yes, everyone know, but no one say. People, they have seen him with his new wife and his new family, but they don't say to me, *why you say he dead*, because they know why. They know he broke my heart, and they understand. You see, we are the same, you and me.'

It took me a long time to get to sleep that night. My mind was churning, and my thoughts were jumbled with the past, today, and tomorrow. I sent Mario a message.

Eve: *I'm sorry x*

Then I lay down and stared at the moon.

CHAPTER 21

I woke up, and for a moment, I forgot Kai was here. I forgot about Mario confronting me in the restaurant, and I forgot about having to face Lydia and Paulo and everyone else who would probably know what I'd done by now because that seemed to be how things worked around here, on this Mediterranean rock.

I had a message from Lydia asking me to go and see her before class. Was I going to get fired twice in two months? That would at least be an achievement, although probably not one to put on my CV.

'Take a seat, please, Eve,' she pointed to the empty chair in front of her. 'How are you?'

'I'm,' I tried to think of an appropriate word to describe how I felt—*ashamed, embarrassed?*—'okay.'

'That's good. When you left the funeral yesterday, we thought maybe you'd been taken ill.' I shook my head. 'So Eve, this is difficult for me to say because your private life is your business, but people are talking.' I nodded. 'The students, they love to gossip, but they are humans, too, and soon, they will forget.' She gave me a sympathetic smile, which made me feel worse. I didn't want her to feel sorry for me. I nodded again, my voice deserting me. 'You can say nothing, but they will still talk, so I suggest you say something, but this is up to you.'

'I'm sorry.'

'Please do not feel embarrassed, Eve. We are a small island, and everyone knows everyone else's business, but really, this is not a big story compared to what goes on with families here.' She smiled. 'Really, trust me.'

'Thank you,' I whispered as I stood up to leave.

'We have been very impressed with your teaching, and we hope you will want to stay with us.'

That was it. No sacking, no warning, no drama. Maybe Kai was right. I was a drama queen.

As I walked into class, my hands were sweating, my legs felt unstable, and I had an overwhelming feeling of fear and dread. I heard a few whispers and some sniggering, but other than that, the pupils acted pretty much the same as they always did. I said good morning, and they sat down and took their books out. Then, there was a heckle from the back.

'How's your boyfriend, miss?'

Before I could respond, several pupils turned around and spoke angrily to the culprit in Maltese.

'Are you getting married, miss? Can we come to the wedding?'

There were more angry Maltese words exchanged until I stood up and clapped my hands. The room fell silent.

'I am aware there are some stories going around about me, but I would prefer it if we could concentrate on learning English and not on my personal life. Any questions?'

There was a chorus of 'No, miss.'

I sat back down and started the lesson on past and present tenses—ironically—and as the minutes ticked by, I began to feel calmer and more in control.

Kai met me outside after my class. He was sitting on a wall, his skin already looking tanned. He was wearing a short-sleeved V-neck shirt and a pair of bottle-green chino trousers. His Ray-bans and slicked-back hair made him look local. I, on the other hand, still very much looked like a tourist. Pale with a few freckles, mousy-brown hair, with maybe a few sun-kissed honey streaks.

'Hello, miss. How was your class?'

'It was fine, thank you. Better than expected.'

'Any detentions, exclusions or bad behaviour?'

'Nope.'

'I'm loving your new look, by the way,' Kai said, looking me up and down. 'What's happened to your homeless vibe?'

'I'm a professional now,' I said, 'and I've discovered linen.'

'Linen—an iron's best friend'

'I do spend a lot of time looking creased.'

'Creased is better than homeless,' Kai said. 'So, were you reprimanded for your colourful personal life?'

'Well, I've still got a job if that's what you mean?'

'See, I told you,' he slung his arm around my shoulders,' I shrugged it off and looked behind me. 'I'm sure your students are way too interested in themselves to care about what their teacher is up to,' he said, offering me his hand and curling his fingers around mine.

We headed to my apartment. Kai wanted to see where I lived. I showed him the market on the way, and we browsed the stalls. He bought a bandana and a samosa. We both got a peanut butter ice cream.

Kai liked where I lived. He said it felt homely, and he especially loved the big window.

'Let's go to the beach,' Kai said. 'It will make us feel like we're on holiday.'

I liked this idea. We would be less likely to bump into any of the students, and the beach was my favourite place to find head space. I went to get changed. I felt tired; yesterday had been a strange day. I'd gone from truly believing my new life was over to thinking that maybe it wasn't. Now, I didn't know if I felt happy or sad.

I pulled on my long linen skirt and a pale-blue cotton blouse. I put on a little make-up and some body spray. I grabbed a cardigan, opened the door and saw Kai sitting in my favourite chair, reading my dragonfly notebook. I lunged forward and snatched it away from him.

'What are you doing? That's private.'

'But those letters are addressed to me.'

'That doesn't mean you can read them.'

Kai laughed.

'Tell me if I'm mistaken, but are you a tiny bit in love with me?'

'Oh my God. No, I am definitely not!'

'Are you sure? Cos reading those letters, it sounds like you might be.'

'Don't be so,' I couldn't think of an appropriate word, 'annoying.'

'Maybe it's just wishful thinking on my behalf,' Kai said.

'You are an obnoxious, cocky, arrogant English man,' I said, for want of anything better to say. 'Wait, what did you just say?'

'Is there any part of you that could ever consider coming back to England and spending the rest of your life with me?' I stared at him, my heart beginning to do somersaults. Was this some kind of joke? 'I mean it,' he said. Giving me the same smile he'd given me the first time we met all those years ago in a grubby classroom.

I looked up at him. This was my best friend, my rock. The person that made me laugh more than anyone else could.

'If you agree to cancel my £8.90 Lime Bike debt, accept that I like the way I dress, and hire me a private jet to get me off this island, then I'll think about it.'

'Two out of three?' he said, coming towards me and very gently kissing me on the lips.

I pulled away reluctantly. I could feel my cheeks burning. I felt like this should be awkward, but it wasn't.

'I'm not sure this is a good idea?' I said.

'Let's go to the beach and discuss,' he said. 'By the way, you might want to change, cos I've hired us a moped.'

I'd never been on a moped before. I clung onto Kai's waist and buried my head in his shoulder as he took us through the tomato fields and down the steep road towards Ramla. It was exhilarating as much as it was terrifying.

When we got to the beach, Kai couldn't get to the sea quickly enough.

'I love the beach,' he said, kicking water at me.

'You're such a kid.'

'Shall we build a sandcastle and live happily ever after?' he said, running ahead before I could answer.

It was a small bay, and we walked all the way to the end, occasionally stopping to skim stones.

'I need to tell you something,' Kai said. He took his jacket off chivalrously and lay it on the sand for me to sit on.

'I was a bit pissed off with you that day in the park. Mainly because I thought you had a boyfriend, which—one—made me insanely jealous, and—two—I couldn't believe you hadn't told me.'

'I've explained all that.'

'Yeah, I know that now, but at the time,' he sighed loudly, 'anyway, that isn't why I didn't return your calls or reply to your messages.' I looked at him. He was digging a hole in the sand with his hand. 'I was actually in hospital, wishing I was dead.'

'What?' I turned to face him, thoughts flying through my mind quicker than I could acknowledge them. 'What do you mean?' I said, a lump forming in my throat.

'You promise not to laugh?' Kai said.

'It doesn't sound like it's going to be a funny story,' I said.

'So, you know, my job is to arrange pretentious events for clients?' I nodded. 'Well, sometimes, my clients just want coffee, tea, a selection of M&S sandwiches, etc...'

'Is this going somewhere?'

'Bear with me.' He paused. 'Sometimes, they want a three-course meal, top wines, aperitifs, the lot.'

'What's an aperitif?'

'Are you joking?'

'Yes, obviously.'

'Very funny. Can I carry on telling you about my near-death experience?'

'Go ahead.'

'So the day after the park, I was at a new corporate catering company, trying out their food.'

'Nice.'

'The food was amazing. Every dish looked like a van Gogh painting.'

'Who?'

'You're not funny,' Kai said, laughing. 'Seriously, the food was crazy. The sauces were greener than—'

'Grass?' I offered.

'Not that creative, but yes, and there were edible flowers, seeds, and berries scattered on top of everything. I actually took some photos to send to you.'

'So what happened? Did you drop your phone in the clam chowder?'

'Funnily enough. No.'

'I can sense there's a "but" coming.'

'But then, I tried the oysters.'

'I knew it! So it was the clam chowder?' I slammed my hands on my table in victory. 'Wait, you ate oysters? I thought you only ate fish if it's battered and served with chips?'

'Normally, I would never have eaten anything so slimy looking, but they smelt so good, and the sauce tasted of melted butter and wine. It was honestly delicious.'

'Can you stop dragging this out? I'm on the edge of my seat here.'

'The next thing I know, I'm being violently sick.'

'Allergic? Or food poisoning?'

'Wait, this is the dramatic bit. When I say sick, I mean I didn't even care that I'd ruined my brown DMs and my light-tan chinos.'

'Wow, it must have been bad.'

'Every time I tried to breathe, it was like a waterfall. Projectile vomit everywhere. Literally, I couldn't stop.'

'I get it, no need to expand any more. Remember, I, too, had a recent vomiting experience. Hence, why I'm stranded on this island.'

'I think my vomiting was worse than yours.'

'Shall we have a vomit off?'

'Let's not.'

'Okay.'

'I remember being on my hands and knees and someone shoving a plastic measuring jug under my chin,' Kai said.

'That's weird.'

'Yeah, and it was a bad choice cos it only held 200 ml, and I knocked it over with my next retch. Anyway, then everything went black.'

'This is a horrible story.'

'I know. It gets worse.'

'Really? But you were okay, right?'

'Obviously not, because I went to the hospital.'

'Oh, yeah. Sorry.'

'I woke up to find myself in an ambulance, and the next time I was conscious, I was in a hospital bed, attached to a drip. I remember nothing of the next twenty-four hours.'

'Wait, so all the time I was bombarding you with messages and phone calls, you were in hospital?' Kai nodded. 'Why the hell didn't you let me know?'

'Because I had no idea where my phone was, or my keys, or my wallet.'

'Maybe you did lose them in the clam chowder?'

'Can you stop with the clam chowder jokes?'

'Soz.' I made a clam impression with my hand, he laughed and ran his hand through his hair. My heart missed a beat.

'I had nothing with me. I'd left it all at the caterers. All I knew was that they'd contacted my office to tell them what had happened and the office had contacted my mum.

'Oh my God.'

'I stayed in the hospital for the next two days, then my mum came to pick me up.' He stopped talking and I waited.

'And you didn't tell me any of this because?'

'Because, when I got home I called the office and they said everything had been returned, except my phone. They said they'd contacted the catering company, but that they were refusing to communicate on the advice of their solicitors. For legal reasons.'

'What the hell?'

'Yeah, they thought I was gonna sue them or something.'

'You should!'

'The last time I remembered having my phone was when I'd taken photos of the food.'

'Ahhh, evidence,' I said, resting my chin in my hand, Inspector Clouseau style. 'I can't believe I didn't know about this. Why didn't you just call me from your mum's phone?'

'Do you know my mobile number?'

'No, but— '

'Do you know your own mobile number?'

'No, but—'

'Can I carry on?'

'Have you nearly finished? This is going on a bit.' I pretended to yawn.

'I'll try and wrap up my near-death experience as quickly as possible.'

'If you could, please.'

'I was in bed for the rest of that week, literally sipping water through a straw, until I finally managed to nibble on a piece of dried toast. Honestly, I was pathetically weak.'

'Nibble? What like a mouse?' I did my best impression of a mouse. Banter had always been our default way of communicating.

'I felt very sorry for myself. I had no way of contacting you; my laptop was still in the office, and I felt the worst I'd ever felt.' He paused. 'And because of the stupid argument in the park, it had somehow become awkward because it had been so long, and I was kind of angry at you for not contacting me.'

'But I tried. Do you have any idea how many times I tried to call you?'

'I know, I wasn't thinking straight.'

'Have you finished?'

'Nearly. I was off work for three weeks, and I thought about you a lot. More than anything else, actually. I just wanted to get better and then come and see you to explain.'

'So why didn't you?'

'I did! I came over twice to see you, and you were out both times.'

'What? When? I never go out.'

'That's what I thought, but then I figured you had a boyfriend now, so maybe you'd been coaxed out of your shell.' He smiled. 'It was around Christmas time.'

'Oh.' I puffed out my cheeks. 'I think I thought you were an ASOS delivery guy.'

'You bought something from ASOS?'

'No, don't be dumb, of course, I didn't. What would I wear from ASOS? My neighbour has an ASOS addiction. It's like AA, but for ASOS.'

'Funny–not. Anyway, my phone never turned up and so as a gesture of goodwill, my office gave me a work phone, but I'd lost all of my contacts, and I didn't know your number by heart. When I tried to log in to my iCloud, I couldn't remember my password, and then it all got super complicated. The HR department said that the National Health inspector suspected my phone had been withheld because of the images of the food,' he stopped to breathe, 'so it became a legal investigation.'

'Are you making this up?'

'No, seriously. I know it's a crazy story. It's still going on.'

'As excuses go, this is pretty impressive.'

'I know, right? So it's nearly Christmas, I've lost about a stone and look like Mick Jagger.'

'Who?'

'I know you're joking. I've been to your flat twice, and eventually, I called your radio station.'

'Really? When?'

'I spoke to that idiot, Gary. He gave me some bullshit about the phone number was for listeners and not for staff's personal calls. I asked him to pass on a message, with my new number. I'm guessing you never got the message?'

'What a bastard.'

'So, when you didn't get in touch, I was pretty gutted and started to think you didn't want to see me.'

'What, after twenty years?'

'I was vulnerable, remember? I just thought maybe our friendship hadn't meant as much to you as it had to me. And that you were in love.'

'You idiot.'

'Then, on Christmas Day, I spent the whole day wanting to tell you about the weird gift my nan got me.'

'Which was?'

'A puncture repair kit in a silver tin.' I swallowed a laugh.

'You don't even have a bike, do you?'

'Exactly.'

'And I bought you a gift. A really nice one.'

'What was it?'

'A cocktail maker, with two glasses, a recipe book, and a bottle of rum.'

'That's thoughtful.'

'You said you'd been out for cocktails, remember?'

'Oh. Yeah. The East Hotel night. Where this mess all started.'

'Finally, I managed to get an appointment at the Apple Genius Bar and managed to access my messages, and that's when I got all your messages.'

'Too much?'

'Bit Baby Reindeer.' I laughed. 'But by then, I'd got your postcard and remembered I had your email address from the time I registered you on the Lime Bike, and that's when I emailed you.'

'Okay, we are definitely coming to the end now.'

'Moments away.'

'Thank God.'

'Then, a week later. Yes, A WEEK, you replied, telling me you're living on an island in the middle of the Mediterranean.'

'Yeah, well, maybe I wouldn't be if I hadn't thought you'd abandoned me. I had nothing to stay for.'

'The end.'

As the sun set, we got a table at the beach cafe and sat outside under the canopy. The waiter brought us out some blankets, and we ordered cocktails and chips.

'That's a crazy story. Are you sure you didn't make it up?' I said.

'Actually, I overheard this guy on a bus talking about a killer oyster, and I thought, *I know what I'll do.*'

'God, you're hilarious.'

'I realised how much I missed you when you weren't in my life,' Kai said, finishing his second cocktail.

'Not the best strategy for starting a relationship,' I said.

'No, and it made me very miserable.'

Kai ordered another two cocktails.

'I have a question,' he said.

'Go on.'

'Why did you start to write your own eulogy?'

'If you must know, I overheard a conversation about someone else who'd done it and thought I'd have a go. I didn't get very far.'

'It was sad.'

'Well, a eulogy isn't meant to be happy, is it?'

Kai laughed and leant back on his chair, but then, he fell back into the sand. I laughed so much that I gave myself hiccups, and the waiter rushed over to help Kai up.

'Sorry. He's a tourist recovering from a traumatic experience involving an oyster,' I apologised.

'Oysters are delicious but can kill you,' the waiter said, walking away and laughing.

'See. I told you,' Kai said.

The waiter returned with more drinks and a complimentary bowl of nuts.

'Oh bum,' Kai said, giggling like a four-year-old. 'I forgot about the moped.'

We got a taxi back to Kai's hotel, and I lay in his arms and wondered if this was the happiest I'd ever felt, but I was exhausted. In the past twenty-four hours, my emotions had been seriously challenged, and I felt like I'd done a round or two in a boxing ring.

I woke in the morning in a pool of sand and sent Kai out for coffee while I showered and washed my hair. I searched through his luggage and found a sweatshirt. It smelt of him, and I wrapped my arms around myself like they do in the movies. Kai returned as I was attempting to dry my hair with the hotel dryer, which had about as much power in it as a ten-year-old camping torch. He was carrying two coffees in one hand and several brown paper bags in the other.

'Breakfast in bed?'

I giggled like we'd just met. 'I have work, remember?'

'But we need to discuss our future,' he said, looking very serious and then breaking into a smile.

'I finish at lunchtime,' I said, taking a bite from an almond croissant.

'Is that my sweatshirt?' Kai said.

'It's what girlfriends do,' I said, the words leaving my mouth before I could catch them.

'Girlfriend, eh?'

'I didn't say that.'

I walked to work, smiling. My life had never been so good.

I was brought straight back down to earth when I saw Paulo getting off the bus in front of me. He stared at me, swinging a dirty rucksack onto his shoulder. I lifted my hand in a half-hearted wave. I owed him an explanation.

'Where is your briefcase?' I said.

'This was my uncle's,' he said.

'Oh.' I smiled at him. 'Can I talk to you?'

He looked down at his shoes.

'I'm sorry I left the funeral early. It was a beautiful service.'

'Thank you, miss.'

'I owe you an explanation,' I said.

'It's okay, miss. You do not need to explain.'

'I meant what I said, you know.'

'I know. Thank you, miss.'

'I have lost people in my life. It's hard, and I'm sorry. There was a misunderstanding.'

'It's okay, miss; you help me a lot.'

I must have looked at my watch a hundred times during my two-hour lesson. All I could think about was Kai. Eve and Kai. We'd been friends for so long, knew so much about each

261

other, had competitions about how sad our lives were, and now we were what—a couple?

In the last thirty minutes of the lesson, I played a game. They were only allowed to speak in English, and if they made a mistake or spoke in Maltese, they were out. Each student had to answer a question and then ask the student sitting next to them a new question.

'Who is your favourite teacher?' one of the students said.

'Miss Eva is the best teacher. Do you agree with me?' she asked the next student.

'I do agree with you. What teacher do you prefer best?' the student asked Paulo.

'I agree she is the best,' Paulo said.

By the end of the class, my head was so big, I thought it might not fit through the door, but my heart felt even bigger.

Kai greeted me with a slush puppie.

'Thought I'd see what you looked like with blue lips,' he said, thrusting it in my hand.

We walked towards the park and sat on a bench, looking out at a waterfall without water.

'I'm going back tomorrow,' he said quietly.

'I know,' I said.

'Soooooo?' I looked at him. 'We should at least try and have a grown-up conversation,' he laughed, 'without laughing.'

'You start,' I said.

He turned his body to face me.

'I have never seen you so happy, or so confident, or enjoying your life as much as you are here.' He reached for my hand. 'But my life, my job, is in England.' He squeezed my hand tighter. 'I'm not going to ask you to come back to England for me because that's not fair.' I gave him a half smile, scared of what he was going to say next, 'and you need to sort things out with Mario.'

'What? Why? There's nothing going on. I told you already. I want to be with you,' I said.

'Even if it means living in Kings Cross with your parents' appalling taste in furniture and giving up the Maltese birdsong for police sirens?' Kai said.

'Yes, but I'm not prepared to get back on that ferry without being put to sleep first.

'Be serious, Eve. Just for a minute.'

'I have six weeks left of my contract at the Language School. I need to see it through.'

'Okay, so you have six weeks to decide what you really want. Deal?'

'Deal,' I said, 'but I already know what I want.'

Later that afternoon, I took Kai to the Azure Window to watch the sunset. It was pretty romantic, and we walked hand in hand along the clifftop. I sat leaning against his chest, listening to the waves crashing against the rocks.

On the way back, we stopped at a pizza van and shared a fungi with truffle oil as the sun went down. I would remember this day forever.

We went back to Kai's hotel and lay on his bed, talking about everything and nothing.

'I've been thinking about your oyster story,' I said, swallowing a laugh.

'I'm securing the movie rights,' Kai said.

'Good idea. So, while I was considering playing the sympathy card and telling everyone you'd died, you did, in fact, nearly die.'

'Yeah, and I bet, you wouldn't have said I was killed by an oyster.'

'Probably not. But how weird would it have been if I told everyone you'd died, and then you did actually die!'

'Incredibly weird. Hilarious, in fact.'

'A great story, though.'

'Or not.'

For the second night running, I fell asleep in his arms, wishing this day would never end.

CHAPTER 22

Kai was calm and collected, but I was struggling to hold it together.

'So are you seriously telling me I came all this way to see you, tracked you down at a funeral, stayed in some dodgy hotel, and you're still not paying me back the £8.90 for your Christmas bike?'

I punched him on the arm.

'Why can't I come to the airport with you?' I said.

'In a word, boat.'

'Oh yeah. I don't like you that much.'

'And I don't want you crying and wailing as I walk through security. It'll be embarrassing.'

'Don't flatter yourself. I'm thinking of going clubbing later,' I trailed off, worried my voice might break.

'Sounds great. I know how much you love to party.'

He took me in his arms and kissed the top of my head.

'We'll talk soon, yeah.' I nodded. 'You've got six weeks to decide if you can live without my daily wit and charm or if a yearly visit is enough. I'll love you forever, whatever you decide, okay?'

'Did you just tell me you loved me?' I said.

'Don't be ridiculous. Of course, I didn't,' he said. Then, he was gone into a crowd of tourists queuing for the ferry.

I wanted to follow him, beg him not to leave, maybe even get on the ferry with him. Show him how much he means to me, but I was a grown-up. I had responsibilities, a job, students who needed me, and now, a big decision to make. I waited until I saw him walk up the ferry ramp, his bag slung over his shoulder, baseball cap on back to front. He looked back at me and waved. I smiled and waved back, confident he couldn't see my tears through my sunglasses from that far away.

The rest of the day was very quiet, and I kept myself distracted with chores. I did some laundry, cleaned up, filled the fridge with food, and planned some revision lessons. There wasn't a cloud in the sky, and I thought of England and its grey, cold skies. If it wasn't for Kai, I wouldn't want to go back. I felt happy here, with people who didn't judge me the way Poppy and Gary had. People who had accepted me and forgiven me without asking questions. Poppy and Gary had known me for five years, and in that time, I'd not taken a single day off sick. I'd always done what was asked of me and never complained about the way Gary treated me. I never asked why they didn't include me in things, never asked for a pay rise, and yet, they'd dismissed me without even giving me a chance to explain. These past few days, I'd learnt that people are allowed to make mistakes, even big ones, and still, they can be given another chance. Everyone does things, sometimes, that others don't understand, but there are reasons they behave the way they do that have nothing to do with the here and now. Some people are so used to carrying around sadness and longing that they don't even realise it's impacting their lives.

Kai: *Hi. I'm back, and I survived the ferry crossing. If you decide to return to grey, wet, cold, miserable England, I think you'll survive, especially if you have someone to hold your hair back if the worst happens.*

Miss you already.

Love

Kai xx

I couldn't sleep. I tried reading but couldn't concentrate. I tried deep breathing and listening to a sleep meditation, but it failed. I tried an alternative version of counting sheep by remembering all my students' names, but that didn't work either. I gave up, got up, and wrapped myself in my duvet like a burrito, then shuffled to my favourite chair. I curled my legs underneath me and stared out into the night sky, replaying the past forty-eight hours. I needed to make sense of it all. I pulled my dragonfly notebook down from the shelf and re-read my letters to Kai.

No one makes me laugh like you do. I think of you as the brother I never had. I couldn't ask for a better sibling.

Did I really think of Kai as a brother? Or had I just said that because I thought that's how he saw me?

I'm spending Christmas on my own this year, as Mad Auntie Jean has volunteered to help at the Soup Kitchen. Don't feel bad; I'll be fine on my own, although being on your own at Christmas feels sad.

What had Kai felt when he'd read this?

I've decided to stop messaging you. I don't know if you've noticed. It's my New Year's resolution, but I still think of you, and I'm still sad and sorry about what happened.

Kai had read these letters, but we hadn't talked about them. I'd told him about how my made-up life had snowballed out of control, and he told me how he was nearly killed by an oyster, but we hadn't talked about us. What did we want and need from each other? We seemed to have blurred the lines and turned a friendship into a relationship, but that risked losing the friendship and the friendship was what I had missed the most. I was confused. The 'I'm in love and don't care who knows it' mood was disappearing as quickly as it had arrived and left me feeling restless.

I woke to a horn beeping outside the apartment, a stiff neck and pins and needles. I heaved myself out of the chair and looked out of the window. Mario was outside, lifting a large suitcase out of his jeep. His mum came to greet him. I noticed how defined his muscles were on his tanned arms. They embraced, and I saw him look up at my window. I stepped back into the shadows.

When I got out of the shower, a note had been pushed under my door.

Please come for dinner tonight.

Maria (Downstairs)

I finally knew her name. I always referred to her as 'my landlady' or 'Mario's mum,' and I hadn't thought of her as a friend until the night she told me about her husband, but Maria had been kind to me since the very first day. She'd brought me strawberries and tomatoes and hadn't judged me when I'd messed up, even though I'd let her and her beloved son down.

It had been a long time since anyone had cooked for me, but I hadn't seen Mario since he tracked me down at the cafe with Kai. He hadn't replied to my apology, so it would be awkward. But after everything she'd done for me and everything I'd done, I didn't feel I could say no.

On my way home, I bought a bottle of wine and then changed into the only dress I had brought with me. A denim A-line that could be worn with trainers without looking too scruffy. I painted my nails and put on some make-up. I'd finally come around to Kai's way of thinking.

If you look your best, you'll be your best.

I spritzed my neck with perfume and locked up, ignoring the voice in my head telling me not to go.

Mario answered the door.

'Hi. Come in. How are you?' He was smiling. There was no awkwardness. I handed him the wine. 'Did my mama tell you I would be here?' he said, opening the fridge and holding a beer in one hand, a bottle of white in the other and offering me both.

'I saw you arrive this morning,' I said. 'Wine, please. It's nice to see you.'

Maria came in, her signature apron around her waist.

'Ahh, you are here.' She kissed me on both cheeks. 'Mario, get your mama a drink.'

'Something smells delicious,' I said. 'Thank you very much for inviting me.'

'You're welcome, isn't she, Mario?'

'Very welcome,' he said.

The table was set with a red and white checked tablecloth and white cotton napkins. A bowl of olives swimming in oil and a silver jug of water were on the table. Maria carried in three plates, expertly balancing one on her forearm.

'Aubergine parmigiana. It is very good,' she said.

It was very good, delicious, in fact, and combined with the wine and Maria's stories about Mario when he was a boy, I was enjoying myself. The main dish was fish paella, which

Maria carried to the table in a large iron skillet and told us to help ourselves. Mario kept us topped up with wine, and the longer the evening went on, the more I relaxed and the less I thought about Kai.

'My mum has made my favourite dessert.' He smiled at Maria. 'I hope you like it, too,' Mario said, getting up to clear the plates.

I got up to help but was promptly told off and ushered back to my seat. The tiramisu melted in my mouth, and when I told Maria it was the best meal I'd ever eaten, I meant it.

'I am going to need to be rolled upstairs,' I said. 'But really, that was the best meal of my life.'

They both laughed.

'My mama is a brilliant cook,' Mario said.

'And you are a brilliant son,' Maria said.

I felt very at home sitting there with Maria and Mario and was in no hurry to leave. It had been such a strange few days, and my emotions had been up and down like the ferry, but this was nice. I had needed company tonight more than I realised and this was a perfect distraction from my thoughts.

'You two must go and have a drink,' Maria said. I protested, asking her to please let me help clean up, but she insisted. So, less than twenty-four hours after spending the night with Kai and crying because he was leaving, I found myself sitting in a bar with Mario, drinking amaretto.

'I am sorry for my mama; she is keen for me to have girlfriend, get married, have a family.' Mario slid off his chair to his feet.

I gasped.

'Don't look so frightened, Eva—I am not about to propose.' He laughed. 'I am going to the bathroom. I laughed, too. 'But it would make her very happy.' He laughed again, and I laughed too, ninety-nine per cent sure he was joking.

'My mama, she tell me she tell you about my papa?' I nodded. 'So I guess we are, how do you say, the same?'

'Quits?' I said, offering him my hand.

'Quits?'

'Equal,' I said, offering him a handshake.

'I didn't mean to lie. I'm sorry,' I said. Mario shrugged. 'It was a misunderstanding, and I didn't know how to explain.'

'It's okay.'

'No, it's not,' I said. I owed him an explanation, and I wanted to make things right. 'When the language school asked me why I'd come to Malta, I thought I needed a reason.' I paused again. 'The real reason is complicated.' I looked away. 'I've known Kai since we were at school. He is my best friend, but we had a fight, and we weren't talking. It was stupid. I don't know why I said he was my boyfriend or that we were getting married. I wish I hadn't. We were just friends.'

Mario ran his hand through his hair.

'I didn't know Lydia would tell your mum, and then she told you, and I didn't know what to do, so I just did nothing.'

'So there was no wedding?'

I shook my head and looked away.

'I thought me saying I had left England because of a broken heart would stop people asking questions. Instead, it made them ask more.' I looked at him, and he was chewing his lips. 'He was my rock, and then he just walked out of my life,' I said. 'So when I told Lydia he'd broken my heart, he had. But just not in that way.'

'So you replaced him with an actual rock?' I laughed. 'And you forgive him, even though he do this to you?'

'Yes. It wasn't his fault.'

'What about your Maltese relatives?'

'It is true my grandmother was Maltese, according to my dad. But he didn't talk to me much about her. There is a photo of a lady in a black dress holding a baby, which my dad said was the only time we met. I didn't know her.' Mario looked thoughtful.

'In Gozo, everyone knows everyone's business.'

'In London, I don't even know my neighbours,' I said.

'But London is full of people, no?'

'Yes, but it's hard to explain.'

'Where you live in London is a busy place? Kings Cross is a famous train station—yes?'

'Yes. And there's also cafes and restaurants and art galleries and shops, but,' I looked into his eyes, 'also, many people who are homeless and struggling to survive, and my flat is not that nice.'

'What about your other friends and your family?'

I told him about Auntie Jean and about Poppy, who was too popular and beautiful to be my friend, and Gary, who was too wrapped up in himself to even notice me.

'Coming to Gozo has made me very happy.'

'So, will you stay?' Mario said.

I hesitated. I didn't know what I wanted anymore.

'I don't know if I can stay. It is complicated now that we have left the EU.' I shrugged. 'But my nan being Maltese could help.'

'I can marry you.' He laughed. 'Then my mama is happy, and the immigration office are happy. My mama, she thinks you are the best thing since...'

'Sliced bread?' I said.

'Sliced bread? I do not understand what you mean, sliced bread?'

We both laughed so much people looked over at us, but I didn't care. I felt happy, and the wine and the amaretto had gone to my head.

'You English say some funny things,' he carried on laughing, 'but I really need to go to the bathroom now.'

How could I be having such a good time? What about Kai? He'd told me he loved me, and I'd cried when he walked away. But already I was getting used to life without him.

Mario sat back down, placing two more drinks on the table.

'So Kai is just your friend?'

'We have only ever been friends,' I said again. I wanted to be honest, but I didn't know what we were. 'It's a bit complicated.' I added. 'But he has gone back to England now.'

We talked until the bar closed and then walked back together in the moonlight, arm in arm. Mario kissed me goodnight on both cheeks and waved to me as I walked upstairs. I didn't ask him to come upstairs, and he didn't offer. I took my shoes off and heard the front door shut downstairs. I lay down on my bed and stared at the ceiling. Somehow, I'd found myself in a love triangle, and I didn't know what to do about it.

I woke to an email from Kai and a message from Mario.

If I let you off the £8.90, will you consider coming home?

Life is boring without you

Kai x

Mario: *It's a beautiful day. Can I take you to a special beach?*

San Blas was indeed beautiful, as long as you were prepared to take your life in your hands to get there. It was at the bottom of a hill that was so steep, we had to abandon Mario's jeep halfway down and walk the rest of the way. This was actually a relief because we'd been driving practically vertically, and visions of the car flipping over were giving me heart palpitations. The beach was small and abandoned and had no signs of life other than a small beach shack, which was closed for the winter. Mario led me to a large fallen tree and helped me up onto the trunk, where we sat together, looking out at the waves.

'Do you remember your dad?' I asked him.

'No, not really.'

'Do you remember him leaving?'

He shook his head.

'I just remember him not being there. My mama told me he'd gone away but would be coming back. Then, one day, she just told me he wasn't ever coming back.' He was picking bits of bark off the trunk and throwing it into the sea. 'My friends at school told me my papa was dead, so I asked my mama if this was true, and she told me no, he isn't dead, but he is dead to us. And that was it.'

'Have you ever tried to see him?'

'I've thought about it, but it would break my mama's heart.'

'What about you?' he said. 'Where are your parents?'

'My parents really are dead. I didn't make that up.'

'I'm sorry,' he said.

'I don't miss them, but I wish I did.' I looked out to sea. 'They weren't unkind, but I don't think they loved me all that much.'

'That is a sad thing to say,' Mario said. He paused, and we sat in silence for a while. 'What about your relatives?'

'I don't have any. Well, I do have one aunt, who is nice but not like an auntie.'

'If you stay here in Malta, I can help you find your family?' I smiled. 'I am being serious, Eva. I know how to do it. We can find your family.'

CHAPTER 23

During the week, I talked to Kai every night. At the weekends, I hung out with Mario. I didn't tell either of them about the time I spent with the other. I felt guilty even though I wasn't doing anything wrong and no promises had been made. I knew I needed to make a decision before I lost them both, but it wasn't that simple. Mario was here, and Kai wasn't, but Kai was my best friend. He knew me better than anyone else in the whole world. He was my go-to person in a crisis, apart from when he wasn't, but he'd explained that. I guess being in the hospital and having your phone confiscated by the FBI was a pretty good excuse not to be there when I needed him.

Mario was kind and offered me the opportunity to start a new life away from London and in a new place where I felt accepted for who I was. I was happy living here and happy when I was with him. But I was happy with Kai, too, and he made me laugh like no one else could. Then, there was my job. It was one of the best things that had ever happened to me. I'd gone from feeling anxious before each lesson and relieved after each class, to looking forward to seeing the students. They made me feel good about myself, and they wanted to learn and were actually improving. I was doing something worthwhile and making a difference in their lives. I felt fulfilled.

The students had a fascination with England, London in particular, and some of them wanted to live and work in the UK. They were constantly asking me questions.

About the Royal family: 'What are they like?'

Piccadilly Circus: 'Is it a circus?'

Buckingham Palace: 'How many rooms does it have?'

Big Ben, 'Is it big?'

'Miss, why do you want to live in Gozo when you have a home in London?' Melanie asked me one day.

'England is very cold in the winter,' I said.

'But Gozo is too hot in the summer, so how do you say, "swings and roundabouts?"'

'Very good, Melanie. You are right. The grass is always greener on the other side.'

'London has green grass? Is this an English saying?' She laughed.

'Yes, London does have grass, but it means people think what they don't have is better than what they do have.'

'Ahhhh, I see, so you stay here in the winter and go home in the summer? Then you can have green grass all the time.'

Maybe that was the answer. Keep Mario as my winter sun and Kai as my British summertime. The best of both worlds.

When I finished class on Friday, Mario was waiting for me outside. He was sitting on the same wall Kai had sat on when he waited for me on his last day. He stood up and jogged over when he saw me.

'I have a big surprise for you.'

'What is it?'

'If I tell you, it won't be a surprise.'

'We're not riding into the sunset again, are we?' Mario shook his head and smiled. His fringe flopped over his eyes, and his cheeks dimpled. 'I don't like surprises,' I argued. 'I am not very good in unexpected situations. I say things I don't mean and act impulsively. Do things I regret.'

'Do not worry, you will say the right thing. Come with me.'

We got into Mario's jeep and made our way up high towards to salt plains near Marsalforn beach. Mario gave me another one of his history lessons, telling me the locals had been collecting rock salt from there for 350 years.

'Is this my surprise?' I said. 'A lesson in salt mining?'

Mario laughed.

'No, a trip to the salt plains is not your surprise, but if you like, we can stop here on the way back from your surprise.'

We drove on for a further ten minutes, the houses becoming further and further apart. We turned onto a dirt track and were greeted by several dogs running alongside us, barking excitedly, their tails wagging so hard that I was worried they were going to injure themselves. I wasn't used to dogs. We pulled up alongside a vineyard that carried on beyond where I could see.

'Are we doing a wine tasting?' I said.

Mario grabbed my hand, pulling me towards a whitewashed farmhouse. He knocked on the door, stood behind me, and covered my eyes with his hands.

'What's going on?' I said, hearing the door open. I was pulled into an embrace and could hear lots of voices talking Maltese. People came from every direction, and the dogs started jumping up at me. It was noisy and chaotic, and I had no idea who these people were or what I was doing here.

'Eva, meet your great cousin, Lucia,' Mario said, pulling his hands away, revealing a smile that was taking up his entire face.

'What do you mean?' I said as Cousin Lucia squished my face and planted a kiss on my cheek.

'I found them. The Sultana family. Your family. They are here in Gozo.' Mario was like an excited puppy. He couldn't stand still and kept switching from English to Maltese, speaking to the people in the room and then to me. I stood still as, one by one, people came up to me, speaking in a language I didn't understand, hugging me and laughing.

'How do you know these people are my family?' I said. I wasn't enjoying this experience one bit and wanted to run back to the car, climb in and lock the doors. I was ushered into a large kitchen, and a drink with floating oranges and what looked like a Scotch egg was pushed into my hand.

'Eat, drink,' I was ordered.

Mario appeared beside me.

'They are very happy and excited.'

'How do you know this is my family?' I said again. 'I don't understand.'

Mario spoke in Maltese to the lady who'd greeted us at the door. My newly discovered cousin got up and disappeared.

'She has something to show you,' Mario said.

Everyone was staring at me. I felt like they were waiting for me to start singing a song or give a speech. I lifted my hand in a half wave.

'Hi everyone,' I said.

Mario translated, and everyone fell about laughing like I'd just said the funniest thing they'd ever heard. My cousin returned, holding a large black book. She put it on the table and beckoned me over. As she turned the pages, I caught glimpses of photographs in black and white, yellowing at the edges. She kept turning the pages until, eventually, she stopped and pointed at a small picture stuck in the top right-hand corner of the page. She peeled back the cellophane and lifted the photo away, handing it to me. I stared at the picture. It was the same picture I'd seen many years before, of me as a baby, being held by a woman dressed in black. I turned it over. Written on the back, in faded scrawling handwriting, it read.

'Nana Sultana with baby Eve, 1995.'

'Where did you get this?' I said. Mario translated. 'Are you really my family?' Mario stepped in again. I had so many questions, but I wasn't ready for this. I wasn't good with surprises, and this one, while in theory could be a nice surprise, it was also a shock, and I didn't know how to react. The excitement of my newfound relatives confused me. They didn't know me; they'd never met me, so why were they so emotional? I felt uncomfortable and under pressure to jump about and scream with glee. I was out of my comfort zone. Mario was sitting next to me, beaming like he was the hero of the moment.

'Please, Mario, tell me how you found them?' I whispered. 'And I don't need everything I say translated. I just want you to answer me.'

He told me how he'd gone to the Public Records Office in Malta and, with the help of a friend, had managed to trace my gran. They'd worked through the family line, and this led them to the Sultana Family, who owned a large vineyard near the coast.

'And then what, you wrote to them?'

'Yes,' he beamed. 'I explain who I am and about you, and they agree they are your family and ask to meet you.' He looked at me. 'Are you not happy? Have I done something wrong?'

'I just wish I was more prepared.'

Another drink was pushed into my hand, and a plate carrying a large slab of cake. A man came over and took my face in both of his hands. With both hands occupied, I was powerless to stop him. Everyone was talking loudly and laughing, and I felt like I was watching a scene play out on a stage in front of me.

'What are they saying?' I asked Mario.

'They say your papa was,' he stopped.

'Go on,'

'They say he leave and not come back.'

'Why?'

'For better life in England.'

So here I was, in Gozo, searching for a better life, a new life, a life that made me happy, and my dad had done the very same thing, but in reverse.

'I never knew that,' I said. 'He didn't talk about his life here with me.'

Mario translated what I'd said. This got a big reaction, and everyone started talking at once. I just didn't know what it was they were saying. I looked at Mario again, pleading with my eyes for him to translate.

'They say, your dad leave his girlfriend here and go to England, where he fell in love with an English girl.'

'He was with someone else? Someone other than my mum?'

There was more discussion in Maltese. Mario explained.

'His mama, she try to persuade him to come back, but he not want to. He say, England is better.' I nodded. 'They only met you once, and your dad, he—' He paused. 'He didn't stay in touch.'

'Oh,' I said again. 'So how are these people related to me?' I said.

Everyone in the room seemed to be an auntie, a cousin, a second uncle, or a nephew. There must have been about fifteen people in total, plus two young children. I was taken on a tour of the house and then taken outside for a tour of the vineyard. Mario was ahead of me, and I didn't understand a word anyone was saying. I nodded and smiled a lot, eventually managing to catch up with him.

'Are you happy?' he said. 'You tell me you have no family, but now you have family.'

He was right. Now, I had a family, and from what I could tell, they were a happy, united family who were very much welcoming me into their home, but I didn't want to be there. I felt like a stranger, and even if we were related, that didn't mean I wanted to be in their lives or that they really wanted to be in mine despite their enthusiasm.

'Can we go soon?' I said. 'You can't force me on these people.'

He looked upset, and I felt bad, but I was unprepared for this, and I wasn't enjoying it. I wanted to leave. 'I'm happy to have met them, but please, tell them we need to leave. I don't feel comfortable.'

Mario spoke to them in Maltese, then he turned to me.

'They say they wanted to meet you very much. They say thank you to me for bringing you.'

We drove back in silence. Mario had been so excited, and I had obviously not reacted the way he'd expected or wanted me to. He pulled up outside the apartment, and I climbed down from his jeep.

'I really appreciate what you did for me today,' I said. He looked down at his feet. 'I've not had a family before. It's going to take some getting used to.'

'It is not good to always be on your own,' Mario said.

'I'm not on my own. I have you,' I said, *and Kai,* I thought.

'Do you want to come in? Tell my mum about it. She was very excited for you,' he said.

My heart ached.

'I have stuff I need to do. Maybe tomorrow.'

I shut the door and made my way upstairs. I threw open the balcony windows and pulled the chair close so I could feel the breeze on my skin. I had a real-life family. A family who had known about me even though I knew nothing about them at all. What did they expect from me? Was it just Christmas cards? Was I now expected to visit? Did I need to become a Catholic, learn Maltese, help out on the vineyard, start drinking more wine? I didn't know what any of this meant or why I wasn't feeling happy. I thought of Auntie Jean telling me I should go and find my family, telling me she thought I'd missed out by not having more people in my life. But here I was, with a ready-made vineyard of relatives that I'd run away from.

I called Kai, but he didn't answer. A message followed soon after.

Kai: *Sorry, in a boring lunch meeting. Thankfully, no oysters in sight. x*

Corrina Bryant

I opened a beer, opened the large window and opened my book. The postcard of Gozo zig-zagged to the floor. I reached for a pen.

Dear Auntie Jean

I hope you are well.

I'm in Malta, and I've met my family.

Thank you for inviting me to the community centre on Christmas Day. I really enjoyed it.

Hope to see you soon.

Eve x

Ps My school friend came to find me, and you were right.

Later that night, I opened my laptop.

To Kai

Guess what? I have some news! I have a family. An actual real Maltese family, and they are not made of milk chocolate and crunchy in the middle. I've met my Great Aunt Sultana and several other members of my family, but I'm not sure who was who. There were lots of them, though, and my cheek got kissed lots of times. Everyone was very excited even though I couldn't talk to them because they didn't speak English. They showed me a photo where my great Nan is wearing black and holding the baby me. It was written on the back in my mum's handwriting, which was weird. To be honest, I couldn't get out of there quick enough. You know me; I'm not a lover of crowds!

I'm also not sure I really want all these people in my life. You don't even like your relatives, do you? Not that I didn't like them, I

284

just didn't feel anything towards them, and I'm wondering if the old me is better than the new me. I think, maybe, I quite like it being just you and me. Please, can you tell me what I should do? They own a vineyard, lots of dogs, and a nice whitewashed farmhouse, if that helps? Although, I don't even like wine that much. They also gave me a strange ball decorated in bread crumbs, which tasted quite nice, but also, a bit strange.

How are you?

Miss you.

Eve x

I felt claustrophobic and like I either wanted to run away or lock the door and play loud music. When I went to bed, I left the large windows open so I could listen to the signs of life below. I tried to recall conversations with my dad about his family in Malta. He hadn't told me anything at all about them, and I had no way of knowing his side of the story. I had so many new questions. *Why did my mum and dad live such isolated lives if they had this large extended family? Were they really happy just with each other's company, never wanting or needing anyone else? Not even me, their only daughter?*

I felt annoyed at Mario and guilty for feeling annoyed. He had no right to do this. It wasn't his past; it wasn't his business, and if he knew me, he would never have put me in this situation. He didn't actually know me very well at all.

CHAPTER 24

Things hadn't been the same between me and Mario since the trip to meet my long-lost family. I was agitated he'd done something so personal and private without discussing it with me first. He couldn't understand why I was so upset. We both viewed what he had done very differently and nothing either of us said was bringing us closer to agreeing.

'I'm sorry. I thought you would be so happy. You tell me you have no family, and I find your family for you.' He held his hands up in the air and shrugged his shoulders. No matter where in the world you come from, body language seems universal.

'I wasn't ready. I have never had a family before,' I said, probably louder than I should have.

'Prepared for what? To be welcomed by lovely people who want to get to know you? What is wrong with that?'

'You don't know me. I don't like being the centre of attention. Especially with people I don't know.'

'They're your family, Eve.'

'But I don't know them. They're strangers.'

'But you can get to know them.'

'I don't want to.'

'Why not?'

And so it went on.

The last few weeks of the term were fast approaching, and I was spending most of my time helping the students prepare for their exams. Lydia needed to know if I was staying next term, and I was feeling the pressure to make a decision. I needed to separate my career from my feelings about Kai and Mario, but everything was connected, and nothing was straightforward.

I emailed my solicitor asking him if the conditions of my parents' Will meant I was allowed to rent the flat in Kings Cross. He said he would get back to me. I needed to know if staying in Gozo meant that I was making myself homeless in the UK. I hadn't made up my mind, and my feelings changed on an hourly basis. Every time I thought of a reason to stay, I thought of a reason not to. When I thought about going back, my heart ached for what I'd miss. Even if I did go back to England, I wasn't sure I wanted to live in my family home in King's Cross anymore. My parents were no longer alive, yet I felt trapped by their wishes, and the whole Sultana Vineyard family thing had unsettled me. I didn't feel like I belonged anywhere.

Today, Lydia was trying again to convince me to stay.

'Eve, you know how much the students like you. Please tell me, what can I do to persuade you to stay?'

It made me emotional just thinking about leaving. I had become attached to my students and Maria, and I loved my job. It was so different from my job at Thames FM, where I never felt valued or even liked. I felt like whatever decision I made, I would regret it. I didn't want Kai to be the reason I left or Mario to be the reason I stayed.

'I have loved working here. Really. It's been the best job I've ever had.'

'So stay. Why would you say that and not want to stay?'

Lydia was right. I had everything. A job I enjoyed, somewhere to stay, real friends, and I got to live on an island where the sun always shines, and the people are kind.

'I will let you know by Monday. I promise.' I said, only just managing to stop myself from saying yes there and then. But I had learnt not to do or say things on impulse, and I needed to speak to Kai first.

Maria had also asked me if I wanted to stay on. She offered me another good deal to stay but said she usually rented it out to holidaymakers in the summer, so she also needed to know one way or the other. Every which way I turned, I was being asked to make a decision. I just wanted to press pause.

Kai and me were still exchanging emails most days, and this was still a highlight of my day. Occasionally, we facetimed, but he had stopped asking me if I was coming home, and when we spoke, we skirted around the issue like it was a stranger's cough curing COVID.

On Saturday night, I was in bed trying to focus on reading a book. Maria never got me the TV she promised me, but I'd read more books in my three months in Gozo than I had in my entire life to date, and I didn't even miss the TV anymore. My phone rang, and Kai's smiling face filled the screen.

'Are you in bed already, on a Saturday night?' he said, a slight slur to his words.

'I'm just getting ready to go clubbing, actually.'

'In your pyjamas and glasses?'

'It's a sleepover party. They're big in Gozo.' His face was red, and his eyes looked glassy. 'Are you drunk?' I said.

He hung his head, giving me a close-up of the crown of his head. 'Sorry, miss.'

'Have you called for a reason or just to be annoying?' I smiled. Kai seemed to think this was hysterically funny and threw his head back as he laughed, banging it on the wall behind him. I heard a loud crack. 'Are you okay?' I said. He lifted his head, and I saw a trickle of blood fall down the side of his face. 'I think you've cut yourself, you idiot.'

He touched his head, then looked at his red hand. He stopped laughing and stared into the camera. 'Please come home,' he said. 'I'm a disaster without you.'

And that was it. The moment I realised the only person I was still lying to was myself. It was time to stop pretending. I was going back to London and back to Kai.

Lydia insisted I have a leaving do, promising me faithfully that there would be no dancing. All the staff came and several of the students, including Paulo. Lydia reserved a tapas bar near the school which had a small outdoor space. Real lemon trees in large terracotta pots had fairy lights hanging from their branches. Wooden wind chimes hung from the ceiling. I wore my linen skirt again, white trainers, and a pale-orange, short-sleeved knit top I'd bought from the market. My large pendant hung between my breasts, and I felt good. I actually quite liked getting dressed up nowadays, but I was never going to admit that to Kai. I planned to continue mocking him for being vain, just as I had done for our entire friendship.

It was a nice evening, and I felt relaxed chatting with the students and marvelling at how good their English was. I answered questions about London, striking a balance between encouraging them to visit and setting them realistic expectations.

'You can pay up to £9 for a pint of beer. That's around ten euros.'

'You are joking, miss?' Paulo said. I shook my head.

'The nice places have expensive beer; the not-so-nice places have cheap beer. But if you come to visit me, I will give you free beer,' I said, and everyone laughed.

The bar was playing local folk music, and the manager brought out some olives, bread with oil, and Padrón peppers. He told us they were on the house 'to say goodbye to the lovely English lady.' Halfway through the evening, Lydia stood on a chair and banged a glass with a spoon.

'As you know, we are all here to say goodbye to Eve. Our brilliant English teacher, who we will miss very much.' She waited for the heckling and cheering to die down. 'I know all of your students will miss you, and we hope you come back and visit us very soon. *Sahha!*' Everyone raised their glasses, and I felt overcome with emotion.

'*Sahha,*' I whispered.

Paulo then stood up on a chair. 'We have a small gift for you, miss,' he said. Max handed him a football scarf, and Paulo beckoned me over. 'This is the scarf of our football team, and you are our *mascotti.*'

'Mascot,' I said, and everyone laughed again. 'This will be very useful back in England,' I said, wrapping it around my neck. Everyone cheered, and I made a quick exit to the ladies, to avoid crying in public.

I had only known these people for a few months, but they had welcomed me and all my flaws into their lives. Accepted me for who I was and did not force me to do things I didn't want to do. They didn't make me feel I needed to pretend to be someone I wasn't. They hadn't questioned my motives for lying about why I had left England, and if anyone felt like the family I never had, it was them, not the Sultanas and their vineyard. I questioned if I was doing the right thing a hundred times a day, but I'd accepted that, too, was one of my flaws. I would always wonder if I was doing the right thing and would never truly know the answer. I'd spent too much time listening to other people's conversations and letting what I heard determine my life instead of making decisions for myself. It was time to make my own choices, and I'd done that based on one thing. I wanted Kai to be in my life.

Saying goodbye to Mario wasn't sad or dramatic. We hugged, and he was kind, and I felt sure I would see him again.

'Me and Mama will miss you.'

'I will miss both of you, too,' I said, and I meant it.

'Eva, please tell me something.' He ran his hand through his thick hair and clenched and unclenched his fists. 'Was I too slow in telling you how I felt?' He sucked his bottom lip under his teeth. I shook my head.

'No, of course not.'

'I was going to tell you how I felt after Paulo's uncle's funeral, but then when I saw you with your friend in the café. I knew.'

'You knew?'

'I saw the way he looked at you.' I opened my mouth to speak, but he continued, 'Then my mama tell me you not come home for two nights.'

I looked away. 'It wasn't like that.'

'And then when your friend—he left, I saw how sad you were.'

I'd been fooling myself. Deep down I'd known all along what I had wanted. I just needed to be sure Kai meant what he said. Plus, I'd quite enjoyed making him sweat a little.

'I try to give you a family here, then maybe you stay, but I know that is not what you want. I am sorry.'

I hugged him.

'It was the nicest thing anyone has ever done for me,' I said, and I meant it. 'I hope you will come to England one day. I have a spare room, so you must come and stay. Maria, too, if she wants to?'

'Thank you. My mama will never leave Gozo, but I will definitely come and see Kings Cross station.'

I laughed. 'I wouldn't come to England just to see Kings Cross Station.'

'Okay, but I will start there.'

I made my final payment to Mama Maria and took her some flowers. She hugged me tight.

'You will always be welcome here any time. If upstairs not free, you stay here with me.'

'Thank you. I will miss you and Mario very much.' I untangled myself from her cleavage. 'I've cleaned the apartment, emptied the fridge, taken the rubbish out, stripped the bed, and left the window open. Is there anything else you would like me to do?'

'Keep in touch. You are like the daughter I never had.'

And you, the mum I wished I'd had, I thought.

On my last day in Gozo, it was raining—for only the second time since I'd arrived. I was wearing my new scarf and not because it was cold, but because I was going to watch my first-ever football match. When I arrived at the ground, I saw Max, Paulo, and the rest of their team warming up. I made my way to the other side of the pitch, where groups of people stood chatting together. I stood next to two attractive women. I smiled and said hello, and they smiled back, then carried on speaking to each other in Maltese. The match started, and I took their lead on when to clap and cheer, although I soon worked out that one of them cheered particularly loudly and with great enthusiasm every time Paulo got the ball. She also flicked her hair to the side and laughed loudly whenever he ran past. Paulo's name was mentioned a lot, but I didn't need to understand Maltese to work out what they were saying.

At half-time, Paulo ran over to me.

'Miss, you are here?'

'Of course,' I said, holding my scarf above my head with both hands.

'It is a good game today. Do you enjoy?'

'It's great,' I said. 'Especially when there is a goal.'

'That is the game, miss,' Paulo laughed.

'I know that much,' I said.

He laughed and ran back to his team. The girls pounced.

'You know Paulo?' the hair flicker girl said.

'I used to teach him English,' I said.

'What's he like?' they said in unison, then laughed hysterically.

'He's very nice, very kind, and good at English.'

'And you come to watch him play football?'

'It is my first time,' I said.

'Our teacher wouldn't do that,' they said.

'Paulo is my friend,' I said.

In the second half, goals were coming left, right, and centre, and at three-all, with only minutes to spare, Max scored the winner. Me and the girls cheered loudly. They grabbed my scarf off of me and waved it about. It was fun and a lot more entertaining than I had expected.

Max and Paulo stood in front of me, sweating, smiling, and singing a celebratory song.

'Thank you for coming, miss,' Max said.'

'I enjoyed it, and I wore my lucky scarf,' I said.

Paulo gave me a high five, and I decided that it was time to do good with my listening skills. I looked at the two girls.

'These two were very impressed, too.' I looked at Paulo. 'The one with the blue jacket speaks very good English.'

Max laughed and slapped him on the back. 'Maybe you do score today.'

Colour rose to Paulo's cheeks, and I stood next to the girls, all of us laughing in the rain.

My taxi was coming at two pm for a six p.m. flight. I was packed and ready and wished I'd booked my cab to come early. It was making me unsettled just waiting. There was a knock on the door.

'What are you doing here?' I said, looking up into Kai's smiling face, then down at the mustard-yellow chinos and deep-red tee shirt with turned-up sleeves.

'That's a nice welcome,' he said, holding out a packet of Sealeg sea sickness pills. 'Apparently, they work, but I thought I'd chaperone you, just in case.'

'You've come all the way here to give me some travel sickness pills and travel back with me?'

'I thought you might be so impressed you'd agree to spend Christmas with me this year. What do you think?'

'Possibly.'

'Although, if you do feel sick, please can you try to avoid my trousers? They're dry clean only and preferably my shirt, too, cos it's new and wasn't cheap.'

'Anything else? Shoes?'

'Definitely avoid. They're not my favourites or that expensive, but I'm just not a fan of shoes covered in vomit.'

'Fair,' I said.

'I will hold your hair and mop your brow if required.'

I smiled at him. My best friend, the only person I trusted with my life.

'The crossing here was very calm and I've spoken to the captain and asked her to arrange the same for the return leg.'

'You didn't?'

'No, of course, I didn't because the captain can't control the sea, but if she could, I would have asked.'

'Really? You'd do that for me?'

'I'd walk on water for you.'

'If you could do that, you could give me a piggyback instead of making me get back on that boat.'

'Good point. Okay, I can't walk on water or turn water into wine.'

'You're such a disappointment.'

I fell into his arms, and we hugged for a very long time. He smelt like home.

As the taxi pulled away, I turned and waved at Maria. I looked out of the window at the market, the shops, the cafes, the churches—so many churches. The tomato fields—so many tomato fields. Kai reached for my hand and gave it a quick squeeze.

'You okay?'

I nodded. I was done running away. Gozo had taught me so much about myself. What I was capable of, but also what I wanted, and as beautiful as Gozo and the people who lived here were, it wasn't home. Kai was my home.

I walked upstairs to the deck. Kai went to get me tea, a chocolate Yazoo drink for himself, and some biscuits. I sat outside on one of the benches and looked out to sea. The sun shone down on the water, making it shimmer and sparkle like a billion gemstones floating on the surface. I turned back and stared at the mainland getting smaller as we pulled away.

'You okay?' Kai said, coming back, arms laden with treats.

'I am now,' I said, taking a packet of biscuits off him.

'I've got something to talk to you about,' Kai said. 'Something to distract you from any feelings of nausea.'

'I actually feel okay,' I said, unwrapping a vanilla cream wafer biscuit.

'How would you feel about me moving in with you?'

A piece of wafer got stuck in my throat, and I started coughing, which turned into a very dramatic choking fit.

'Is that a no?' Kai said, whacking me on the back.

'Why would you want to move into a dark, cold, old-fashioned, tired-looking two-bedroom flat in Kings Cross that often has no hot water?' I said, tears streaming down my face as I tried to breathe.

'We could turn it into a warm, bright, modern flat and call a plumber? If you want to. I'm quite handy, you know?'

'Really?'

'Yes, and it means I could buy some overalls.'

'Ahhh, that's why you want to move in?'

'We could get matching his and hers. And I got my Food Tech GCSE, remember?'

'Ahh yes, thanks to the beautiful Miss Dubois.'

Kai went quiet, and I put my sunglasses on and leaned against the railings as Gozo disappeared. The sun covered the island in an orange glow like a blanket. I thought of London.

The smog, the grey, cold, damp streets where people walked past the homeless without seeing them and lived next door to people they never spoke to. Where not a minute goes by without hearing a police siren. Was it too late to change my mind? Did I want to live with Kai? Was it too soon? I'd known him since I was eleven, and I'd been in love with him since I was thirteen, so it wasn't like I'd be rushing into things. I turned to face him, to say *yes, yes, please move in with me,* but the moment was lost by the sound of Kai retching over the side of the boat. I watched brown creamy chocolate Yazoo projectile into the sea. I reached deep into my jeans pocket and pulled out a scrunched-up paper napkin covered in pizza sauce. Kai took it and wiped his mouth.

'You okay?'

'I know you want to laugh.'

'I'm laughing with you, not at you,' I said, bursting into fits of giggles.

'Next time you run away, I'm not coming to get you.'

'There won't be a next time,' I said.

CHAPTER 25

The first thing I did when I got home was draw back all the curtains and open all the windows. It was a cold day in London, and the air had a chill, but the flat smelt stale, and the air needed replacing. There was a small pile of post—not much, considering I'd been gone three months. Most of it was junk mail. There were no messages on the machine. I turned the tap on, and the water spluttered, struggling to escape, and then the pipes creaked into action. I filled the kettle and turned it on. I opened the fridge and stared at a jar of jam, a bottle of ketchup, mayonnaise, and a nearly empty tub of Lurpak butter with the yellow sticker still on.

An hour later, the washing machine was on, and I was back from Sainsbury's with enough food and provisions for the next few days. I had a very cold shower, pulled on my joggers and a baggy jumper, and lit a fragrance candle called *warm orange*. I put a bottle of wine in the freezer and cleared a shelf in the bathroom. Then, for the first time in over two years, I opened the door to my parents' bedroom. I sat on their bed and breathed slowly. Even when they were alive, I'd never come in here. Not even when I was young. The last time I'd be in here was when I'd bagged up all their clothes, stripped the bed, and cleared away the surfaces of their knick-knacks. None of them had any meaning to me.

My mum's jewellery box was one of the few remaining objects. I moved off the bed and sat at the dressing table, wiping the dust off the mirror with my hand. She had nothing of value. A small gold-plated watch with Roman numerals on the face, some pearl earrings that weren't real, and a heart-shaped locket on a tarnished silver chain. I picked the locket up and turned it over in my fingers. I had no memory of her ever wearing this. I flicked it open and saw a tiny photo of me as a little girl. I was staring straight into the camera, not smiling. My hair was neat, and I was wearing a pinafore dress. I remembered this day. I didn't have a single photo of the three of us together, which symbolised our family because we weren't a proper family unit. We were disjointed, all three of us living in our own worlds under the same roof. I closed the door behind me and sat down on the sofa. Another cloud of dust filled the air.

By the time Kai arrived with his laptop, some clean clothes, toiletries, and an Tesco Meal Deal, I'd beaten all the cushions half to death, and the flat was smelling and feeling fresher.

'Did you miss me?'

'Did you brush your teeth?' I said.

He breathed in my face. 'Fresh as a daisy.'

I showed him where I'd made space for his stuff.

'This feels very grown up and serious,' he said.

'We're just seeing how it goes, yeah? Checking if we actually like each other, and if I'm capable of living with another human being,' I said.

He smiled. 'How confident are you feeling?'

'Fifty, fifty.'

'I'll take it,' he said.

Later, we sat at the table and talked about how the flat could look if we had lots of money to spend. Then we had a conversation about what could be done for £250. We gravitated towards the sofa, and I lay with my head in Kai's lap while he stroked my hair.

'I wish I didn't have work tomorrow,' he said, 'cos we could go to Ikea and get domesticated.'

'I wish I did have work tomorrow,' I said.

We hadn't discussed my employment status, and while I owned the flat as long as I lived in it, I still needed money to live. We'd agree Kai would cover the bills, but I certainly wasn't going to rely on him to feed and clothe me as well.

'I'm thinking of applying to be a teaching assistant,' I said. 'I think my job in Gozo will help me get an interview, but the money isn't great.'

'Why a teaching assistant and not a teacher?' Kai said.

'Because I'm not qualified to be a teacher.'

'So get qualified,' Kai said, lighting a spark inside me, which started to flicker gently.

We slept in my bed, even though my parent's bed was bigger. I just didn't like being in that room. Kai curled himself around my body, and I held his hand, looking at our fingers entwined in the street lights.

'I'd really like to make love to you right now,' Kai whispered.

'I'd like that, too,' I whispered back, 'but only if you promise never to stand me up at the aisle.'

'I promise. As long as we don't have oysters at our wedding.'

'Deal,' I said.

In the morning, Kai left for work, and after I'd floated in and out of the shower, I started researching teacher training courses. I felt overwhelmed, underqualified, and deflated.

Maybe this wasn't my path after all. I tackled some more laundry, and as I methodically folded each item, I came across Gary's Thames FM tee shirt and Poppy's *loungewear* that she'd lent me the day I stayed at her luxury apartment. With nothing else to do, I put them in a bag and headed to Hammersmith before I changed my mind.

On the train, I overheard a couple argue about money.

'You can't keep buying clothes you don't need,' he said.

'I do need them,' she said.

'No one needs that many clothes. You've got nowhere to put them; the flat looks like a TK Maxx store.'

'I'm sending most of them back.'

'Then why order them? It's ridiculous.'

'Because I like to look good. What's wrong with that?'

They sat in silence, both facing away from each other. Then he turned back around.

'I don't think we're happy anymore,' he said.

'I'm happy,' she said.

I waited for his response.

'I don't think you are. Not with me, anyway.' The train pulled into the next stop and he got up and got off. She stayed on, and the doors shut, and the train pulled away. Had I just witnessed a breakup? I felt sad for both of them. But this was one conversation I wasn't going to highjack. I was in love for the first time in my life, and I wasn't going to do anything to jeopardise that.

I went to the Really Good cafe and ordered a latte. It felt like a lifetime ago when I was in there, buying Poppy a latte, not getting myself one because I couldn't afford two. The barista remembered me.

'How have you been? We haven't seen you in a long time.'

'I've been away. Working abroad.'

'And you came back in winter? Why?' He laughed at his own joke.

'It's a long story,' I said.

I took a seat in the window and looked across the road. The lights were on, and the Thames FM sign was lit up. I felt nothing.

I warmed my hands on my coffee, trying to weigh up the pros and cons of going to see Poppy. I didn't know how I would feel or how she would react. We used to be colleagues, then friends, then neither. I owed her an apology, I knew that, but it had been a long time ago, and three months had passed. Maybe it was best to leave things as they were.

An older couple sat at the table next to me.

'We paid all that money for her education, and she wants to go to drama school,' he said.

'It's her decision,' she said.

'She's making a mistake. She's bright. She could do anything.'

'It's her life. She's young, and she's got time.'

'She's following some crazy dream. It's going to get her nowhere.'

'But at least she's giving it a shot.'

'What's that supposed to mean?'

'You know what it means.'

'I never stopped you.'

'But you didn't encourage me either.'

'You can't live your life through her.'

'I'm not. I'm making sure she doesn't make the same mistakes I did.'

They sat in silence, both lost in thought. A mum who wanted her daughter to follow her dreams, a dad who wanted his daughter to reach her potential. Two unhappy couples on the same day that I finally admitted to myself I was in love.

I looked back out across the road and saw Poppy come out of the building, followed by Gary. They looked exactly the same. Poppy was wearing white jeans, a leather jacket, and a baby-pink beanie hat. She looked cool and pretty as always. Gary was smoking, wearing all denim. I slunk down in my chair and pulled my jacket high up around my face. Gary put his arm around Poppy. She looked up at him, and he kissed her.

'What the hell?' I said out loud.

I picked up my coffee and left. I'd been back in the country less than twenty-four hours, and already, I was listening in to stranger's conversations and following my old boss down the street. Had I learnt nothing from my previous mistakes?

They stopped outside the grotty pub. Gary opened the door and followed Poppy inside.

Gary and Poppy together. I couldn't get my head around it. She used to bad mouth him to me all the time. We'd joked about his hygiene habits, and I'd complained to her about how rude he was.

I crossed the road and stood outside the pub, trying to build up the courage to go inside when all I wanted to do was walk away. I pulled open the door.

Gary and Poppy were sitting in the corner. She already had a glass of white wine in front of her. He was holding a beer. Their heads were bent close together. As I walked towards them, Gary caught my eye and quickly pulled away. Poppy turned around and met my gaze.

Corrina Bryant

'Eve! What are you doing here?'

'Hi.' I placed a Tesco bag for life on the table. 'I just wanted to return these.' Poppy looked inside the bag. 'Your t-shirt is in there, too.' I looked at Gary. 'I've washed it.'

'You look really well.' Poppy said.

'I've been working abroad. Teaching English.'

'Is that the truth or another load of bullshit?' Gary said.

'Gary!' Poppy said, glaring at him.

'I'm going for a piss,' he said.

'Do you want a drink?' Poppy said.

I shook my head and waited for Gary to be out of earshot.

'So, how long have you and Gary been together?'

'Together?' Poppy threw her head back and laughed. 'We're not together.'

'I saw you,' I said. Poppy looked down at her hands.

'A couple of years,' she said, taking a large gulp of her wine and avoiding my gaze. 'You would have known this already if you'd come to my dinner party.'

It didn't take long for my memory to catch up with my thoughts.

'So all that time, when he was treating me like something on the bottom of his shoe, you and him were—' I stopped. 'Wait, so Gary was your secret boyfriend? Oh my God.'

'Why don't you join us for a drink?'

'I need to go.' I turned towards the door, then turned back. 'I wanted to apologise to you.' Poppy went to speak. 'I just wished you'd let me explain.' Gary slid back into his seat. There was an awkward silence. Poppy gave me a half smile. 'By the way, did you ever find out who complained about the

304

panto tickets? Because,' I looked at Poppy, 'I always thought it must have been you.'

I walked towards Baron's Court, knowing this would be the last time I would see Poppy or be anywhere near Thames FM. It was a part of my life that was over.

When Kai got back later, he handed me a bag.

'I got you a present,' he said.

I unpacked several mini sample pots of paint, a small paintbrush, and a bottle of white spirit.

'Weekend entertainment?' he said.

'Ahhh, about that,' I said. 'How do you feel about my Aunt Jean coming over?'

'Mad Auntie Jean?'

'Yes, but maybe don't call her that to her face.' I paused. 'Although, to be honest, I don't think she'll mind if you do.'

'I like her already.'

I picked up one of the samples.

'Pink?'

'Fusion Pink. It's the 'in' colour apparently.'

By Sunday night, the lounge had been transformed. The woodwork was an antique white, and the walls a rosey pink. The sofa had a large cream throw covering it, and the cushions were bagged up and ready to be donated to the recycled textiles bin.

'I think yellow for our bedroom,' Kai said.

'Our bedroom?'

'And a white black-out blind. It will make the room look bigger and brighter, and I can fit it.' He paused. 'But obviously, it's up to you. It's your flat.'

I walked over to him and hugged him. 'It's our home, and as you know, I'm very bad at making decisions.'

'But you do look very good in overalls,' Kai said.

'Overalls are very on-trend.'

I walked in, feeling a familiar sense of dread and fear. Everyone else looked younger than me and seemed to know where they were going and what they were doing. I looked around for someone to come and rescue me.

'Are you okay?' A young girl wearing a staff ID badge and holding an iPad approached me.

'I'm here for the teacher training open morning.'

'Did you register?'

I nodded.

She showed me to the main lecture hall, where the welcome talk was about to begin.

The three-year course combined study with practical work placements. Employment opportunities were high, and this was a job where you could make a real difference in young people's lives. An ex-student, now working as a qualified teacher, who had studied the course, introduced herself and offered to answer questions. I watched her, listened to her answers, smiled at her stories of the kids, laughed at tales of nightmare parents, and felt excited when she said that no two days were ever the same. She was honest and open and admitted she was always exhausted by the end of the week but finished by saying it was the best job in the world.

In the foyer afterwards, I picked up the course brochure. It was all there in black and white. The modules, how to apply for a student loan, and the teaching specialities. Primary, Secondary, Special Needs. I wanted to apply there and then. I wanted to buy the books, a notebook, a new fluffy pencil case, and maybe some Doc Martens. Become a student again.

'Are you thinking of applying?' One of the course leaders from the talk approached me.

I nodded.

'Fantastic. Primary or secondary?'

'Secondary, I think.'

'I thought you looked brave,' he said, smiling. 'Have you any experience with teenagers—other than being one yourself?'

'I've been teaching English abroad. To young adults.'

'Great. You know what to expect, then. It's not easy being young in today's world.'

'No, it's not,' I agreed.

'It's not easy being old either.' He laughed.

'I think we all just want to...' I stopped. I felt like I was going to cry, which was ridiculous and embarrassing and the very worst thing I could do in this situation.

'Go on,' he said.

I took a deep breath and thought of my students in the language school. I thought of Paulo and Lydia. Maria and Mario, Poppy, Gary, Greg, Auntie Jean, and even my parents. '...feel like someone is listening to us.'

He smiled.

'I look forward to seeing you in September.'

The End

Printed in Dunstable, United Kingdom